OUR FAMILY TROUBLE

OUR FAMILY TROUBLE

A Domestic Thriller

DON WINSTON

TIGERFISH

This is a work of fiction. Names, characters, businesses, places, events, and incidents are either the products of the author's imagination or used in a fictitious manner. Any resemblance to actual persons, living or dead, or actual events is purely coincidental.

ISBN13: 9780692838082
ISBN-10: 0692838082
Library of Congress Control Number: 2017901191
Tigerfish, Los Angeles, CA

Cover design: Steven Womack

"Do Not Go Gentle Into That Good Night" by Dylan Thomas
From THE POEMS OF DYLAN THOMAS, copyright © 1952 by Dylan Thomas.
Reprinted by permission of New Directions Publishing Corp.

Author photograph: Owen Moogan

For RW

re-ve-nant \ ˈre-və-nənt \ *n* [F, fr. prp. of *revenir* to return] (1827): one that returns after death or a long absence — **revenant** *adj*

—*Merriam-Webster's Collegiate Dictionary,* Tenth Edition

"And much of Madness, and more of Sin,
And Horror the soul of the plot."
—*The Conqueror Worm*
Edgar Allan Poe

Prologue

"**A**nd how old is Campbell II now?" the ob-gyn asked with a smile, thumbing through her files. "Nine months, is he?"

"He's fine. He's wonderful," replied Dillie Parker with pride, holding her son on her lap. "But no 'II.' Just...plain ol' Campbell." She propped him up straighter, which he didn't protest.

The doctor looked up across her desk and winked at the toddler. Then she scribbled the correction on her file. "Hard to believe just a year ago you were in the home stretch."

"Seems like a lifetime ago," said Dillie, laughing. "I definitely remember sweating through the Indian summer. I love the early nip we're having this year."

"That's an adorable outfit," the doctor said as she wrote, tipping her head toward the boy.

"My mother will be thrilled to hear that," Dillie said. "It's the fourth one she's sent this month."

"Is that sweater Ralph Lauren?"

Dillie shook her head. "It's Khaki." To the doctor's confusion, she clarified: "My grandmother. She's a knitting fiend. If you sit still too long, she'll knit a sweater up around you."

The doctor smiled and said, "It's a gift to have a knitter in the family." And Dillie nodded and said, "Khaki is most certainly a gift."

"And you, Dillie?" the doctor asked.

"Me?"

"How are you doing?"

Dillie glowed. "I've never been happier."

"Yes, I can tell. The first few months are typically the most challenging."

Dillie tipped her head with a knowing stare. "Truer words are rarely spoken."

She and the doctor laughed together. The doctor scanned the file again, made a simple notation.

"You're over the first hump," said the doctor as she scribbled. "It's especially big with the first child. Until you hit your stride, which you seem to have done."

"Oh, it's still challenging," said Dillie.

The doctor looked up. "Yes?"

Dillie nodded and shrugged.

"In what way?" the doctor asked.

Campbell squirmed in his mother's lap, and she hoisted him back to a sitting position.

Dillie shook her head, dismissing it. Her fingers fanned across her son's stomach, keeping him on his perch.

The doctor sat still, waiting.

"Oh, you know," Dillie said with a good-natured wave off. "In the normal way. It's nothing. It's just a little different from what I...expected."

"What is?"

Dillie laughed out loud, looking to the ceiling for the answer.

She opened her mouth, collecting her thoughts. "Well…I don't know," she said, searching. "The main challenge, I guess, is that Rupert's been traveling so much. For work. You know Rupert, right?"

"Certainly," said the doctor.

"Yes, of course. He's been here with me. And everybody knows Rupert, it seems." She paused and glanced up at the doctor and then away. And then: "It's just been such a busy time for him, and there's really nothing he can do about that. I mean, it's just his job. But the timing's bad, and so that's been a challenge. Which it would be for anyone."

"It's difficult when the husband has to travel for work," agreed the doctor. "I see that often, as you can imagine."

"Right, when the husband and *father* has to travel for work, and I totally get that it's a high-pressure job, so I try not to let it get to me. And I shouldn't complain. I mean, I have Lola…our baby nurse…but it's just not the same…."

"You still have a baby nurse?" the doctor asked.

Dillie nodded sheepishly. "Extravagant, yes. I'm very lucky that we can…I mean, that we can afford to…well, we had a nanny. Two actually. But they didn't…" She looked past the doctor, inspecting the far wall and its matrix of diplomas. Amherst. Hopkins. "They just didn't work out. So we still have Lola, who is really wonderful, and loves Campbell."

"That's good," the doctor said. "A baby nurse can get pricey."

"Yes, and it's silly, I realize. I'll have to find another nanny soon. If I…can. But Lola is so attached to Campbell, and Rupert doesn't mind the extra expense. At least he says he doesn't. Probably eases his guilt…"

"I see."

"...for traveling so much." Dillie smiled and shrugged. Campbell squirmed, and she pulled him back up to her lap. She glanced out the window, past the tilted blinds, onto the Park Avenue sidewalk. Two older society ladies in light wraps passed side by side and disappeared. Probably on their way to lunch at Swifty's, or shopping on Madison.

"You know, I'm just tired a lot," she finally said. "I think that's my problem. I get punchy. Rupert says I should put Campbell in the nursery, with Lola. I mean, that's why we pay her. So when he cries, it won't wake me up."

"Perhaps you should," said the doctor.

"Yes, but he doesn't cry. He *never* cries. Which Rupert would know if he paid attention to his son. Or to *me*, for that matter. He used to..."

"Campbell doesn't cry?"

"I mean, I *hear* him, but it's not...at least it doesn't seem...It's something else. I don't...And the other noises, you know. I just don't get much sleep. That's the problem, I guess." She stopped, ransacking for her next thought.

The doctor sat still.

"Noises?" she asked.

Campbell started to slide, and Dillie turned him around and held him against her shoulder. She patted his back.

"Oh, you know," she said, rocking him in her seat. "Those old prewar buildings, especially those warehouse ones, no matter how much you renovate and modernize, I mean, the exterminators can't find them; they insist they see no signs of them anywhere, but..."

"What do you hear, Dillie?"

"...and I can't put traps around the crib where they...and Rupert's no help, of course, so I stay up all night looking for them. And I have deadlines, too! I *do* have a career, you know. You think they care if you...? They just don't care."

Dillie stopped herself. She stroked Campbell's back, now fast asleep. She forced a single, quiet laugh.

"Where's that hump I'm supposed to get over?" she asked.

The doctor started to scratch on a pad.

"Are you...happy with your boy?" she asked.

"I...beg your pardon?"

The doctor signed her name at the bottom, tore off the sheet, and slid the prescription across her desk.

"We've talked about postpartum depression...," she said.

"Oh, this is just postpartum bitchiness," said Dillie, sliding the prescription back, pinning Campbell with the other arm. "I don't need happy drugs. Really."

"See me in one month," the doctor said. "Depression is common, of course. But we don't want postpartum psychosis."

Dillie stared at her. Campbell breathed into her neck.

"No," she said, holding an off smile. "We don't."

PART ONE

NƎW YORK

one

DECEMBER

"**L**ola, could you do me a favor and turn down the television? Just a little?" Dillie called out, spiriting through her apartment hallway while the NY1 morning traffic and weather report echoed.

"Got it," Lola called back from the kitchen in her unhurried Jamaican patois.

"Thank you!" Dillie said, and then into her cell phone: "Rupert, where's this thing you need?" She padded down the gallery hall and into his home office overlooking Grand Street at early rush hour. "Is it still snowing in Chicago?" she asked him as she woke and searched his PC, following his directions. "God, I need coffee before working Windows," she joked, clicking through folders of data.

She found and read off the information he needed. "No clue what any of that means," she said. "Just give 'em hell."

She whisked into her own home office next door—clean, white, organized—found and plugged her earbuds into her phone, dropped the phone into her robe pocket, hands free. Then she grabbed her charging iPad, scrolled through e-mails. "How do you pronounce Oliver's wife's name again? I'm sure I mangled it last time, although she had the grace to ignore it. She's bringing their little one today. Do you think I should have name tags?"

3

She swept into the corner living room flooded with winter light from the floor-to-ceiling windows on both sides. Checked the adjacent dining room and decided the adult food would go on the circular mahogany table and the children's on the sideboard. The white wine and juice boxes would live together on the bar. She racked her brain for the whereabouts of the oblong, stainless ice bucket. She'd forgotten the last time she used it.

The cake, of course, would go dead center on the round table, once the waiters had cleared the finger food. She'd lift him up and help him blow out the candle.

"No, I haven't heard them the past few nights....The new traps are working, I think....Yes, of course I got the ones he can't get into. I did all the research....And I only put them out on the back landing anyway....Can you imagine if one ran across the room during the party?" She giggled at the thought. "Hostess of the year!"

Abruptly remembering something from her mental to-do list, which had grown the night before when she was trying to sleep, she darted back down the hallway, to a hidden closet between contemporary art pieces, where she reached up to a roll of toilet paper and hurried toward the metallic-glazed powder room off the foyer. She pushed an errant earbud back in, traded out the half-spent roll, straightened the hostess hand towels, and approved the fresh cake of gardenia soap. She frowned at a dead bulb in a sconce, unscrewed it, and scurried back to the supply closet.

"Yes, he's still asleep. He was snoring, in his own little way. All bundled up and tucked in. Facedown, like you. Too cute to wake him, but I probably should." She traded out the offending bulb in the powder room. "He's gotten so active, I swear he'll be climbing out of his crib soon, although Dr. Pearson said not to worry about that just yet.... Well, don't beat yourself up. We won't tell him you missed it. He can work that out with his therapist in twenty years."

Another thought struck her, and she pivoted back to the foyer coat closet. She cleared out the Burberrys and parkas, all sizes, and scooped up boots and umbrellas to make room for her guests. Her arms piled, she hurried back toward her bedroom.

"Booray, what are you so giddy about? You need to go out?" she asked their three-year-old yellow Labrador retriever, who stood in the middle of the living room, facing away, wagging his tail. Back to her phone, she said, "I think the dog's getting funny in the head. Empty rooms excite him these days."

NY1 blared out a report on the latest terrorist attack in Europe. It grew louder to the point of distortion.

"Lola?" Dillie called out. "It won't turn down," Lola called back. "Can you just turn it off please?" Dillie said, having vowed to shield her son from the world's unraveling as long as possible. Sometimes it seemed futile.

"The kitchen TV's acting up," she said to Rupert. "It's still under warranty, right?"

She tiptoed into her room, past the crib, dumped her coat-closet stash on the bed.

"I hate to wake him, but he'll never nap otherwise," she said into the phone, pivoting back to the crib under the solar-system mobile. "Good morning, Campbell," she softly cooed, bent over his bed, gently rubbing the blanket covering his back. "Such a sleepyhead this morning, aren't you?"

Campbell yawned into the mattress, opened one eye and yawned again. "It's your big day," she told him. "Do you know what day it is, little mouse?" She loosened the blanket, which was still tightly wrapped around him. He felt hot.

"I think you're too toasty in this bed," she said. "You're a toasty little burrito." She unbuttoned the top of his pale blue pajamas, which Lola must have buttoned incorrectly the night before, as they were one off.

"Let off a little steam. That's better," she said as she took the phone from her pocket, tapped the camera app. "Here, monkey. Can we give Daddy a birthday smile? Just a little...?" She gently turned him over onto his back, aimed the camera.

Campbell beamed up at his mother with alert, happy eyes.

Dillie yanked back her hand.

She stood up, dropping the phone into the crib.

"Oh my God," she said.

"Lola!" she cried out.

● ● ●

She found Lola in the kitchen.

"How did this happen?" she demanded, carrying Campbell in his diaper.

Lola looked at the child, at Dillie. "You tell me," she said.

"Excuse me?"

"He didn't have that last night," she said.

"What are you suggesting?" Dillie said.

"He didn't have that last night," Lola repeated.

Dillie took a breath, settled. "Lola...if he fell at the playground or something, you can tell me. I won't be..."

"He didn't fall at the playground."

Dillie stared at her. The doorbell rang.

"We'll…discuss this later," she said.

Lola reached for Campbell. "I'll dress him."

Dillie pulled him away, took a step back.

"No," she said. "I'll do it."

• • •

She would have ignored her mother's call were it not the first birthday of her first grandchild. Instead, she thanked her for the new outfit and toys and pack of educational DVDs, but added: "I have guests coming soon, Mom. For a party."

The caterers set up chafing dishes in the dining room. Dillie and Lola were finishing their morning kitchen tasks so they could turn the room over to them. Campbell, dressed in a Christmas-red turtleneck and little jeans, sat watching his brand-new *Baby Mozart* in the sitting room by the window.

"Khaki read about it in your magazine," her mother, Vivian, informed her. "Develops spatial intelligence, so they say…."

Lola rinsed and sterilized baby bottles and little bowls and spoons.

"He loves it," said Dillie, grabbing a clean bottle from the drying rack. "Thank you. And please thank Khaki for me." Her tone indicated a wrap-up, which she already knew was futile.

"I keep looking for your byline," her mother barreled on. "Aren't you working on a profile of some luminary? Your own piece, I mean? Is that still in the cards?"

Dillie pinged from one side of the kitchen to the other. Lola, in the way, turned off the stove, decamped from the room.

"It's very much in the cards," said Dillie, reaching for the Enfagrow soy powder in the cupboard above the range. She double-checked the expiration date on the side and unscrewed the lid.

"I didn't see it this week," said Vivian. "Should I look for it again next week?"

"You can, but you won't find it." She carefully measured the powder with the scoop, dumped it into the bottle.

"I do think they are underutilizing you at that magazine," said Vivian, and Dillie said, "Well, that may be."

"There's just no style to what they have you doing. I don't mean flourishes. I'm all for simple, declarative sentences, but those blurbs they have you writing are so antiseptic, so clinical. Don't you agree?"

Dillie filled the bottle at the sink. "I'm sorry you find my pieces antiseptic."

"You're missing my whole point, Dillie. I realize you must pay your dues as you toil through the ranks, but honestly, how many baby steps are you going to take before you venture a full stride?"

Dillie screwed on the nipple cap. It was off-thread. She unscrewed it and tried again. "Mom, I need to feed Campbell."

"Yes, do that. Don't keep my hungry grandson waiting. Oh, and I gave a deposit to Ensworth Preschool. Just to hold a spot. You'd be shocked how competitive it's gotten here. It is not the Nashville you knew. It's not as treacherous as New York, of course, but I declare..."

"Not sure why you did that," said Dillie, finding powder clumps in the bottle, shaking harder. "Since we're not moving home."

"Delphine, you cannot raise a child in that city. You cannot school him there. On top of everything else, where is he supposed to play? And I know for a fact Rupert can peddle his wares wherever he pleases. He admitted as much to me last Christmas, even though he didn't realize it."

Dillie's arm was getting tired. She switched hands, kept shaking. "Mom, can you rant later? I have guests coming soon."

"Yes, you made that clear as soon as you answered the phone. Oh, did you see that horrible story in the *Post*?" Vivian had subscribed online to the *New York Post* ever since Dillie moved and liked to hector her with its daily freak-show stories. "That girl walking her dog near you? Somewhere on the mean streets down your way, I'm sure, because I looked it up on the map that linked from the page. Just a few blocks away, over by that park on the edge of that dangerous section. That gang hangout. I trust you don't let Campbell play there, although maybe all the parks there are gang-infested."

Dillie checked the formula: milky and smooth enough. Campbell could handle a few powder clumps.

"So this girl was walk-walk-walking her dog"—Vivian always spoke more frantically when she feared the conversation was nearing its end—"I think it was a terrier mutt of some kind. They had a photo, sort of mangy-looking, but I'm sure he meant the world to that poor girl. I got the impression she had no one else in her life. It must be hard to be lonely in such a big city. Where was I? Oh, the dog. With its whiskers and big brown eyes, did you see the photo? So the dog, this terrier mutt, oh, Dillie, it suddenly has a seizure, like an epileptic. A neighbor when I was a girl had an epileptic dog, and it's so unsettling, so eerie, nothing funny about it at all. And, of course, there's nothing you can do but let it run its course, and then the dog was always so exhausted and confused. Because it would be confusing, wouldn't it? It would be embarrassing, too, naturally. But this girl, the mutt's lonely owner, reaches down to soothe and comfort it....Are you listening?"

Dillie stood in the sitting room, next to Campbell, both transfixed and amused by the musical and repetitive DVD that was honing their spatial intelligence. She stroked his hair. "I'm here," she said. "But not for long."

"And, Dillie, she seizes too! The girl suffers her own epileptic seizure, while she's petting her seizing dog. There were witnesses! Hordes of them. It's all in the paper, probably gangbangers and dope pushers, although that's me editorializing. But what's a fact is they saw it and it wasn't epilepsy at all!"

Dillie stared at the little toy circus seals balancing beach balls on their noses as they ascended yellow stairs and then spiraled down the red slide, only to start their journey anew at the bottom. Sisyphus seals. In sync with a Mozart sonata she knew but couldn't pinpoint.

"A live current of electricity had traveled up from the bowels of the subway, through the wet sidewalk. It had rained earlier, they said, and this bolt shot up through the cement and electrocuted them both. Just stopped their hearts cold. Dead! Freak! Too big, too crazy, that town, with so much going on aboveground and underground. For a child. I mean, think, Dillie. Think!"

A metronome with a red crab attached to its arm *tick-tock*ed back and forth. She didn't have time for this.

"I think you should cancel your subscription," said Dillie, bending down to feed the bottle to Campbell, still engrossed in the dancing toys.

A dark hand yanked the bottle away before it reached his mouth. Lola clutched it with two fingers and hurried past Dillie back into the kitchen.

"What?" asked Dillie, taken aback.

Without answering, Lola unscrewed and emptied the bottle into the sink drain, flushing it down with a full blast of water, which she let run.

She pulled a fresh garbage bag from under the sink, dropped the bottle and lid into it, tied it tightly closed.

"What...are you doing?" said Dillie. "I checked the expiration date."

Lola grabbed another garbage bag, turned back to the box of d-CON rat poison sitting next to the stove.

Dillie froze.

Lola sealed the poison in the new bag. Wiped down the counter with a sponge, threw the sponge away and washed her hands. Reached up to the cupboard above the range, took down the canister of Enfagrow soy, placed it on the counter. She stared at Dillie.

"...all I know is stuff like that doesn't happen here," Vivian prattled on in the distance.

"I...have to go now," whispered Dillie to her mother, pulling down the earbuds. They dangled at her side.

"Ms. Parker?" one of the caterers called from the powder room. "Just so you know, there's no hot water."

"...thank you...," said Dillie, to Lola, not the caterer.

Lola took both garbage bags from the kitchen, toward the trash chute in the back hallway.

two

Mindy was the first to arrive, with her new baby Eloise. "She's beautiful," said Dillie, forcing cheer. "Welcome, Eloise!"

"She's been a bit colicky," said Mindy, still out on maternity leave. "That's why I came early. I hope you don't mind." She'd clearly been dieting, if not fasting, having lost nearly all her baby weight.

Greer and Tabitha came together soon after, with their children. Aline, Eleanor, and Tristen arrived on the same elevator, busy and noisy with theirs. "Settle!" Eleanor ordered her rampaging three-year-old. "What did I tell you downstairs? Do not touch the paintings!"

Lola manned the video security panel by the front door to buzz the guests in downstairs. She took coats and hats and hung them in the cleared-out closet.

"He doesn't have a fever, does he?" asked Aline when told that Campbell was sleeping off a bit of congestion. Dillie said, "No. He just needs a little extra rest."

"That's good. Then we can stick to Monday's playdate with Jerusalem."

Dillie turned. "Who?"

"Jeremy," said Aline, and then laughed. "My son."

"Oh yes. Yes, of course."

The apartment was filled with Mylar balloons of giant 1's and Winnie-the-Pooh characters—the classic A. A. Milne ones, not Disney. She'd decided against a clown or even Santa Claus, lest they frighten the young toddlers. Another year.

"Your home is so lovely," said the charming wife whose name she often mangled. "Thank you, Sagitha," said Dillie, confident she'd nailed it. "I'm so happy you could come." And then she thought, *Sangita*, and wondered if that was it, which needled her, as she genuinely liked this woman and meant no disrespect.

Her dear friend Victoria, a publicist for the Shubert Organization, blew in an hour late, apologizing needlessly for a Stockard Channing/Sutton Fraser photo shoot that ran long. She'd left behind her toddler, Beckett, who'd contracted pinkeye at preschool. "I'll wash my hands again," she promised over air kisses.

"Use Purell," said Dillie. "There's no hot water."

"Is Rupert not paying the bills? Should we take up a collection?"

"The super's on it right now."

Victoria eyed her. "What's wrong? You seem spooked. And you're missing an earring, my lamb."

Dillie shook her head, reaching up to her naked ear. "I'm fine. Just a party, you know. All the kids." She removed her lone earring, palmed it.

The children in paper hats sat slack-jawed in the room off the kitchen, too besotted with *Baby Mozart* and "A Little Night Music" to pay attention to the party, the cookies, their juice boxes.

"I would have given you all of mine," whispered Victoria, pointing at the screen. "Those fucking things still give me nightmares." She scoured the room. "Where's the birthday boy?"

"Napping," said Dillie. "He's a bit cranky today. Just like me on my birthday! I'll bring him out later."

Dillie circulated. The mothers, mostly in chic office attire, roamed the living and dining rooms and the gallery hallways, admiring Rupert's collection of contemporary art. They chatted and nibbled and sipped dry chardonnay on their supposed lunch break. 'Tis the season.

"Where are you applying?" asked the wife of one of Rupert's coworkers. "For school."

"Well, he's one," said Dillie. "We haven't thought about it just yet."

"Oh," said the wife, and another said, "You know Lily's daughter got wait-listed at Spence, and her grandmother's on the board." To which the wife said, "Sacred Heart is fine and all, but still embarrassing. You've got to start so early." Another piped in: "We're testing at Dalton in January," and a slightly older mother said, "Oy. Good luck with that one."

The music blared too loudly. Dillie rushed to the audio system concealed in a hall closet to correct it.

"Is that a real Ruscha?" asked Rupert's lawyer's wife. She'd clearly had a boob job since her last child and was dressed inappropriately as always, especially for a first birthday. Dillie stared at the gas station painting while she searched for a non-snippy response and said, "I assume it is. Much of Rupert's collection predates me."

"And this one is simply stunning," the vixen added, pointing to the vast city night scape that spanned the dining room wall. "Who is it?"

"Rupert gave that to me after I had Campbell. I think he found it in London." She smiled and shrugged. "I should know the artist, shouldn't I?"

The tart gazed at it and nodded. "It does remind me of Rupe. Where is he, by the way?"

"*Rupert* is in Chicago," said Dillie, not liking the too-familiar pet name, or this guest. "He'll be glad to hear you like it."

Her phone vibrated in her slacks pocket. A welcome release.

"I'm sure that's him calling now," she said, reaching in and pulling away. "His son's birthday, you know. If you'll excuse me..." She whisked the phone up to her ear.

"Hello?" she said.

There was silence on the other end.

"Hello?" she repeated, moving to the hallway, away from the noise. "Hello?"

A crackle of static and a smacking of lips. Someone eating something. Chewing with an open mouth. Or pretending to, so exaggerated were the effects. Almost taunting.

Dillie plugged her other ear, strained. "Yes, who is this?" She migrated farther from the party. "Lance, is that you? Really, I'm in the middle of your nephew's birthday. Hop to it."

The lip smacking morphed into choking. A gasp, a gag, a grating of the throat. It grew louder, desperate.

Dillie checked the caller ID. Unknown, which was typically Khaki on the family's landline, but couldn't have been with this. She tired of the prank, even as it chilled her.

Movement at the far end of the hallway by her bedroom caught her eye. Two number "1" Mylar balloons had traveled down, bumping against each other at the ceiling. They moved with erratic rhythm, animated by conflicting air currents from somewhere.

Her bedroom door stood open.

Dillie pocketed her phone, moved quickly down the hall, into her room, targeted the crib.

It was empty. The side panel unlatched and open.

She looked around her room, under the bed, in the closet, the bathroom. "Campbell?" she called out. "Campbell?"

She ran into Lola as she hurried from her room. "Have you seen Campbell?" she asked. "Did you take him?"

"No," Lola said.

"Someone let him out. Where is he?" she said, rushing down the hallway, into the dining room, past a floating Piglet and Eeyore, swatting them out of her way.

At the living room door, she cratered.

The wives and mothers stood in a messy circle. In the center, in his diaper, stood Campbell.

His back was bruised and purple, his arms and legs scratched and scabbed. He rotated, delighted to be the center of attention. He turned toward his mother.

His face was marred with cuts and lacerations on one side. He beamed at her.

The guests looked from Campbell to his mother and then mostly away.

Dillie rushed at him, grabbing a gray cashmere throw draped over a chair. She threw it around him, swaddling, and lifted him into her arms. She held him close to her breast.

"An…accident," she told the mothers with their chardonnays. "He…fell. On the playground. Yesterday."

She backed away from them, out of the room, and fled down the hall.

"Ms. Parker?" called a man in a beige worker's uniform from the foyer. "The hot water should be working again, I think."

She stopped and turned, scouring for the super's name. "Yes... thank you... Ernie."

"Little Campbell okay?" Ernie asked.

"*Yes*, he just needs to rest." She moved to go.

The super stepped nearer, his head slightly down. "Close call last night, huh?" he said with a lowered voice.

Dillie halted, turned again. "...last night...?"

Ernie got closer, with delicacy. "I never forget to put the trash out, you know. Thank God the trucks woke me up and reminded me. It was... well, the damn driver just didn't see him, I'm sure...."

"What... are you talking about?"

"If I may say so, ma'am, a Dumpster's not the safest place to play. Especially at three a.m., as tired as you were. Especially on the night when the dump trucks come."

"I don't...," she said, and then stopped.

"You were so tired, just sitting on the stoop. Really out of it, and I remember what that was like with my little ones. If you want, next time just wake me up. I can help you with him if he can't sleep. Really, I can, when your husband's away."

"Yes... we should," she thought she said. "Thank you."

Ernie smiled. "No harm done. Tykes spring back fast. I'm just glad I was there to, you know, stop them. Before they, you know..."

But Dillie had stopped listening.

She wandered away from the super, toward her bedroom, cradling her son. Lola followed from the foyer, shielding them both from the party.

Dillie looked up at her.

"Please get rid of them," she said. "Tell them Campbell is...
under the weather." Lola nodded and turned to go. Dillie touched
her arm. "No. Ill. Tell them Campbell is ill."

● ● ●

That night she decided to let Campbell sleep in Lola's room for
the first time, since he was now one, lest he grow too attached to
his mother.

three

Everything about Campbell had been a surprise, starting with his conception.

She and Rupert hadn't planned on starting a family right out of the gate. Dillie was still proving herself as a staff member at the *New Yorker*—with staff *writer* ambitions—and didn't want to take time off so soon. Rupert was in the prime throes of his hedge-fund career and too often on the road to consider fatherhood. They expected to enjoy at least a few years of young, carefree marriage in the city before hunkering down. Dillie targeted thirty, which seemed the gateway of other professional women she admired. Neither too early, nor too late.

So she was startled when her careful planning went awry and she became pregnant in their first year of marriage. As her mother would say: "If you want to make God laugh..."

She miscarried in the first trimester. Her OB was concerned that what she called an "incompetent cervix" would only worsen over time. Dillie and Rupert had to recalculate their life's schedule. Rupert, five years older, pushed for sooner than later, not only to increase the chances of success, but also because his father, in spotty health back home in London, yearned to meet his first grandchild.

"It's not like we need the second income," he told her, stating the obvious, when she worried anew about leaving the workforce right as she was seeding her writing career. "And frankly, you know, it's not much of an income anyway."

And likely never would be, she knew, and had since setting her sights on a magazine job during a *Vanity Fair* internship before her senior year at Duke. She'd successfully networked each floor of the Condé Nast building that summer and was thrilled by the *New Yorker* offer, however paltry, that came her way after graduation. It was that very job, and the social engagements it entailed, that led her to Rupert, by chance, at a charity dinner in the Met's Egyptian pavilion her first fall. Different tables, but that was scarcely a barrier once they'd spied each other during cocktails. Dillie was taken off the market, more or less, much faster than she'd anticipated, or could resist. Such was his British charm.

His Gramercy Park bachelor pad was more than spacious enough to build a life together, but Dillie was leery of ghosts of girlfriends past, of which she knew he'd had plenty. They'd considered buying but waited to see if the market settled or, she suspected, if Rupert could lure her farther uptown. As their wedding date neared, they found, through one of Rupert's colleagues, a much larger apartment on the border of SoHo and Chinatown, above a tony hair salon and across from a French cooking school. It was an obscenely priced rental (especially absent a doorman), a newly renovated and vast warehouse space carved into bedroom suites, home offices, and gallery spaces for Rupert's art, with an ample expansion pad of sorts for future family growth. *Throwing money out the window*, her mother always said of rentals, and this one in particular. *Month after month after...*

"I know you can *afford* it. That's not the point," she pestered on one of her phone calls. "I just question the wisdom of giving so much *power* to one city. I declare that town will drain it all out of you if you're not careful." And Dillie thanked her and cosigned the lease that day.

Her job at the *New Yorker* was prestigious, she felt, and promising, albeit not nearly as glamorous as her friends and family back in Nashville thought. Nor was it challenging, not at first, and not four years later. What started with dues-paying secretarial grunt work eventually led to proofreading restaurant reviews and "Talk of the Town" pieces and culminated, for now, in a staff position writing blurbs about Broadway and art shows for the calendar section, although even these were synopses of previous articles written by others higher up the food chain.

Ironically, it was her marriage to Rupert—certainly one of the city's more eligible bachelors—that both lent her cachet at Condé Nast and hampered her advancement. They enjoyed her company, she felt sure, and she was a conscientious worker, but no one seemed inclined to give her a boost. That she was now wealthier at twenty-six than her betters would likely ever be no doubt bred a jealousy that dampened her prospects further. The *New Yorker* worshipped wealth and privilege almost as much as they resented it.

Her first potential break came from a supervising editor who mentored her and suggested she write, on spec, a profile of Robert Moses's longtime secretary. If it passed muster, the editor promised to push it up the ranks at the magazine, with hopes of publication. Dillie had thrown herself into research, tracking down the children of the now-dead secretary, but the piece had stalled out after the miscarriage and the ensuing conflict over when to try again.

Surprisingly, her mother was in no rush for a grandchild. "Twenty-six seems awfully young for a modern woman," she said. "Plus it's wise to make sure the marriage sticks before you bring a child into the equation." Dillie ignored the dig of the second part while agreeing with the first, in spite of herself. Unimpressed by Rupert's money, Vivian had long been dubious about his fitness for husbandry and fatherhood, based on nothing but first impressions and instinct. "The playboy of the Western world," she'd deemed him early on in a good-natured but jeering jab to his face.

While Dillie steeled herself for the roller coaster she'd eventually have to reboard, she found herself, surprisingly, expectant again, less than a year later.

"That's stupendous news!" Rupert cheered upon returning from Shanghai late one night, startled to find her waiting up for him after the doctor's confirmation.

"It is," Dillie agreed, still shell-shocked and fretting over the Franklins' dinner party the previous week, when she'd had more wine than usual, unaware her child was growing inside. "Yes, it is."

They celebrated with a quiet weekend in Quogue, keeping their big news secret through the first trimester. This one, it seemed, was a keeper. Congratulations, joy, and endless advice from other mothers followed across the months. Dillie's cervix proved quite competent after all, and her pregnancy was, more or less, seamless and uncomplicated. Everything went by the book.

But the biggest surprise about Campbell was his gender. Up until the last moment, Campbell was a girl.

● ● ●

The twenty-week scan suggested it, and the twenty-four confirmed it. If Rupert was disappointed at not getting a son, he masked it well.

Vivian, on the other hand, was ecstatic.

"We're over the moon!" she squealed. "A baby girl! Is there anything more precious in this world than the thought of a baby girl? Khaki is positively pawing at the door to run out for provisions. Oh, Dillie, we were on tenterhooks, just waiting to hear. It's such thrilling news for us all."

Victoria hosted a boozy shower (at least for the others) in the fifth month, and they converted a guest room into the nursery with a spare bed. They interviewed baby nurses together, and Dillie steered Rupert away from the young Swedes and Swiss he preferred and settled on the more experienced—and expensive—Lola, who came with the agency's highest recommendation. Her soulful, steady demeanor countered Dillie's high-strung tendencies; nothing, it seemed, could ruffle her.

Dillie's only complication arose late in the game. The sixth month brought an occasional spiking pain, which her doctor diagnosed as minor placenta previa but assured her was not cause for alarm. They decided on a scheduled C-section, which would mitigate any risk during labor. The pain, while sharp, was sporadic and became less frequent as the month wore on.

"I had something similar with you," her mother reassured her. "But my doctor thought it was due to twins. Are you certain you're not having twins, too?"

"I am positive," Dillie assured her back, "that I am not having twins."

By month seven, she was in no mood for social engagements or much of anything else, but rose to the occasion for her favorite fall event: the New York Public Library Lions dinner, where she could witness her literary heroes receive their medallions of honor. Victoria helped her find the perfect formal maternity dress—centered around a masking wrap—and Dillie joined Rupert's colleagues at his firm's table in the Celeste Bartos Forum. Her imminent due date was, naturally, the main topic of conversation and celebration.

"You're one of the blessed ones," said Sagitha from across the table, for everyone's benefit. "You've gained no weight at all."

"Have you named her yet?" asked another wife, and Dillie said, "We're whittling down our list." She shot a quick glance to Rupert to remind him to keep it secret, to which he smiled and nodded. Waiters replaced salad plates with dinner.

She felt a sharp pain during the medallion ceremony.

It wasn't a crisis, but when it struck again during the tribute to Jonathan Franzen, she excused herself to the ladies' room.

"I'm fine," she whispered to Rupert, squeezing his hand as she heaved herself up as inconspicuously as possible and ducked through the tables, eyes down.

The ladies' lounge was unattended and empty, a lull during the ceremony. Dillie dabbed cold water on her temples and beheld her enormity in the mirror with both amusement and satisfaction. It would all be over soon, she knew. And worth every minute.

The pain seized her again, more lancing than before. She crumpled and caught herself on the counter. Arms embraced her from behind.

"I'm okay," Dillie insisted, clutching her middle. "Really, it's just…" She looked up to her savior in the mirror's reflection. A grand, regal Indian woman in a richly embroidered sari and festooned with her own medallion. A famous author, a lion, a luminary whose name she would have known if not flummoxed by the pain, which, notably, had subsided and then evaporated with her touch.

"Are you quite all right, my dear?" she purred with a calming British tongue through a warm, motherly smile. She waited until Dillie was stable before releasing her with bejeweled fingers. She smelled of rich, patchouli perfume.

"I am," said Dillie, sheepish, nodding at the medallion. "It's an honor to…collapse in front of you!" The woman laughed but held her concern. Dillie waved it away. "It's just…placenta previa, they call it." The woman nodded in understanding, and Dillie added, "It's a little pesky at times. But it passes. I'm not concerned."

"Your first child?" the woman asked. Dillie nodded and said, "Do you have any?"

"Oh yes," the exotically beautiful woman said, beaming. "It's a grand wonder." She glanced down. "And quite soon for you. When is he due?"

"Twenty-three days, seventeen hours, forty-two minutes," Dillie answered to both their laughter. "But it's a 'she.' I'm having a girl."

The woman bunched her brow, inspected her again. "Oh, I don't think so," she said with a calming assurance. "A beautiful baby boy, I think."

Dillie's first instinct was to drop it. She didn't.

"Well, I've had all the tests," she said delicately, so as not to seem contrarian. She laughed again and said, "We've even painted the nursery pink!"

The woman laughed with her and said, "Then he will be very modern." She waited a brief moment and said, "Show me your hands." Puzzled but obedient, Dillie held them out.

The woman nodded. "Yes, you offer them palms down. You see?" Dillie nodded, still not understanding.

"And your belly," the woman added, gently running her hand in circles on it. "Compact. Rounded. Like a…"

"…basketball?" Dillie said, a flash memory from some gender-guessing article she'd read and dismissed along the way. The woman smiled, her eyes brightening, making progress.

Outside was applause. For Franzen, or one of the others.

The woman lifted her ribboned medallion over her head, carefully turned Dillie back to the mirror. "Now look," she said, reaching around to dangle it just in front of Dillie's stomach. It spun and rotated.

"It moves in a circle," she said, locking eyes in the mirror. "With a girl, it would tick-tock, like a pendulum." Dillie looked down, slightly hypnotized by the circling ornament and the woman's intense attention. It enveloped and soothed her, like an embrace.

When she glanced back up, the woman's face was stuck in a grimace.

"What?" Dillie asked. "What is it?"

The woman shook her head, dismissing it. "Life has been too easy for you, that's all." She pulled back the medallion. The examination was over.

"Is something wrong?" Dillie pressed. The woman donned her medallion and smiled again. "Challenges make life interesting," she said. "Overcoming them makes it meaningful. It's how we find out who we are."

Outside, the emcee announced the next recipient. More applause.

The woman leaned in, gently held Dillie's face, left a soft kiss on her forehead. "I wish you well, my dear," she said. "Everything is about to change." And she was gone from the room.

Two more women entered, stopping first at the mirror. Dillie stood still, digesting. "But I don't want things to...," she said to the now-gone seer. "Wait!"

She hurried back to the ceremony, scanned the room, table to table. The woman was nowhere.

Rupert held her chair upon her return and leaned in with a concerned look. "I'm fine," Dillie whispered, patting his hand. "I'm A-OK."

They left before the final award, to the table's generous understanding, given her special, exciting condition.

● ● ●

So Dillie's shock was tempered and half-baked when, coming to after her C-section, she saw the nurse smiling over her with a reddish-pink newborn swaddled in blue.

Rupert was ecstatic. Vivian was speechless.

"Did you hear me, Mom?" Dillie asked in the phone silence from her hospital bed.

"I heard you," said a halting Vivian, calibrating her response. "I'm just...puzzled...as to how such an error could have been made. I've never heard of such an error."

"He's very beautiful," Dillie added, gingerly cradling him. "And healthy." She added, with a laugh, "Thank God we picked an all-purpose name."

"And you're certain there's no mistake?" Vivian asked. "No mix-up of any sort? That does happen, especially in overcrowded hospitals."

"There's no mistake, and the hospital is quite orderly," Dillie teased. "Should I send him back?"

"Well, I'm thrilled for you both," her mother finally said. "Certainly I am. I just hope you're in good hands at that place. And Khaki will have to knit new booties, of course. In the appropriate color."

"I bet she'll have them finished by the end of this call," Dillie said, cooing at her beautiful new baby boy.

Lola was a godsend from day one. Their temporary, three-month arrangement was extended when two separate replacement nannies didn't work out: the first too skittish and flaky, and, Dillie suspected, likely on drugs of some sort. The second was far more promising, but her mother died within the first two weeks, prompting her return to her homeland of Trinidad. Fortunately, Lola was newly available again and agreed to come back until a permanent replacement could be found. So expert and thorough she was, Dillie kept putting off a new round of interviews. Rupert heartily endorsed the extra expense, deeming Dillie's peace of mind priceless.

All was joy for the first many months. Dillie took to mother-hood naturally, almost effortlessly, which surprised her. Whatever reticence or apprehension she'd felt prebirth quickly evaporated when she held Campbell in her arms. His was a weightless, sunny delight. With Lola's support and gentle counsel, Dillie mastered the art of new parenthood. Perhaps more heartening, so did Rupert.

Vivian's pre-Christmas visit, just days after the birth, was both jubilant and frictionless. She cradled and cooed, fawned and, one late afternoon, even wept at the glorious beauty of her first grandchild. "I promised your father I wouldn't fall to pieces," she whispered when Dillie found her by the window, rocking the baby and dabbing her eyes. "Don't blow the whistle on me."

It wasn't until the following September, after a stormy winter and wilting summer, that Dillie began to splinter.

four

There was no trigger she could pinpoint. Perhaps it was the additional burden of Rupert's absence when he was put on a new deal after Labor Day that often kept him in Chicago, leaving her a single parent during the week. Or the stress of her deadlines when she returned to the *New Yorker* full time, pushing harder to make up for lost time.

Her anxiety spiked when, assigned to a longer blurb on the Joffrey's upcoming fall season, she lost a week's work the day before the issue locked. Her edited and proofed article, which she'd saved on both her computer and in the cloud, was one morning on neither, and thoroughly corrupted in an old e-mail, prompting a frantic and embarrassing *mea culpa* to her boss. Fortunately, Glen's files were orderly and pristine, and she forwarded the latest draft to Dillie, who pulled an all-nighter whittling it back into shape. Campbell mercifully slept through the night, as was his nature. But the mishap—unprecedented and surely due to her own bleary Mom-brain—still mystified and rattled her. The AWOL document never resurfaced, permanently lost in the cyber ether, through glitch or incompetence.

Her stress compounded when Rupert's father suffered a minor stroke, derailing their weekend apple-picking excursion to Warwick and leaving her alone for another ten days, as Rupert made a last-minute return to London. Luckily, the old man expected a full recovery, but the episode saddled her with more urgency to introduce Campbell to his paternal grandfather before it was too late. She vowed to take him as soon as he was old enough for the transatlantic flight.

But her breaking point came with the sudden infestation of rats.

At first she thought the faint noise was coming from her downstairs neighbor, a producer of an early-morning news program who she knew rose long before dawn. It began quietly, a light scampering across the floor, which could have been a new puppy, although she'd never seen or heard it before. It was easy to dismiss the first few nights, and such was her usual exhaustion that she had no trouble returning to sleep.

It soon became clear the noise was not an echo or refracted sound from another apartment. The rodent was in her bedroom. Nightly.

It announced itself with a spastic scratching in the corner of their wooden floor. It moved diagonally across the room, silenced by the thick area rug, only to scratch anew when it reached the far side. Dillie bolted in bed as it scurried underneath, switching on the lamp and squinting at its final destination as her eyes adjusted to the light. It must have disappeared into a never-knew-existed hole by the wall, or else was hiding under her dresser. In any event, the light and sudden movement had scared it off.

It became bolder by the night.

Sometimes it would start overhead, above the ceiling, racing across the top. It would pause in the middle of the room, often long enough for Dillie to think it had gone away, only to resume its trajectory across and then down through the inside of the wall.

When it finished doing whatever it had come to do, it would retrace its steps up and over and back down from where it came.

Ernie apologized and scheduled exterminators, who found no signs but laid out extra traps in the back hallways and near the garbage chutes.

"No, I haven't had any problems," said Beatrice from the seventh floor when Dillie asked her in the elevator. "We had one a couple years ago, a real monster," said the youngish fashion designer on three when she passed him coming in as she was going out. "But not since. I'll ask Aaron when he comes home, but I think he would have said something."

"Thank you," said Dillie. "These old buildings, you know." And the designer nodded and said, "These old buildings. But they've got them in new ones, too. And they carry that awful virus."

She quizzed the younger maintenance men, on all shifts, to find out if other residents had reported a similar issue. It wasn't that she didn't trust Ernie; she just expected him to downplay the problem. The men were no help.

The nightly intrusion never woke Campbell, whose crib Dillie pulled closer and closer to her own bed. Nor did it faze Booray, who stirred only when Dillie moved about the room, searching. She feared he might be losing his hearing, much too soon.

"No, I haven't seen or heard that," said Lola daily, when Dillie asked anew after nights of increasingly little sleep. Still, they worked together one morning to seal the pantry food in plastic, lidded containers.

She checked the exterminator's traps every morning in the service hallways and deemed them useless. She researched online and ordered a humane poison that, according to the reviews, caused little pain while getting the job done. More importantly, it could be baited in tamper-proof containers. She added these to the arsenal by the garbage chute.

The intruder stayed away when Rupert was in town, which more frustrated than relieved her. On those nights, she slept even less, lying in wait for any noise, so she could rouse him and prove it was real. It never came.

When it started gnawing at the legs on Campbell's crib, her battle escalated to war.

Gone was any pretense of sleep, as she sat sentry all night, coiled in bed, flashlight in hand. She moved Campbell to her bed, but he was restless and cranky there, and the commotion confused and excited Booray, who stood bedside, wagging his tail. Her only option was to put him back in his crib and stay up to watch and listen.

Lola shook her awake the next morning. Campbell was wailing. Booray had wet the floor. Her alarm was blaring. Dillie shot up, running late for a breakfast meeting with Glen.

In spite of the gnawing and scraping at the crib's legs, neither she nor Lola could find any marks. Lola changed and fed Campbell; Dillie walked Booray, calling her editor to apologize and learning that her breakfast was actually scheduled for the following day.

She was slow to take the medications her doctor prescribed at her October visit, but once she stopped nursing in the eleventh month, finally relented for the much-needed homeopathic sleeping aid, which she was assured was non-habit-forming and without harsh side effects. It did the trick, and for the first time in weeks, she slept through the night to her six a.m. alarm.

Then the horror of Campbell's first birthday arrived. Rats became the least of her concerns.

That afternoon, hours after Lola had ushered out the shocked party guests, she returned to Dillie's bedroom.

"I'm fine," Dillie said automatically. She stood in the middle of the room while Campbell napped in his crib, fully covered to mask his injuries. The whole day a torment of mystery.

Out the window, Crosby Street darkened. "But I think...," she added, rubbing her arms, "...it's time Campbell slept in his nursery."

Lola nodded and went to lift the sleeping Campbell into her arms.

"The books say," Dillie continued, "after the first year, the child should sleep in his own room."

Lola smiled and moved toward the door.

"That's what the books say...," Dillie repeated.

"Yes, ma'am," said Lola.

"Lola?" she said, stopping her at the door. "There has to be...I mean, I couldn't have..." Her eyes met Lola's, open and pleading.

"Everything will be just fine," Lola assured her. "Good night."

Dillie found the bottles her doctor had prescribed, in a canvas tote bag at the back of her closet. She inspected each label and, using her finger, poked through the protective foil.

Lola woke Campbell long enough to feed and bathe him. She read him *Runaway Bunny* while rocking him back to sleep in the now-blue nursery. She carefully lay him in his spare crib for the first time, tucking him in with a still-unused cashmere blanket. She kissed her fingertips, touched them to his head.

Then she went, very lightly, to her own single bed. With knowing hands, she reached under and pulled out a light brown suitcase, which she placed on her mattress. She fished the key from her ring, unlocked and gently sprung both latches, catching to keep them silent.

Lola lifted the lid and reached inside, sorting.

five

The winter, spring, summer, and following fall marked a blessed return to normalcy.

Whatever angst or disturbance that had plagued Dillie in the months leading up to Campbell's first birthday evaporated between Christmas and the new year's first big snowstorm.

The rodent traps—which Ernie had warned might take a while to prove effective—made a difference even before Christmas, itself a welcome gift. Now Dillie slept through the entire, silent nights, along with the rest of her family, waking fresh and charged for the busiest of seasons.

Most importantly, Dillie became, again, the mother she'd been at the beginning. Just as the Indian literary lion promised, it was a grand wonder.

Her funk, she'd read on blogs, was most likely a delayed postpartum depression, a compounded buildup from those exhausting first few months of interrupted sleep, late-night feedings, the emotional seesaw of glee and anxiety, not to mention the hormonal upheaval as her body tried to acclimate and right itself. This, she learned with substantial relief, was more common than widely acknowledged. Many new mothers—especially those who jumped back into their careers too quickly—lived in denial that the crush of depression could land several months late, just when they thought they'd gained their sea legs. The younger ones, she'd read, tended to overestimate their stamina and ability to fight on all fronts at once. *Guilty*, Dillie realized and accepted.

Perhaps the biggest relief was the demystification, the knowing what had triggered her odd behavior. With her doctor's assistance, it was all soon forgotten, leaving her to refocus on life, work, and especially motherhood. She attacked them all with a welcome, multitasking urgency.

She kept to the same daily schedule, almost like a ritual: waking early with enough rise-and-shine clatter to alert Lola, who would open the nursery door so Dillie could lift a beaming Campbell from his crib. After a brief, bonding playtime and breakfast (whipped up by Dillie), she'd get ready for work, squeezing out a few last moments with Campbell before heading downtown. She'd check in by phone throughout the day, dash back for a quick lunch and visit, and, at five-thirty precisely, rush home to feed and bathe him, read him to sleep, and gently tuck him in. Her night would then often continue with work-related parties, the occasional art opening, and on her favorite mellow nights, a late dinner with Rupert at Café Cluny. On weekends, whenever possible, she resumed her volunteer tutoring for adult literacy at Hunter College.

Lola stayed on, voluntarily trimming her salary—insisting, really—down to normal nanny levels. Dillie tweaked her work schedule to accommodate Lola's Sunday/Monday days off, when she would decamp to her other life in Queens, returning early Tuesday refreshed and with her gorgeous braids newly redone. When Rupert was out of town, they kept each other company over five-dollar backgammon (Lola was unbeatable unless she chose otherwise) and their shared crush on Anderson Cooper.

Lola seamlessly became part of the family, not only indispensable, but increasingly beloved.

February brought Dillie's first career breakthrough, when Glen sparked to her pitch for a six-thousand-word feature on Shirley Jackson's storied history with the magazine. It would be on contingency, and she still had her fact-checking day job, but it dangled the promise of her first byline and membership in the elusive "contributors" club.

Rupert wrapped up his Chicago deal in mid-March and begged off from further travel until a new London venture percolating for the fall. In the meantime, he shouldered his husband and father duties with a passionate zeal that surprised even Dillie.

Campbell was an effortless delight—robust and good-natured and always healthy except for a late-April two-day fever that peaked at 101 yet failed to zap his cheery disposition. Dillie kept him on a strict vaccine schedule, like his pediatrician suggested.

Just before Memorial Day, Rupert dragged Dillie uptown to check out a Rosario Candela prewar on Fifth Avenue, newly on the market, although she felt they were too young for the Upper East Side. "But it has a doorman," he said. "And park views."

"We might as well move to Stepford," she joked, closing the door on the notion.

In late-June, Victoria and her husband took them to the much ballyhooed *Applause* revival at the Golden, which they found energetic but overrated. But they all agreed the new girl playing Eve had chops and a future. "Did you catch her Tony speech last week? About her dead father?" said Victoria. "Totally wrecked me."

July and August brought weekend trips to their rented Quogue home, farmers' markets, and blissful beach days complete with a photo shoot for their Christmas card. Booray and Campbell adored each other, which made for a perfect family picture of near-total blondness.

With Labor Day came the return to the grind and start of the fall social season, as Dillie raced to rewrite her piece, according to Glen's first round of edits, alternating between her little workspace at the *NewYorker* and the roomier freedom of NeueHouse. Glen had targeted a Thanksgiving publication date—a high-profile issue with luxury Christmas ads—and Dillie checked, refined, and shaped her story with admirable precision. She would not blow her debut.

Dillie could do it all, she realized with relief and pride. Certainly she had help, with a loving husband and devoted nanny, for which she was grateful. She knew how fortunate—privileged, really—she was. But her earlier anxieties that motherhood and career would overwhelm, as perhaps they had for a brief, harmless spell a year ago—just a blip, she now acknowledged—were gone and nearly forgotten.

At the end of September, deeming them no longer needed and wary of toxic buildup, Dillie stopped taking her meds altogether.

● ● ●

"I'll be vewy, vewy quiet," Dillie whispered in her best Elmer Fudd, riding Rupert piggyback toward the kitchen in the early-dawn quiet before another work trip. "Nobody will know." Booray bounded along, tail swinging.

"You want the TSA to nail me for human trafficking?" Rupert joked back, pulling his luggage behind. He gently shrugged her off, but she clung, on tiptoes to kiss the back of his neck. He spun and wrapped her in a hug.

"One week to nail this down," he reminded her, brushing her unkempt hair off her forehead. And then their fall Vermont getaway, at the peak of tree beauty—a belated anniversary trip, complete with their beloved son. "Can I get that in writing?" she asked.

He held her face. "You know why I do all this?" he asked rhetorically. Dillie nodded with a deep understanding and said, "So you can buy more paintings." He nodded with her before breaking the act with a sudden tickling. She squealed a giggle, quickly stifled. Booray barked once.

"Ssh!" she ordered them all, pointing back toward the nursery with a finger wag.

Rupert checked his phone. "The car's here," he said, springing. He leaned in for a quick kiss, which Dillie held, running her hands down his arms. She pulled back.

"Where's the watch I gave you?" she asked of her anniversary present, a shamefully expensive Tiffany CT60 made more palatable with the credit card miles she'd accrue. And the midnight-blue dial was unique to his collection.

"In my locker at the racquet club," he said, heading for the door. "I'll grab it on my way to the airport. I'm already late." She turned him one last time.

"I love you, Rupert. So very much."

"You really want me to miss this flight, don't you?" he teased, enveloping her. Booray, confused if he was coming or going, barked again.

From the Dropcam feed on Dillie's laptop perched on the kitchen counter came Campbell's chirping warble.

"Drat, I think we woke the boy," said Dillie, watching him rustle in his crib. "It's too early."

Rupert hurried out the door to the elevator.

"Go! Go!" Dillie said, smacking his rear end. "Give your father my love. I hope he's feeling better."

She closed and locked the door, looked around the kitchen now bathed in morning. Campbell chirped again on the monitor, expectantly. She padded down the hall to the nursery, listened, heard the shower running just beyond. She lightly rapped on the door.

"Lola?" she whispered. "Can I come in?" After a pause to respect her privacy, she slowly cracked the door, peeked in. Campbell stood in his crib, beaming, waiting.

"Good morning, little man," she said, going to him.

She stopped short.

Canopied through the air above his crib, on clotheslines, were dozens of bright satin pouches. Some were topped with dismembered doll heads, others adorned with plucked feathers of all sorts, strings of beads, and dangling metal crosses, like grotesque Christmas ornaments.

A sharp scent turned her to the dresser. A cluster of charred incense sticks, fanning out from a wooden holder, ashes pooled in a reservoir. She sniffed closer and recoiled: a dense and biting aroma that smelled like sage mixed with vinegar.

The shower stopped.

"Lola?" Dillie called out.

A silence, followed by a rush of activity. Sliding shower door, a scramble for towels.

"Coming...," Lola said from inside. She flung open the door, tying her terry-cloth robe, nervously patting her braids. "I was just going to bring him out to you—"

"What is all this?" Dillie cut her off, pointing.

"Just decorations," said Lola, racing to untie one end of a clothesline from a brass hook in the wall. "I put them up at night. Campbell likes them."

"Well, *I* don't like them. And I don't want *him* to like them. They're freaky."

"They're from a different culture, yes." Lola nodded, avoiding Dillie's stare as she spooled the lines around her arm like a hose.

Dillie pointed to the dresser. "And this?"

Lola shrugged. "Just incense."

"You've been burning sticks in my son's room?"

"I extinguish them before I go to bed."

"I'm more worried about what he's breathing in."

Lola seemed offended at the suggestion. "It's organic and non-toxic. Certainly."

Dillie looked around, bewildered. "I think I'm most worried about the...weirdness of it all."

"I take it down each morning," Lola insisted. "I didn't expect you this early."

Dillie inspected one of the doll heads, decapitated from a Barbie and sewn right onto the pouch. "What *are* they?"

"*Paket congos*. Just charms, really. They give the home a good energy."

"They give me the creeps," Dillie said. "Please get rid of them. All of them."

"And they keep away bad things," Lola added with care.

Dillie looked at her. "We don't have bad things." Then: "How long have you been doing all this?"

"Since his birthday."

"You've been surrounding my son with these…horrors…for ten months?"

"And haven't things been nicer?" Lola said delicately. "No more close calls? Late-night wanderings…?"

Dillie stiffened, as if slapped. "Lola, I had a…condition. I explained it to you. I needed a little help, which I got. It's over."

Lola pulled closer, shielding Campbell, and spoke in her ear. "It is not you, Dillie. A *diab* is stalking your child."

Dillie forced a laugh. "A…what?"

"An evil," Lola went on, her eyes wide. "A demon. Playing with your mind. Incredibly powerful, more powerful every day…"

Dillie heard her. "Lola, please don't do this. You're a nurse. A medical professional. What has gotten into you?"

Lola held firm. Exasperated, Dillie grabbed the coil and wadded it into a ball. "No, Dillie," Lola begged. "Please!"

Dillie threw it out the door, down the hallway. "Goddammit, did you have to pick this week to show your lunacy? I can't…"

"You must believe me," Lola insisted, grasping her arm. "It will come back, like a virus, stronger than ever. It wants your *son!*"

"Stop it, Lola!" Dillie screamed.

Over Lola's shoulder, Campbell still stood in his crib, smiling at them both. Dillie calmed herself, went to lift him out. She held his head against her shoulder and moved toward the door before turning back.

"Lola, you told me you wanted to stay on. If you've changed your mind, just say so."

"I haven't," Lola said.

Dillie looked down, hesitant to pull rank on her friend and yet unable to avoid it. "I can't have…your black magic around my son.

We'll interview when Rupert gets back." She carried Campbell into the kitchen for breakfast. While his oatmeal cooked, she wrapped the clothesline in a white plastic garbage bag, tied it securely, and dropped it down the chute.

It was Wednesday, the twenty-sixth of October.

six

The hot water went out the next morning, midshower, before an early meeting with Glen.

"I thought the tankless never ran out," Dillie said, shivering and sudsy in her robe, as Ernie tinkered with the unit in the utility room.

"They do require maintenance," he said, flushing the reservoir and adjusting the temperature. "Especially with the city's hard water." He promised to bring in an expert to make it right before Campbell's bath that evening. Dillie sponged off the soap residue at her sink, grateful she hadn't washed her hair that morning.

Glen went over her final tweaks and edits for Dillie's piece—all astute and supportive but surprisingly many, considering the fact-checkers and first-round proofers had already signed off. Dillie nodded and tried to keep up, determined to turn it around quickly before her deadline the following Thursday. Glen droned on, more exacting than usual.

"Is everything all right?" asked Glen, startling her. "Yes," Dillie replied, nodding more emphatically. "You seem a little scatter-shot," Glen added.

Dillie waved it off. "I'm fine," she insisted. "Rupert's gone again, and just a few issues with the nanny, that's all. Well, that and the hot water. That's why I was a little late. No biggie." She paused, and then opted not to elaborate.

"We can push the piece, you know," said Glen. "We just need to decide right now."

Dillie shook her head. "Absolutely not. I've got this. And I really appreciate your help."

Although Lola's stunt had unsettled her—spooked, really—she still left Campbell in her care. After all, she'd been a saint from the beginning, not only for her expertise, but also for her soothing demeanor and increasingly as a trusted confidante. Dillie could scarcely imagine the family without her. And certainly Campbell would miss her, as one of the first faces and voices he'd ever known.

There was nothing dangerous about Lola—she was remarkably normal, if not blasé—but the charms, spells, and voodoo, regardless of her native culture, were unacceptable. She hadn't revealed her religious fervor during the interview process, or at least Dillie hadn't picked up on it, not expecting something quite so exotic. And while she'd always intended to expose Campbell to different religions, she hadn't planned on this one, with its hexes and curses and what next? *Chicken blood? Snake dancing?* she thought, quickly pulling back from the dark humor of it all.

Dillie found the realization of Lola's true self destabilizing, the intensity of her delusional passion particularly disturbing—*diab?* demon? coming after her son?—while at the same time needing her that week more than ever. Still, after putting in daily face time at the office, she worked from home and cared for Campbell more closely, using Lola as babysitter only when necessary. And even when home, she kept a watchful eye on the Dropcam feed trained on his crib from her laptop.

On Thursday, her home Wi-Fi went down just as she was trying to access the latest draft of her article in the cloud. When resetting the modem and restarting her laptop didn't work, she called her provider and waited on hold while they checked for service interruptions in the area, of which they claimed there were none.

"But my work is there," Dillie stressed, increasingly panicked. "It's proofed and fact-checked," which the operator didn't understand, repeating his apology for the inconvenience.

The Genius Bar on Prince Street was able to retrieve them—five identically named files, which they advised her against and she insisted she hadn't done—and she copied them over to a flash drive to sort through later, in order to find the correct and most up-to-date version. She held tightly to Campbell, who smiled back at the technicians and customers, curious at the noisy goings-on and happy to be on an outing with his mother.

In her rush, she'd left the coffeemaker on, which should have turned off automatically but hadn't, burning dry and cracking the glass carafe. She threw the whole contraption down the trash chute, no longer trusting it and wondering—but not asking—why Lola hadn't smelled it roasting itself up. Unless she was suddenly unhelpful, borderline vindictive, after Dillie threw her witchcraft decorations down the same trash chute two days earlier.

Glen texted her, making sure she'd gotten her earlier e-mail, which she hadn't because of the down Wi-Fi, but she hadn't gotten it on her phone either and apologized and asked Glen to resend, now that that everything was, apparently, working properly again. Ditto Victoria, whose e-mail about the Grace Church School junior kindergarten application had landed in her spam folder.

"The earlier the better, my pet," Victoria advised when she called. "So we can prepare the battlefield. Which it is."

"I'm on it!" Dillie said, both grateful for Victoria's influence at the school and slightly irritated the process required such ludicrously advanced planning. Campbell wasn't even talking yet, so *nursery school* admissions testing seemed grossly premature. "Life in the big city," her mother would say with contempt.

On Friday, what had been a slow drain in her bathroom sink became a full backup, apartment-wide.

"I'm so sorry," Dillie said to Ernie when he came to rooter it. "I should have called at the first sign." The clog relented a bit but was stubborn, and he scheduled a plumber to check the main line later that day. "You're really earning your keep this week," joked Dillie, more sheepish than annoyed at the latest apartment debacle, as if she were somehow responsible, which was preposterous.

The weather turned on Saturday, bringing an early winter bite to the city. "Bundle up, little mouse!" she told Campbell, tying the hood on his new Brooks Brothers safety orange parka before a trip to the Flatiron Home Depot to restock lightbulbs that had burned out in the living room, the kitchen, the bedroom closet. "Aren't the new ones supposed to last longer?" she asked the salesperson, who advised her to keep her receipt.

She and Campbell Skyped with Rupert twice a day, at his London office in the morning and at his hotel before dinner. The transatlantic wizardry scarcely registered with Campbell, although he did perk to his father's voice and always gravitated to the keyboard buttons. "Careful," Dillie said, gently diverting his curious fingers. "You'll cut off Daddy." His trip had been extended by a day, which meant canceling dinner with Greer and Emerson (fine by her, with her deadline looming). At least his father was doing better, a relief to them both. Still, she wanted Rupert back, and he promised no more work delays.

"Miss you! Love you!" she said before signing off, puppeteering Campbell's hand in a goodbye wave.

Lola had snapped back to her typical quiet efficiency, although she seemed more conscientious than usual. She even volunteered to forgo her days off, with Rupert away. "That's generous of you, but we'll be fine," Dillie assured her, feeling both confident and accomplished after submitting her final piece to the magazine two days early. Lola nodded and roamed the living room, dining room, and the landing by the back stairs. She appeared to be checking for drafts by the windows and doors—Dillie simply ignored her—before returning to the nursery to pack her bag for home.

On Saturday evening, after Lola had left for her weekend, the weather dropped another several degrees.

"Thank goodness we're toasty together inside," Dillie told Campbell before bed, rubbing noses while he giggled.

seven

Early Monday morning, Dillie's copyeditor called in a panic. "I don't understand," Dillie protested. "I'm sure I sent the right one. I know I did."

She had to admit her error when the copyeditor returned the file. It was at least three drafts old, before Glen's latest rounds of notes. Baffled, and now panicked herself, she promised to find and send the correct version by the end of day. "Please don't tell Glen," she pleaded. "I know I have it here somewhere."

She should have rushed to the office to handle this, but Campbell had woken up moody and flush, and she feared he was coming down with something. It would be unprofessional to haul a cranky and possibly feverish toddler to work, and her emergency babysitter was booked for the day on the Upper West Side. She was tempted to call Lola, who could have been there within the hour, but she didn't want to admit that she was overwhelmed, that a series of inexplicable and unfortunate events had hit so suddenly. She fed Campbell and sat him in front of *Postcards from Buster* in the alcove off the kitchen. She needed coffee but had thrown out her machine—a rash, impulsive tantrum she now regretted when she could have easily replaced the ruined carafe at the Sur La Table down the street. Instead, she boiled water for tea and realized she'd forgotten to take Booray out, which explained the accident on the kitchen floor she quickly cleaned and disinfected.

"My bad, Boo," she admitted, without apology, lest he think this the new normal.

Her laptop slowed to a near-freeze as she searched through her old files, knowing she had saved the correct one—inconceivable she hadn't—but the spinning disk on her screen stuck. Another call to tech support (she didn't have time for the Genius Bar, especially with a temperamental Campbell in tow) helped her pinpoint the "runaway" apps that were eating up her memory. "I didn't even know they were running," she told the tech. "I don't even know what they are." With his help, she unchecked and uninstalled what needed to be, but even after the reboot was unable to locate the most recent draft of her article. The closest she could find was one draft old, which confused and infuriated her—how and when did she delete the one she needed?—and the tech carefully talked her through saving it in three different locations, so it would not happen again.

She thanked him profusely, although she already knew the process; she'd been doing all this *for years,* and blamed her apparent sloppiness on the combination of the looming deadline and the pressure of her magazine debut coupled with taking care of Campbell by herself and the annoying sporadic chirp of the hallway smoke detector that needed a new battery but was too high to reach without a ladder she didn't have and didn't want to bother Ernie about, since he'd just been there to replace the lightbulbs that had died prematurely. She didn't want to be *that tenant*, so the chirping continued on its own schedule and when she least expected it.

A jolt of memory took her back to last fall—roughly this time—when it had seemed like she was under mysterious assault from all directions to the point she'd feared she was losing her mind. She stiffened with the horror that it could be happening again, a relapse into whatever mental illness had plagued her right when she felt on top of the world. She dismissed it outright: That was entirely different. She'd been suffering from a diagnosable, clinical condition—more common than most mothers chose to admit—and had been successfully treated and cured. Postpartum did not flare up late in the second year, and in any event, her current headaches were garden variety compared to the last ones: mere tech glitches, all explainable, snowballing the way glitches often did and no reason to fall apart or panic. Surely she'd developed stronger coping skills than that. In fact, she thought with sudden relief, she could likely trace her missing draft back to her Rupert Skype calls, with Campbell banging away at her keyboard, inadvertently sending the file deep into the cyber hinterland. Or perhaps Mercury was very much in retrograde, if she believed in such a thing.

The door buzzer rang from the street level, jarring her. On the security cam by the front door, she saw the FreshDirect deliveryman with their Monday groceries, which he brought up in cardboard boxes and unloaded on the kitchen counter. "I'm sorry, I think this is the wrong order," she said after a cursory glance at the seaweed wraps and odd spices and a sugary cartoon cereal she'd never feed her child, but not the almond milk and organic yogurt she needed for his oatmeal, which was also missing. The deliveryman apologized and promised to return later with the correct order.

Vivian called, as she usually did on Monday mornings after yoga, but Dillie let it go to voice mail as she scrambled to compare files that differed only slightly and struggled to remember which changes she'd made in which draft. She finally decided the only solution was to start from scratch, transposing the entire article, piecing together the different drafts with the edits from memory and based on prior e-mails—all doable, with time and concentration, both of which she'd have to carve out today. She called to explain the situation to Glen, apologizing profusely, again refusing to postpone the piece, and swore she'd turn it around by the next morning.

The door buzzer rang again, but not the groceries she was expecting. It was their UPS man, trying to deliver a large package to the Connors on five. She rang him in and had fresh thoughts about the benefits of a doorman to prevent these distractions and intrusions.

By lunch she'd finished just over a third—the task was less daunting than she'd feared, as her latest edits and tweaks were fresh on her mind—and every few minutes she saved it anew, on two separate flash drives, in the cloud, and in e-mails she sent to herself on different accounts and one to Rupert with the subject: *Please Keep.*

She canceled Campbell's afternoon playdate with Jeremy, which she felt bad about, although his mother took it in stride. "Don't sweat it," insisted Aline. "Work comes first. It's gotten a little chilly anyway." Campbell would still get his playtime, Dillie vowed to herself, but a multitasking one later so she could keep on schedule. Whatever funk he'd woken up with had worn off, replaced with his typical sunniness, his color and temperature back to normal. It was as if he'd pulled himself together to help bolster his mother on her no-good day.

After his post-lunch nap and with her fresh draft nearly done, Dillie bundled him up in Khaki's latest knit creation and strapped him into his stroller.

• • •

The Washington Square tot playground was more crowded than she'd expected, although the afternoon sun had warmed things up a bit. She kept Campbell close to her bench but let him wander to other children and nearby activities, while she proofed on her iPad. It was easy to keep his orange parka in her periphery as she read and made notations. Other young mothers and nannies, many she recognized from previous visits, looked after the flock and encouraged their play while gently diffusing any minor dustups.

"Come here, Campbell," she called to him, wiping his nose before sending him back out to the sandbox. "Share, please," she chided when he became a bit territorial with his space. "Let others join you."

Her article seemed stronger than she remembered. It read faster and tracked better, perhaps benefitting from her urgency and focus. It crackled. She hoped Glen would notice.

"Back this way," she said when Campbell stubbornly obstructed the miniature slide that a little redheaded girl was trying to dismount. "Let her off, please."

The girl's dark-haired mother (the father must be fiery red, she thought) laughed and introduced the curious toddlers. "May I?" she asked Dillie, indicating the five-step ladder up the minislide. Campbell was a regular on it, and Dillie smiled and nodded, proud that he waited his turn. "Thank you," she said to the mother, who monitored him with the others. She looked vaguely familiar, although Dillie couldn't place from where. Either they were on the same schedule here, or had potentially seen each other at any number of events around town. She was slightly older with a distinguished Roman nose and strikingly stylish in her dove-gray overcoat, the season's color among the smart set. For a flash, Dillie fretted she might be the wife of one of Rupert's colleagues, or even a colleague herself, but that would be a doubtful coincidence and surely her memory was sharper than that. Most likely, she simply looked like many other young, professional mothers in the city juggling family and career, as was she. Dillie hoped she herself came across as centered and unruffled as this put-together woman with a lilting, unhurried laugh.

She highlighted a string of typos in the middle of her piece, to fix when she returned to her computer. She traced the errors back to the UPS doorman interruption earlier that morning.

The dark-haired mother had migrated with the children's brigade over to the toddler-sized jungle gym next to the swing set. Her other child—an older blond boy—threw a serious wrench into Dillie's imagined redheaded father. Perhaps a recessive gene, or even adopted children. Dillie focused on her article, determined to finish proofing before leaving the playground, even though her iPad was dangerously low on power. She could have sworn she'd recharged it.

A sharp wind caught her attention. Clouds had covered the afternoon sun. Dillie checked her watch, later than she realized. She slipped her iPad into her satchel. "Time to go, Campbell!" she called out, looking up.

The dark-haired mother gently pushed Campbell on the swings across the way.

Dillie glanced around for her redheaded daughter and blond son. They were gone.

The dark-haired woman pushed again. Campbell giggled.

Dillie stood, looked around the jungle gym, the slide, the sandbox, the benches, and trees. The woman's children had vanished. Her protective instincts sharpening, she had to alert their mother they had wandered off. "Excuse me," she said, moving toward her with a rapid wave. "Hello?"

Just beyond the playground fence, the redheaded girl walked away toward the arch, hand in hand with an auburn-haired woman who was clearly her real mother. In the distance, by the fountain, the blond boy followed his nanny and younger brother in protest, kicking rocks.

Dillie looked back at the swings. The woman, smiling, spooled and unspooled Campbell in a shallow twist. Gently, safely, just a slight, controlled movement that thrilled him nonetheless. She laughed with him.

Dillie moved more quickly, arrived at the swing set edge.

The woman slowed down the swing to a stop and held it steady by the chains.

"Yes?" the woman asked her. "Is something wrong?" She spoke with crisp British diction.

"I panicked for a moment," Dillie said, laughing at her own overreaction. "I thought those children were yours. But they're not. Obviously."

"Oh?" said the woman through a puzzled smile. "Which?"

Dillie was about to explain, then waved it off. "My error. They're gone now. With their families." She laughed again.

"Oh," said the woman, still holding the chains. "That's good." Campbell kicked his feet, wanting motion.

The white-skied air smelled wet, threatening rain. Dillie went to Campbell in his seat.

"Thank you," she said, lifting him out. "For looking after him." He stiffened, resisting.

"My pleasure. He's a beautiful boy."

"He is, thank you." Dillie nodded at her with an awkward grin and wondered if she should prompt Campbell to wave goodbye. She decided against it and turned to go.

"He has his father's eyes," said the woman.

Dillie stopped, turned back. "I beg your pardon?"

"Yours are blue," the woman added, nodding at Campbell. "His are hazel."

"Oh. Yes," Dillie said. "Indeed they are. Take care."

"Enjoy him now," the woman called out when they reached the playhouse gate.

"Be a good boy, Campbell!" she cheered as they passed the fountain.

Dillie held him tightly, hurried along.

● ● ●

Campbell splashed both hands in his bubble bath, dousing Dillie.

"Careful!" she said, giggling with him as she knelt by the nursery's tub, rinsing him off with the hand shower.

She noticed for the first time Lola's exotic bath salts, oils, and aromatic candles on thick, wooden pillars perched around the tub's edge. She always felt a bit uneasy violating Lola's personal space, but it was Campbell's bathtub, too, with his own toys and soaps, and Lola never seemed to object. Dillie also wondered for the first time if the salts and oils and candles held any mystical powers in Lola's mind, like her charms and incense did. A moot point soon enough, she realized, although today's adventures made her value Lola more than ever. She'd be tough to replace.

"Eyes closed," she said with a shielding hand, gently spraying the baby shampoo from his hair.

The British woman from the playground with the glassy smile had spooked her on the trip home, while making Campbell's macaroni dinner, and still now, which Dillie realized was overblown. Her own children must have been there somewhere, either by the seesaw or the spiderweb rope-crawling contraption for older kids. Perhaps she'd brought along her nanny to look after her children, freeing her up to play with the others. Or maybe she could tell that Dillie was preoccupied with work and was simply lending a hand to another busy mother who could use it, in a neighborly, it-takes-a-village spirit. Surely she hadn't been lurking, childless, in a public playground, which the posted signs clearly prohibited. "You can never take your eyes off a child," Vivian had warned her whole life, one of her many wisdoms that Dillie had to admit was dead-on.

Had the woman even been wearing a wedding ring? Dillie hadn't thought to look, so distracted she'd been, although that wouldn't have solved much anyway.

"Sorry, sweetie! Sorry!" she cried when the hand shower shuddered and spat a blast of scalding water. Fortunately, it hit her first, so she could divert it in time. Ernie needed to adjust the water heater, or fix the valves. Or something. They spent too much on the place for these sketchy, third-world hiccups.

After ten minutes of *Corduroy*, Campbell went down easily, still clinging to her in his sleep as she laid him in his nursery crib and tucked him in. As always, an effortless, loving boy, although she steeled herself for the terrible twos certain to kick in any day.

Dillie focused on the last few paragraphs of her article, newly confident that it was vastly improved and, more importantly, almost done. The disastrous glitches that had started her day in a frenzy now seemed an easily overcome obstacle. In two days, her family would be complete again, on their way to a Vermont fall getaway, celebrating her debut in one of the nation's most prestigious magazines set to land on newsstands and in mailboxes worldwide. Including her mother's.

Lola slipped in at 8:17, quietly, with her overnight bag and braids newly perfect. Booray bounded up, thrilled to see her again.

"How was your weekend?" Dillie asked, before turning back to her work. She could sense Lola drinking in the mood of the apartment. If she were expecting chaos, or worse, she'd be flatly disappointed.

"It was good. And yours?"

"Just fine," Dillie said into her laptop. "Uneventful."

eight

Dillie unloaded on him before he could finish his sentence. "Rupert, no! C'mon! You promised this wouldn't happen."

Her day had started out smoothly enough. After staying up until midnight finishing her article—and spellchecking, proofing, riffling through her notes one last time—Dillie had saved it in all the right places and was relieved to find it in perfect condition the next morning. With a final glance-over, she confidently hit "send" to her copyeditor and to Glen, to land on their desks before they arrived at work. As it swooshed away, Dillie took only a moment's relief and satisfaction before getting ready to run to the office herself.

By lunchtime she was itchy again, having gotten no response from either. She wasn't looking for praise or validation—needy writers didn't belong at the *New Yorker*—but wanted to make sure they'd received it. Glen was out of the office, and her copyeditor, on the phone, shot a do-not-disturb glare when she poked her head in. Not surprising, thought Dillie, as her own late submission had no doubt increased her workload.

There were no congratulations from colleagues, no acknowledgment of her first milestone as a writer at the magazine. She made an unsatisfying round of the floor, lingered a bit longer in case Glen returned, and then, free of her staff duties for the week, left at one thirty. At least the security guards wished her a good day.

Their cleaning lady had called in sick again, a too-common occurrence that suggested she'd have to replace her, as well. A problem for next week, after their much-needed getaway that was, at least in her mind, a celebration of her months-long accomplishment.

Her anxiety spiked midafternoon when she still hadn't heard from Glen. It needled her more than it should have, and she blamed her insecurities on the stress buildup of the past few days, the release of which had made her abruptly emotional as the day wore on. And her gnawing headache was, no doubt, due to her skipping lunch.

So when Rupert called with the news that the deal had been delayed by another two days, scuttling their Vermont trip, Dillie snapped.

"There's *no one* there who can cover for you?" she demanded into her hands-free while rinsing a sinkload of dishes that Lola, had she not picked this day to be unhelpful, could have already done during Campbell's nap. "I don't know why I expected you to come through this time, since you almost never do."

His explanations, apologies, and pleas fell on deaf ears. She'd heard it all before.

"Goddammit!" she shrieked, yanking back her hand when the faucet sputtered and shot out a rush of near-boiling water. The coffee mug she dropped shattered on the floor, spraying shards across the room. "Ernie has to fix this stupid thing! I almost burned Campbell last night in the tub!"

Down the hall, the smoke detector chirped once. Overhead, the kitchen one did the same.

"And we need new batteries, everywhere really, and I can't reach that high," she went on, unloading.

Her phone beeped in another call. Out of area. Likely Khaki from the landline, for her periodic great-grandson update. It was a call she could never ignore. She told Rupert to stay on and clicked over.

The lip smacking didn't wait for a silence. It seemed in progress when she answered it, like a recording on a loop.

"Khaki?" she asked, and then demanded, "Who *is* this?" The smacking became a choking, a gasping, but calm and taunting, not desperate. "Khaki?" The gasp reverted to a grating of the throat, at a leisurely pace, beginning the cycle anew. Dillie hung up on not-Khaki, irritated and rattled by whatever prankster had resurfaced from almost a year ago with terrible timing.

"Will you call Ernie this time so I'm not the one nagging him," she went on to the waiting Rupert, "or do I have to run this house, our son, our life completely and totally alone?" She caught her breath, to keep going.

Her phone beeped in another call. Glen.

"I gotta go. I submitted my article today, Rupert. Did you know that? Did you remember? Just stay there forever. I really don't give a damn anymore."

As she clicked over, a newly wakened Campbell warbled a greeting on the Dropcam monitor. He stood in his crib, wanting attention, hands on the railing.

"Lola!" she called out. "Can you please...?"

"I've got him," Lola called back from the nursery.

"Glen, hello!" she said with pent-up gusto, struggling to settle her voice. "Look, I'm so sorry it was late. My computer or something had a meltdown, Rupert's still out of town, and I've been having some staff issues..."

On the laptop monitor, Campbell banged the railing like a drum, cried out for attention.

"*Lola?*" Dillie called again, covering and uncovering the mouthpiece. "Sorry, Glen. Campbell's perilously close to being able to climb from his crib. That's a brave new world I'm not quite ready for...." She laughed, hoping Glen would join her, which she didn't.

On the monitor, Campbell raised his arms as Lola lifted him from the crib and out of view. Dillie turn her attention back to Glen and listened. "Oh good!" she said. "I'm just glad you got it, after all these glitches....I can make any more changes or tweaks, anything you want, really, but I think I've...Yes, I'm around Friday. Certainly, that'd be..."

The front door lock clicked. It opened with a notifying beep-chime. Lola walked in from the outside hallway, dressed in her hat and overcoat. She carried her grocery bag into the kitchen and set it on the counter.

Dillie stared at her, dropped her phone, sprinted from the room, down the hall, burst into the nursery.

Campbell sat happily on the carpeted floor, alone, surrounded by his Mega Bloks and wheeling his chatter toy telephone back and forth. He smiled up at his mother.

Dillie scooped him into her arms, held his head against her shoulder. She scanned the nursery, stormed into the empty bathroom, checked the closet and the window, closed and locked.

"What is it?" Lola asked from the nursery door, still in her coat. "What's wrong?"

Dillie spun to her. "Where were you? Weren't you just in here?"

Lola inspected her. "I ran out to get his oatmeal. I told you."

"I thought you were back."

"I am back."

Dillie turned in the room, looking and listening.

"Is there a problem?" Lola asked.

"No...no, of course not. I just thought..." Dillie stopped herself, unwilling to tell more. "There's no problem." She took a breath, pointed at the crib. "He can get out on his own, you know. We have to be careful."

"I've never seen him do that."

"He *can*, I'm telling you. It's a...new thing."

"I'll keep an eye on that."

Dillie nodded, still clutching Campbell tightly. She rocked him as she stood, calming herself. She kissed the top of his head. And avoided Lola's stare.

"Oh God!" she said, remembering. "Glen!" She rushed from the nursery, still holding her son.

● ● ●

She clearly hadn't seen what she thought she had.

No one had been in the nursery, or the apartment. She'd inspected every inch of it, for any sign of entry, from the front to the back door, chained and dead-bolted. She'd checked all the windows, which were also locked and, being on the third floor, inaccessible.

"No, I wasn't in your apartment today," said Ernie, when she went to his little first-floor room off the lobby. "I always knock, you know." "Oh, I know," Dillie insisted. "I just thought maybe I hadn't heard you come in, if you were there to fix something. You're always welcome, of course...." She stopped herself from overexplaining and then laughed and dismissed, lest he think she was accusing him of anything. In any event, she would have heard the door chime, which they both knew, so she shrugged and thanked him and left.

She'd simply seen a shadow—from a passing cloud, most likely—on the monitor and, distracted and charged up as she was, mistaken it for Lola's back at the crib and assumed she'd lifted Campbell out. And Campbell—strong, adventurous, fearless boy that he was—had cleverly figured out how to escape the crib on his own. Both Victoria and his pediatrician had warned this was coming.

And her laptop had been across the kitchen counter, at an angle. She'd looked at it from a distorted view—a glance, really—while multitasking with the broken coffee mug and Glen's unexpected call and her own frustrations with Rupert's extended trip. It was also possible her laptop's video was glitchy (like the rest of it lately), or the Dropbox feed had frozen up and then sped up, as it often did when it lost and regained connection with her (newly spotty) network. Indeed, upon rewinding it, she didn't see anyone lift him up at all, such was the gap in the feed. He'd simply raised his arms when he'd heard his mother's voice in another room—but not Lola's, since she wasn't there and which Dillie assumed she had heard but obviously hadn't—and then, impatient and moving out of frame to the foot of the crib, must have climbed up and shimmied down the leg to the floor. Everything else she'd thought she saw had only been what she'd *imagined* would happen, as it normally did.

The wait at the Apple Genius Bar was too long to fix her iPhone screen that had cracked when she'd dropped it in the kitchen, leaving Glen on hold so long that she'd finally hung up and e-mailed details for their lunch tomorrow. A celebration, Dillie suspected, of their two-year mentorship that had finally born fruit right at the deadline. Had there been any problems, any last-minute tweaks or edits, Glen would have alerted her. Instead, they would toast the milestone like friends and professional colleagues, and then Dillie would come clean on all the week's screwy mishaps that Glen would surely understand and even find amusing, having been a working new mother not so long ago. And Dillie would pitch her more story ideas that had been brewing.

As she battled through the hoards on Spring Street, she again dismissed the needling fear that the week's screwy mishaps were at all comparable to her problems of the previous year, even though they'd grown thornier at just about this time. Then, too, she'd had escalating bouts of confusion and anxiety, progressing to paranoia and ultimately what she could only describe as hallucinations. But that was a medical condition, as she'd explained to Lola and now explained to herself anew, that could in no way be responsible for the physical breakdowns around the house or the temperamental computer hiccups that had nearly derailed her magazine debut. *When it rains, it pours,* her mother often said.

Sur La Table was mobbed, mostly with tourists, although kitchenware from a chain store seemed a misguided souvenir from a New York vacation. She scoured the coffee section, pinpointing the right machine to replace the one she'd scorched and ruined, and lined up at the cash register.

She'd call Rupert before dinner and apologize for lashing out. It wasn't his fault the deal was delayed. She needed the same respect for his career that he'd always had for hers, especially since he brought in the lion's share of their income. Behind his British charm that made everything seem effortless lay a relentless worker in a pressure-cooker job. The least he should count on was the unconditional support of his wife, not the hounding harpy she'd been today. And his stiff upper lip never betrayed, even to her, the stress he shouldered with his father's deteriorating health. If either in their marriage was entitled to a meltdown, it'd be Rupert. Yet he was always the most stable, dependable, and endlessly giving. She vowed to match him and never again punish him for something as petty as a weekend trip. The leaves changed in Vermont every fall, and Campbell would enjoy them even more a year older.

Movement in her peripheral caught her eye. An insistent wave across the store, trying to get her attention. Dillie turned toward it.

It was the dark-haired British woman from the playground. She stood near the juicers, poking her head above the crowd, smiling.

Dillie quickly looked down at her coffeemaker. The woman must be waving at a friend nearby. The greeting was too warm and familiar for a stranger. She couldn't be sure, now that she wasn't looking, that it was even the same woman.

The line stalled. A tourist's debit card had been declined. She fished around for another card, voicing her confusion. Dillie stood still.

She glanced up without raising her head. The woman looked right at her, waving more frantically. The same eyes, Roman nose, dove-gray overcoat. Surprised and thrilled to see her.

This was silly. Dillie nodded in recognition, with a tight, polite smile—surely all that was required from such a passing, non-acquaintance. It wasn't. The woman, blocked by others in the aisle, held up a wait-a-minute finger and started to weave her way toward her. It seemed important.

Perhaps Dillie had left something behind at the playground. She did a quick mental inventory: iPad, wallet, keys, Campbell's things, all accounted for. Anything else was expendable.

The line was at a standstill. Dillie didn't need the coffeemaker after all. She could find it cheaper online, or switch to K-cups, like everyone else. She placed the box on a shelf by the door, wormed her way outside, and hurried into the crowd always gathered around Starbucks.

She made her way home in a roundabout way, via Broadway and White Street, in order to check out the new jewelry at Ted Muehling. *Not* to make sure she wasn't being followed.

nine

It wasn't a celebratory lunch.

"We think you should take a leave of absence from the magazine," Glen said shortly after kisses and pleasantries at the Blue Water Grill on Union Square.

Dillie had gotten there early, after a morning of organizing her pitches and a wildly expensive blowout at Laicale. She'd slept fitfully and finally gave up at five a.m. but still felt refreshed and charged. To her relief, Rupert had texted on his way to Heathrow, and then again when his flight was delayed. She'd responded "safe travels" at takeoff and then, "I do love you, jackass," which prompted a rare, tongue-wagging emoji.

She'd requested the perfect table along the wall, one-third down the room, far enough from the front door but appropriately distant from Siberia in back.

She sat speechless.

"Just for a few months," Glen went on. "A break would do you good." There was neither hostility nor reprimand. It sounded like a reward for good performance.

"Oh, I don't need a break," said Dillie lightly, declining an invitation.

"Well, it's not an option. We've made our decision."

The "we" stung. How high up did this go?

"Glen, please. I know I missed a couple deadlines, by just a couple days...."

"Three, actually," said Glen, sharpening. "By over a week. It's getting harder to defend you. Please respect me, too."

The room grew warmer and more crowded. She should have picked a table away from the heat vent.

"Of course I do," Dillie insisted. "I just..."

"You're just distracted and scattered lately, for whatever reason, and think you can do it all, and I love you and have a magazine to run. It's that simple."

The waiter brought their iced teas. It seemed pointless to order anything else.

"Glen, I worked my ass off for this. We did it together. You *know* it's a good piece."

"Oh really?" Glen pulled a clipped stack of pages from her bag, placed it on top of Dillie's menu. *"This?"*

Dillie saw her byline at the top. Perplexed, she looked back at Glen.

"Read the first paragraph to me, if you would," said Glen. "The first sentence, really."

She started, couldn't. The words made no sense. Dillie flipped through the sheets. A chaotic jumble of letters in perfect sentences that were impossible to decipher.

"What...is this?" Dillie demanded, thumbing to the end with a trembling hand.

"I wondered the same thing. That's your article, Dillie. Exactly as you submitted it."

Dillie squinted at a line. It wasn't English, nor any other language she recognized or likely existed. It seemed like a code.

"Just out of curiosity, we sent it to a linguist," Glen continued. "Apparently, it's a combination of Creole and Pidgin, but a variation more commonly used over a century ago. It's quite an impressive achievement, if we published in the West Indies. In the 1800s."

Dillie released it, patted her neck with her napkin. She felt a trickle down her back. "I...didn't write this. I didn't send this."

"Shall I show you the e-mail?" asked Glen. "I didn't believe it myself, of course. I assumed there was something wrong with my computer. But it was the same, office-wide. I told everyone it was just another glitch, to cover for you."

Dillie shook her head, unable to speak.

Glen softened, leaned in. "Dillie, what is going on? Can you tell me?"

"I...don't know." It was broiling in here.

Glen put her hand on hers. "Is it something with Rupert? Or Campbell?" She squeezed her hand, leaned in, hushed. "Are you... taking any medications, or anything you shouldn't?"

"I'm not taking anything!" Dillie said, too forcefully. She looked down, to mask her confusion. The room had gotten so crowded. The words she'd written stared back up at her.

"Okay, okay," Glen soothed, patting her hand. "You needn't tell me right now. But it would be wise for you and your family to address whatever it is. Sooner than later. These things only get worse, you know." Her face was slightly pitying, and skeptical.

Dillie nodded, feeling a tear collect. She looked up at Glen, nodded again. "Yes. I will."

Over Glen's shoulder, toward the back of the room, the woman from the playground sat alone at a table along the wall.

Dillie locked onto her. The woman peered around, people-watching. Her raptor profile was unmistakable. Scanning back, she caught Dillie. She laughed and smiled with surprise.

"Oh my God," Dillie muttered.

"What? What is it?" said Glen.

"She's stalking me. That crazy bitch is stalking me."

Glen perked up in her chair, and Dillie said, "No! Don't look. Sit still."

"Okay, Dillie," said Glen.

"She was playing with my son. On the swings. My God, how could I let her?"

"Okay, Dillie," Glen repeated.

The woman, still smiling, started to stand.

"No!" Dillie said.

"Ssh," Glen insisted, leaning in again. "You're all right, Dillie." She signaled the waiter for the check.

"What the *hell* does she want?" Dillie reached for her purse, not taking her eyes off the woman in her dove-gray overcoat, who navigated toward her.

Dillie pushed back from the table, sloshing their iced teas.

"Stop it, Dillie. Please," Glen said, avoiding the splash, steadying the table.

The woman paused for a server to move by, kept approaching.

Dillie bolted up, grabbing her coat from the back of her chair.

"We need to get you help, Dillie," Glen said in full voice. "There's no shame in that."

"What is it?" Dillie hissed at the woman. The room quieted, listening.

"Stop it, Dillie," Glen ordered. "Please let me help you."

The smiling woman neared.

"Stay away from me!" Dillie shouted, backing away, bumping the guest behind her.

Glen, giving up, settled back in her seat, waiting for the storm to pass.

Dillie, pushing past the crowd at the entrance, tore out the door.

The stunned room looked after her, paying no attention to the smiling woman in the gray overcoat who calmly followed.

● ● ●

The Union Square subway station was its usual screechy beehive. Throngs of neighbors, tourists, and NYU students knit through one another on the mid-level, targeting their stairs to the scramble of lines that merged below.

The woman wandered along the curving, downtown four-five-six platform. She'd caught a glimpse of Dillie scurrying across the narrow Broadway sliver and down into the station. Although Dillie had disappeared by the time she reached the mid-level, the woman seemed to know which platform to pick. Unhurried, she meandered, looking around with her pleasant, steady gaze. The congestion seemed to give her peace; she had not just missed a train. Upstairs, a lone saxophonist played.

"What do you want?" came a voice from behind. She spun to Dillie, calm but coiled.

The woman's smile warmed to a professional level. She extended her hand. "Delphine, I'm Madeleine."

Dillie ignored the hand. "What do you want?" she repeated.

On a distant track, a train rumbled into the station.

"Can't we go somewhere?" the woman asked loudly, cupping her ear. "Somewhere quieter?"

"Tell me now!" Dillie shouted over the noise.

The woman laughed and shook her head with embarrassment. Then she took a breath and shrugged. "Rupert promised he would tell you. I assume he hasn't."

The name threw Dillie, but she didn't flinch. "How do you know Rupert?"

The question pleased the woman, who seemed prepared and well rehearsed. "We met on a plane. The day your son was born."

Dillie shook her head. "He was with me."

With care, the woman shook her head, too. "Are you sure? Do you remember?"

Dillie didn't, at least not all of it. His red-eye *had* been late that morning, again. She stood still and stared.

The woman's smile grew a tinge of pity. "Do I need to say it? Do you need to hear it?"

An uptown train one track over thundered into the station.

"This can't really shock you," the woman yelled above it. "Can we be adults about it?"

A loudspeaker garbled through the air. The train's doors ding-ed their closure.

"We love each other," she went on. "He hasn't told you. So I have to."

"I don't believe you," said Dillie simply, meaning it.

The woman reached into her coat pocket, fished out a watch with a midnight-blue dial. She held it out to Dillie. "He left this behind," she said. "I thought I should return it."

Against her will, Dillie snatched the Tiffany CT60. Turned it over to the engraved inscription: *To my favorite dad: Love, Dill*. Just as she'd had it done.

A six train quietly approached their curved platform, seemingly out of steam. It squealed to a long, slow stop. The platform grate engaged to cover the gap.

Masses poured from the train, around and between the standoff.

"Do not contact me again," Dillie said, clutching the watch as she turned to board.

"But your son...," the woman called after her.

Dillie stopped and whirled on the platform. "Stay the *hell* away from my son!" she spat.

The doors dinged and closed. The pokey train inched away from them.

The woman's face reached its most comforting and radiant as the crowd cleared. She unbuttoned her overcoat. "But someday," she said, "he'll want to meet his sister." She peeked it open to reveal the bump at her waist. She looked down at her belly, caressed her hand across it, and looked back at Dillie in a plea. "Don't you think?" she asked with a motherly smile.

Dillie backed up a step. And another.

She turned, threading through the newly gathered crowd, and raced up the stairs toward an escape beyond.

The woman exhaled, buttoned her coat around her. Her smile drained. She focused on the grimy floor and blinked erratically. She leaned to one side, nearly tipping over, bumping against a youngish commuter in a peacoat before righting herself.

"I'm sorry," she said, abruptly pale and feverish. She backed away and chirped an embarrassed laugh. "I'm so sorry."

She looked around the underground cavern, track to track. She patted her face, to blot the sweat. Steadying on a spilled-over trash can, she took a deep breath and centered herself.

Light danced along the tile wall as a new train approached down the tunnel.

The woman careened toward the track, stumbling on the yellow line at the platform edge.

"Whoa!" a round man in a black hoodie and Rangers cap called out, yanking her back. "Easy!"

She forced another laugh. "I'm sorry," she said, patting his hand in gratitude. "I'm so sorry." She backed away, then jerked her head as if summoned by a familiar voice. She shook it off. There were only strangers here.

The train's light shined and grew along the wall. The brakes screeched. The platform vibrated.

She turned in a tight circle, disoriented and seemingly lost. She palmed her damp, matted hair. Dizzy and nauseous, she squinted and pointed up at the signage. "Uptown?" she slurred with a stubborn grin, to no one. "Downtown?"

She held her spot, calming, and rocked her head in a sad *tsk*. She moved toward the staircase, gripped the banister, and took a step up with care before stopping. Thrummed her fingers on the railing, caressed her round stomach. Then with a jolt she lurched back toward the platform edge, pushing through.

The express shrieked into the station at barreling speed.

ten

Perhaps the most painful shock was that she wasn't shocked at all. Off guard, unsuspecting, yes. Not shocked.

She'd known of Rupert's reputation before they married. While not quite gossip-column-worthy (he wasn't so prominent), she'd heard smatterings of his pre-Dillie escapades from well-intentioned friends that grew sharper and more specific the longer they dated. Their arched eyebrows and pursed lips softened once Dillie and Rupert announced their engagement. She had, to their surprise—and not a little envy—seemingly tamed him. Or else had been foolishly blinded by his rakish charms.

But Dillie was tough to fool. And his womanizing past became a private joke between the couple, an understanding that whatever had happened when he was "most eligible" among the twentysomethings was a normal passage of youth on the way to finding his permanent life mate. Dillie herself had had plenty of flings and boyfriends—both tawdry and more serious—before taking a calculated risk on a man she grew to love and trust completely. To prove they were in on the fun, "They All Laughed" had been their first dance at their wedding.

On the steps back up to Union Square, she summoned an Uber black, a rare indulgence. There'd be no slinking home in a dingy taxi.

She'd never had an inkling of fear that he would cheat. Even during her pregnancy and after, when she couldn't have felt less desirable, she never worried that Rupert would stray. If nothing else, he prided himself on his originality, and sleeping around on a pregnant wife was simply too cliché.

Her driver was close. She fought through an agitated mob flooding up from another subway exit on Union Square East, waved him down, hopped in. He inched through the swelling swarm blocking Broadway, continued on.

Dillie certainly knew couples whose infidelities were an open secret—Tabitha came to mind, or turn-the-other-way Aline, whose financier husband's transgressions with a barely of-age Marchesa model had been a recurring whisper on "Page Six"—but those marriages smacked of arrangement, a hushed agreement as long as the shenanigans didn't cross over to flagrant embarrassment. It seemed special dispensation for the New York wannabe billionaire boys club. Dillie and Rupert had no such deal. They mocked it.

So it was extra piercing, galling, *humiliating*, to discover he'd fallen in line with the others. More than their marriage, he'd betrayed their kinship and decimated their uniqueness. He'd made them common.

A harmony of sirens forced them to the side by the Strand bookstore. Ambulance, fire truck, a blur of NYPD blew by on Twelfth toward Fourth Avenue. Dillie burrowed into the dark upholstered seat.

Don't pet that dog, her mother had warned of the Millers' terrier mix at their church picnics. Defiant young Dillie had proved her wrong, beguiling and befriending the skittish mutt as it curled on her lap under the park elm. Until, with no warning, it snagged its teeth into her palm. *Told you*, her mother said on the race to the ER for stitches. *Listen next time.* Rupert's treachery stung more deeply, but the lesson was the same.

The sirens headed uptown. The driver continued on.

Of course the woman was lying, Dillie realized with a burst of relief. A disgruntled ex-girlfriend from his pre-Dillie past, or even an outright fraud. A stalker in this city of crazies who had targeted Rupert through any number of ways: a casual encounter, his photo from one of the many galas they'd attended, his LinkedIn profile. What proof did she have, besides her claim they'd met on a plane (low-hanging fruit) and a second-trimester bump that could have been anyone's? She wasn't even Rupert's type, had he been inclined to wreck his family and life by taking on a mistress.

Dillie tightened. The watch. "Madeleine" with the raven hair and Roman nose and pregnant belly had the watch she'd given him just weeks ago on their anniversary. A watch he took off only before showering or bed. With the same engraved message she'd personally written after much thought and careful calculation so it would fit.

Unless the crazed woman with the sickly smile had stolen it. Stalkers had taken more extreme measures, to be sure. But that would mean she'd been there, with him, before he showered or before bed. And Rupert was missing his watch the last time she saw him. "At the club," he'd claimed, one of his endless lies.

She faced the reality: It was all true.

And unfixable. An affair, or two, would have destroyed her trust and likely ended their marriage. Devastating, heartbreaking, but recoverable.

A child changes everything, her mother had always lectured, most recently days before her wedding. "Until then you can always cut your losses. No harm, no foul. But after a child, your wants don't matter. You're stuck. So choose wisely."

Broadway was jammed in SoHo, per usual. "I'll walk from here," said Dillie, springing out.

And now Campbell would be saddled with a half sister, a blood relative, less than two years younger, through his life. A perversely modern family forced on him, derailing a normal childhood even before he learned to talk. Rupert's gift would keep on giving, long after they were both gone. Her heart also went out to the unborn girl, to be raised by a crackpot stalker who targeted married men and smiled as she shattered families.

She pivoted on Spring, away from the tourist hoards, threading through the permanent cluster by Balthazar. Considered/reconsidered a chardonnay at the bar, opted for a clear mind, carried on down cobbled Crosby.

"Can This Marriage Be Saved?" was Vivian's favorite family parlor game when Dillie was a little girl. After dinner she'd read aloud the column from *Ladies' Home Journal* with a gleeful voyeurism, laying out the case from both warring spouses before canvassing her captive audience by the fireplace. Her father and toddler Lance would ignore her, Khaki would fight a smile and keep to her needlework, but Dillie would lean in for her mother's verdict. "No chance!" Vivian would cackle at sorry tales of ungrateful husbands, frigid wives, and the ultimate torpedo: what she delicately translated as "carrying on" with feigned shock. Slapping the magazine on her lap, she'd bellow: "Doomed!"

That's what Rupert had done. He'd doomed them.

Lola was waking Campbell from his afternoon nap when she walked in. "I can take him for the rest of the day," said Dillie, scooping him into her arms.

"Is everything okay?" asked Lola, stepping back into the nursery.

"Yes, of course," Dillie replied, carrying him out. "Why wouldn't it be?"

When was Rupert planning to tell her? He couldn't wait much longer; the clock was ticking. And his plan: Straddle two families? Endure the inevitable divorce and then marry Madeleine? It was inconceivable he hadn't thought all this through before he plunged headfirst into a longtime affair. Not a fling or a tryst, but a relationship.

And when did they get together? Dillie knew his schedule. He rarely worked late, although he traveled often for work. Did he concoct "business trips"—even his father's stroke—to spend time with his girlfriend, away from his own wife and young son? With this many strata of lies, anything was possible.

Had he cheated on her ten, fifteen, even five years into their marriage, it would have been agonizing enough. But they were practically newlyweds. The "salad days," her mother called them. Why had he proposed in the first place? It struck her, with a strange tinge of victim's relief, that she had married, not a philanderer—someone who cheated because he found her inadequate—but a debased con artist. A sociopath. An unwell man.

But as sick as he was, he was still a calculating, self-obsessed menace.

"Lola, can you take Booray out for a quick walk?" she called from the kitchen while making Campbell's dinner of mac and cheese and organic corn with kale, happily his favorite green. "He's antsy."

A sharp fear pierced through: If Rupert was having unprotected sex with his now-pregnant, mentally unstable lover—and possibly, probably others—what lurking diseases had he exposed Dillie to over the years? And by extension, when she was nursing, his own infant son at his most vulnerable? It was an unconscionable, reckless endangerment—abuse, really—crossing over to criminal negligence. She'd call her and Campbell's doctors for a thorough examination, right before her lawyer, which she didn't have. Victoria would find her a blistering one.

She checked the flight-tracking app on her phone. Rupert was two-thirds over the Atlantic. She wished for a safe landing; a downed plane would be unsatisfying.

Dillie shielded herself from Campbell's bathtub splashing, his favorite sport. She dried and powdered him before dressing him in his fleece pajamas.

There would be outrage, pity, and ultimately solidarity from her New York friends. They would rally around her. Even the men couldn't possibly side with Rupert; his indiscretion was too flagrant and sloppy. It tarnished them all.

She read *Panda Bear, Panda Bear* while Campbell palmed the pages out of order. When he fell asleep against her chest, she gently tucked him in and caressed his cheek.

"You in for the night?" she whispered to Lola, who had settled in. Lola nodded and said, "Good night, Dillie," eyeing her as she soundlessly closed the door.

Her mother would be the wild card. She'd lambast Rupert's cheating but also, drip by drip, pin blame on Dillie for the whole disaster. It would creep in, after the shower of love and commiseration and anger: the passive-aggressive musings of how Dillie could have so misjudged her mate before bringing a child into a sham family. With the final verdict that Vivian herself had failed as a mother, for her daughter to make such a colossal and life-wrecking blunder. She'd spread the guilt around, which would only amplify the enormity of Dillie's fiasco.

Dillie poured the chardonnay she'd denied herself all day.

Glass in hand, she wandered the long white hallways of Rupert's art collection. Contemporary, multimedia, the occasional sculpture on pedestal. Most of it preceded her; all would outlast her. He could keep it.

She migrated to the dining room. The giant nighttime cityscape painting spanned nearly the entire wall. Rupert's present to her after Campbell's birth, perhaps out of guilt for launching his affair on the same day. Dillie snickered at her delusion; he felt no such guilt.

She returned to the kitchen, poured herself another glass. Scrounged through the utility drawer next to the oven, plucked out the tape measure and a capless, ballpoint pen. From the cabinet above, she lifted down the brown leather box of Wüsthof steak knives that Rupert's Cambridge roommate had given for their wedding. Rarely used, equally sharp, she picked one at random.

She dragged a heavy, armless dining chair to the wall. Another, and another, to form a makeshift bench in front of the cityscape. Starting at the top left corner, she hooked the tape measure on the canvas edge and unspooled it across, inching her way down the chairs. Checked the end mark, made a mental calculation.

Back to the starting edge. Using the pen and tape measure, imprinted a series of dots along the top in equidistant intervals. At the end, realized her division was slightly off, dismissed it. Close enough.

Dillie climbed down and took another gulp of wine.

Once more to the top left of the painting, this time with the steak knife. Into the night sky, just east of an acrylic star, she pierced the knife tip to the wood frame beneath. Steadying the handle with both hands, she pulled straight down—slowly, precisely—ripping through the cloth fiber with the serrated edge. The knife caught and slowed on the thicker paint layers of skyscrapers and windows, but with careful persistence, she sheared her way through the tight fabric to the bottom.

Booray, delighted by the game, scampered forward and back and woofed a single, expectant bark. "No," Dillie scolded, waving him back. "Quiet."

Two inch by two inch, she repeated the pattern, alternating slices across the top and bottom, as she made her way across with increasing speed and efficiency. The precision was surprisingly taxing.

She stepped down from the chair, found her balance and moved to the far side of the room to survey her artistry. The painting hung in ribbons, half hanging downward and touching the floor, the other half dangling from the top, in perfect symmetry.

Dillie summoned the camera on her phone. Adjusted the room lighting to showcase the violent massacre of her handiwork. Took three photos in quick succession and then shared them.

Glass and bottle in hand, she retired to the corner of the living room, where she sat, on the floor, watching the students at the cooking school down below on their smoke break. Booray sidled next to her, and she stroked his head, thinking, waiting.

eleven

The front door clicked and turned. "Hello?" Rupert called out. Booray bounded up and practically doubled in half, so over-joyed he was at his return.

"Dill?" said Rupert, leaving his rolling bag in the foyer.

He went to the dining room painting first, having expected it from the photo. It looked more horrible live. He backed away, past the tape measure, the steak knife.

She sat in the corner, facing out, bottle half drained. Knees to chest, relaxed and focused on the night world outside.

"I called from the airport," he said. "You didn't answer."

She didn't now.

He pointed back to the cityscape. "Who did this?"

"Madeleine," Dillie said, not turning her head. It came out growly and phlegmy. She cleared her throat and repeated it.

"Who?"

She tipped her head back, catching a smile. "What's the matter, Rupert? Can't keep them all straight?"

Rupert listened, pondered, gave up. She was impenetrable.

"Part of me wants to get to the bottom of this," he said. "Another thinks I should just leave for the night."

Dillie turned back to the window.

"We need to get you help, Dillie. Real help. Where's Campbell?"

She whirled. "In the nursery. With Lola. Where he's staying."

Rupert backed down, turned to go. "I'll call tomorrow."

She waited until his steps crossed the kitchen.

"Your watch is on the counter," she called back, her trump card. "Your anniversary gift. In case you're missing it."

"I'm not," Rupert replied. "I'm wearing it."

The front door closed with a controlled *thud* and *click*. The apartment was silent again, except for Booray's confused steps room to room. Dillie sprang up.

The non-confrontation confounded her. She knew Rupert's tricks of avoidance, the sheepish timbre of his voice when caught in the wrong. He'd played none of them. He seemed, instead, genuinely concerned for her. And guiltless. Not only had her blows not landed; he didn't realize she was throwing any.

She picked up the orphaned watch. Moments earlier the symbol of betrayal, now of her disorientation. She grabbed the kitchen counter to steady herself. Lightbulbs needed replacing; it had gotten so dark.

She knew why, careening down the hall, newly narrow and tilted, Booray at a cautious distance. Inside her bathroom mirror, she scrolled past the Haldol and Trilafon—on hand, but not her current regimen—and plucked the Lithane, which she'd forgotten in the day's upheaval. A no-no with wine, but she wouldn't be operating heavy machinery. And Campbell was safely tucked away, with Lola looking over them all.

A "mood stabilizer," her doctor termed it. The right prescription for her day.

She paused, weighed her options, and added a Lunestra. There was no other way.

They hit quickly and mercifully. The cocktail she needed, just for tonight, with nothing on her schedule tomorrow or the next. Booray, knowing better, hopped onto the bed, and she let him.

Whoever suggested Times Square for Campbell's second birthday party had led her brutally astray. Victoria? Eleanor? Even worse, why had she agreed, when she'd already reserved the upstairs at Dylan's Candy Bar and would forfeit her deposit? The December weather was blustery and cruel—even Mickey and Spidey had taken shelter in the bank's ATM vestibule—yet the pre-Christmas tourists still swarmed and gaped at the frenzied light storm above. Dillie struggled to keep the dinosaur-themed tablecloth down, but the corners blew up and over the Magnolia Bakery cake, matting the icing. More challenging was keeping tabs on the toddlers in her charge.

Dear, unflappable Emma had come up from Nashville to pitch in and did her usual mother-hen job corralling the youngsters, like she had for Dillie since her earliest memories. A comforting presence and godsend, as always. But even she seemed overwhelmed by the chaos in the middle of the square.

The cutting of the cake focused the kids' attention and gathered them 'round. Emma passed the little plates and diffused any spats. She held the last plate and looked around. "Are we missing one?" she asked with a tinge of concern. Dillie licked her finger and scanned.

A dark-haired woman led one of the boys away, threading through the crowd.

"Hello!" Dillie called out. "Excuse me!"

Madeleine looked back at her and smiled. She held the blond boy's hand tighter and kept moving toward Broadway.

"Stop!" Dillie cried above the noise, pushing through the mob. "Stop her!"

The toddler turned to her voice.

"Adam!" Dillie yelled, racing to him. Vivian would be over-joyed after so many years.

Madeleine waited on the sidewalk until the light turned green. Adam grinned at his sister and fanned a tiny wave. Madeleine led him off the curb as a taxi sped toward them.

"No!" Dillie screamed.

A loud buzz rattled the air. Booray howled an alarm.

Dillie thrashed awake, bolted from under the covers. The clock pulsed 3:12 a.m.

Another buzz. Booray howled again, more insistent.

She squinted off her haze as she padded toward the door. Rupert's luggage still sat in the foyer. He must have left his keys, as well. She pushed the video on the keypad. The grainy view offered an empty sidewalk.

"Hello?" she said into the mic. "Rupert?"

Nothing. An unconscionable hour for a false buzz. "Hello?" she repeated.

Large eyes filled the screen, peering at her. *"Delphine, I'm Madeleine,"* the intercom warbled. Dillie released and sprang back. The feed played on.

"Rupert promised he would tell you...."

Dillie backed up farther and stopped. Lola, tying her robe, rushed in from the nursery. "Who is it?" she asked.

"A...friend of Rupert's," Dillie stammered, deadened with confusion and panic. "She's stalking me!"

"Do I need to say it? Do you need to hear it?" A single eye took over, focusing on her.

"Go away!" Dillie screamed at the eye. "Go away!"

"It is no one's friend," Lola said, hurrying to the keypad.

"And your son..."

Lola killed the feed.

"How dare she come to my home!" Dillie said, regaining her rage.

Lola faced her, calm. "Delphine, it is not what you think it is. It wants inside. That must not happen."

"Of course, I'm not going to let her inside!"

The doorbell rang, inches from them. Booray bellowed anew.

Dillie raced to turn the dead bolt. "I'm calling the police," she said loudly. Lola shook her head and said, "They cannot help you."

It rang again, insistent. Booray howled.

From her robe pocket, Lola pulled two familiar jewel-toned satin pouches. She walked toward the incessant ringing and held them against the doorframe.

"Don't let her in!" Dillie said, shielding the hallway to the nursery.

Ignoring her, Lola whispered against the door, a repeating chant in her native tongue. She dialed up in speed and intensity to match the pattern of the constant ringing. Her chant morphed into a singular phrase, which she sustained in one breath, propelling it through the door. She sweat.

The ringing reached a climax and then lost steam, growing more sporadic until it trickled to a weak effort. And stopped.

Lola rested her head on the door for a moment, recharging. Then stepped back, glistening, and pocketed the bright bags. "It is gone. For now."

"What?" Dillie demanded, shaking her head as she pointed. "She's there. Waiting."

Lola clicked the dead bolt, reached for the knob. "Don't!" cried Dillie.

Flinging open the door, Lola revealed the empty landing just beyond. The hallway table, mirror, the closed elevator. Nothing more.

Lola paced outside. "See?"

She hit the elevator button, waking it from below. It arrived quickly, as Lola turned to Dillie, her back to the door sliding open.

"Lola! No!" Dillie screamed.

Without looking, Lola stepped into the vacant elevator. Leaned down to grab the morning papers, stacked by apartment. Brought them back inside, locked and bolted the door anew.

"We must hurry," she said, tossing the papers on the kitchen counter. "It will be back."

Dillie succumbed to the hyperventilation she'd held at bay. "What is happening?"

"The *ang* guarding your boy needs help," Lola explained. "I can cast permanent protection. For the sake of your child, I beg you…"

Flummoxed and disoriented, Dillie stared at her. "Lola, what are you…?"

"Your boy is special," Lola insisted. "That's why it wants him. I won't be here much longer. *Please…*"

Dillie stood silent, helpless.

Lola looked past her. Dillie turned to Campbell standing in his pajamas in the hall. He yawned and smiled at his mother. She scooped him up, pivoted back to Lola, the authority in the room.

"Do it," she said.

Lola went to her, embraced them gently. Kissed the top of Campbell's head. "I must cleanse for the ritual. We will protect him, Delphine. It's time." She hurried down the hall, untying her robe as she turned in to the nursery.

Dillie carried Campbell into the kitchen, still rousing her mind and wishing she'd skipped the Lunestra. Nothing Lola said made sense. Her cryptic warning that she was leaving them—right now? today?—was a fresh shock and horribly timed, given the immediate chaos. She'd picked the worst and weirdest moment to abandon them. Surely Dillie had misheard her.

And whatever hocus-pocus she was planning from her bag of tricks would not drive Madeleine away. Even if they'd scared her off from the front door—the police threat, *not* Lola's nonsensical chanting, had done that—she'd be back. She'd grown unhinged and fearless. And possibly dangerous.

Campbell wriggled. She considered his high chair, then opted to set him on the floor, out of window range. He looked up at her, curious and expectant. "You're okay, little mouse," she said, her voice trembling. "We're just up a little early today."

Against her better judgment, she peered down onto the street, looking. No sign of anyone. She snuck to the next window for a wider view, hiding by the frame. Having gained access to the building, Madeleine was still inside somewhere. Waiting.

Her mind sharpened. This was unacceptable. Terrified in her own home, hiding her child, interrupting his sleep with a traumatic energy that would surely imprint on his subconscious.

She would call Rupert. Their own clash could wait; their son's safety was priority now. He'd brought Madeleine into their lives; he would get rid of her, tonight. Dillie grabbed the cordless, squinted to remember his number. Madeleine smiled up at her from the kitchen counter.

Dillie dropped the phone.

Peeking out from the stack of papers—under the *Times*, the *Journal*—the *New York Post* teased Madeleine's beaming face in full color. Dillie slowly slid it from the pile, revealing her full-length photo next to the wailing headline: "MOTHER OF HORRORS! Pregnant Tourist Killed by 4 Train."

Madeleine stood with expectant pride and glory, sheepishly grinning at the camera for a candid family shot in an unguarded moment. Cropped just out of frame was the husbandly arm around her shoulder, the raven-haired toddler son clutching her free hand. She caressed her belly as she had on the subway platform, but against a decidedly non-New York background of fall foliage. She radiated joy, contentment. Stability.

Dillie clutched the paper, too paralyzed to follow the invitation to page three.

Above her head, the smoke alarm chirped once.

In the nursery, Lola tucked her braids under her shower cap, turned on the water and let it run. She reached into the under-sink cabinet and with knowing, childlike hands, pulled out three heavy wooden pillars. With apparent strategy, she placed them on the sink's far ledge, the little chest of Campbell's bath toys, the toilet tank by the shower door. She stood in the middle to survey, then adjusted them to form a semblance of a triangle.

On top of each she set a charcoal-black pillar candle, burned a quarter down, the rims curved inward. From a green glass vial with rubber dropper, she anointed each wick with a thick, clear oil. Striking a wooden kitchen match, she lit each candle, then doused the match under the faucet. The candles crackled in the oil and settled to a slow, even burn.

Lastly, she unwrapped from tissue a worn cake of dull black soap and perched it next to the candle on the center of the toilet with care, lest it slip off.

She slid the heavy shower door closed and faced the water, tweaking the temperature.

The kitchen smoke detector beeped three times in quick succession and then went silent. Dillie scoured for any source of fire and breathed easy. A glitchy ceiling appliance was the least of her concerns. She went to lift Campbell off the floor.

The detector screamed a steady alarm.

Lola, wetted down, cracked open the shower door and reached past the candle to the black soap. It slithered from her grip, but she caught and clutched it in time. Yanking it back to the shower, her knuckle knocked against the candle pillar, set it wobbling at the base.

She quickly closed the shower door, frothed the soap under the warm water. The wooden pillar tipped over, fell onto the door track, the flame washing out. In a rush, Lola lathered.

The siren was deafening. Dillie left Campbell on the floor and checked the kitchen, the oven, the outlets. Booray reared and barked at the haywire alarm.

The hallway detector joined in, at a higher pitch. Panicked, Dillie scoured and sniffed. Nothing. The piercing harmony was unendurable and inescapable. She dragged the kitchen dining chair underneath, climbed and reached, falling well short. She stepped down, clear of Campbell, and raced to the utility room.

Lola was scrubbing her face with the rich lather when the shower sputtered and briefly trickled. Then, with a slight trembling from the wall, it spat and gushed a stronger stream. She adjusted the temperature to cool it down. It grew hotter.

She turned the knob to cold, but the water was unresponsive and became uncomfortable. Lola hurried to rinse, as the water turned scalding.

She'd finish in the sink. She shut the shower off. It surged instead. Lola reached for the door. The pillar blocked the track.

The flood thickened, boiling. Lola flinched from the pain, smashed into the sliding door. She grabbed the handle and pulled; her force had derailed it, the frame jamming on the pillar at a few inches. Lola wriggled her hand through the slim opening, straining to dislodge it, hopelessly out of reach. She shook the door, immovable. The water hissed and tea-kettle-whistled, as steam overtook the room.

Dillie held the broom like a bat, swatted at the shrieking alarm. Booray woofed and wagged at the game. She pushed the bristles around the edge, struggling to pry it from the ceiling. They bent and broke, useless. Her brain throbbed; the screeching was torture.

She looked down. Campbell had moved a safe distance, toward the hall. She flipped the broom around and banged at the detector, to destroy it.

Lola thrashed about her cage. She flailed at the nozzle, deflecting its scorch upward. The shower head broke from its riser, clanking into the tub. The pipe exploded in the wall, flooding her with scald. She clawed at the tiles, freed from melting caulk, clattering one by one to the floor. The water now felt icy; she knew it was not. Her bursting blisters and slackened skin told the truth.

The steam morphed darker, mixing with smoke from her own flesh. Screaming was pointless.

Lola slipped on the loose tiles, foamy from the smelted soap. Her forehead struck the tub edge first, and she thanked her god as the room clouded to black. The boil rained down, filling the tub around her.

Dillie struck over and over, smashing the detector to shards that sprayed through the air. She aimed for the exposed circuitry with a double bash. The alarm fell silent. The hallway alarm petered out and died with it. Her arms ached and legs trembled, but the relief was instant, blissful. She was drenched from her panic, the apartment stifling and jungly.

She carefully stepped down and grabbed the counter to brace her buckling knees. Booray bounded to her, all a-wag.

Dillie looked around the room. "Campbell?" she called out, her senses sharpening. "Lola, do you have him?"

He stood in the fogged-over nursery, facing the bathroom door, ajar. Just beyond, the water was loud and angry. Dingy steam whispered through the cracks. He drew closer, placed his hand on the door. Warm.

"Lola?" Dillie said from another room. "Campbell sweetie?"

He pushed it open and peered in as acrid, gray smoke billowed out, engulfing him. It stank and stung his eyes, but he didn't blink. He stepped into it.

"Campbell?" His mother's voice drifted from the hallway, drawing closer. "Come to Mommy, Campbell!"

"...*Campbell?*"

PART TWO

NASHVILLƎ

one

"Yep, it's Dillie. Sorry to miss you. Tell me everything...."

She glanced back at Campbell buckled in his rear-facing car seat, riveted by the passing scene of hills and trees, so foreign to his urban youth. Booray perched next to him, stymied by closed windows but excited nonetheless by new sights and smells. Dillie turned to her father at the wheel with a weary glance of appreciation for taking the scenic route from the airport as the countryside rolled by, heading away from Nashville proper and into Williamson County.

"Ms. Parker, this is Dr. Perry's office. We had you scheduled for an appointment today. As you are aware, a 'no-show' fee will be charged. Please call to reschedule at your earliest convenience. Thank you very much."

The Range Rover slowed to a roll in the downtown Franklin historic district, the turn-of-century, Disneyesque village that seemed even more congested since her last trip home. Tourists and soccer moms with quilted parkas and strollers mixed easily with inked hipsters in skinny jeans and ear gauges along the sidewalks, crisscrossing Main Street between shops, cafés, and churches. Trendiness made strange bedfellows.

"Dillie, it's Glen...I...don't know what to say. Except I'm here for you...to listen, for anything. Please call...when you're ready. You're in my thoughts, Dillie. And prayers."

They cruised through the adjacent residential section of pristine Victorian and renovated Federal brick homes whose front gardens, though now barren, held the memory and promise of meticulous care.

"My lamb, just making sure you landed okay. And it was not an imposition on any level. You and Campbell are always welcome to stay here, you know that. I just hope you got a little sleep with my cretins giving me fits. Give my best to your mother and please, please, please reach out soon and often. And always."

Farther out, past an expanse of rolling hills dotted with Angus cattle grazing on remnants of grass. White, split-rail fences stretched on for miles.

"Dill…I'm handling everything. I'll take care of it. Just take care of yourself…and our boy. And know I love you more than life itself. We'll figure it all out. I love you, Dill…."

They turned off the main road to a gravel drive, past newer, nondescript and decidedly modest houses. Dear Mrs. Hatcher waved from her mailbox at the familiar Rover and then brightened at Dillie in the passenger seat. She forced a smile and waved back as they continued on.

"Sorry. That mailbox is full and can no longer accept messages."

They steered around young children on bicycles—recent transplants Dillie didn't recognize—and slowed at the gray stone arch, waiting for the motorized wrought-iron gates to swing open. Rolling through, they passed the verdigris copper plaque: River Kiss.

Dillie breathed out. She was home.

• • •

She'd dialed 911, and then Rupert. He'd arrived first, followed by the paramedics, police, and firemen. The commotion woke Ernie, who shut off the building's water on their orders.

Dillie had initially rushed to grab Campbell from the bathroom to protect Lola's privacy before the calamity hit her. The stench struck first: a putrid, scorched odor, a pot left far too long on the stove. She dashed Campbell to the hallway and shut the bedroom door. The horror lay in the tub.

She instinctively reached in to scoop the naked, limp Lola from the heat-spent water pouring from the broken wall. She lay her on the tile floor and called to her, needlessly. Her sightless eyes stared ahead; her charred skin cracked open in lesions the length of her body. Her still face betrayed neither pain nor hope.

Rupert, then the professionals, took over. Dillie, calm and focused, rocked and soothed Campbell on the living room sofa as the morning city woke beyond the window. Ernie took Booray out for a walk. A makeup-less Victoria blew in to babysit Campbell in the master bedroom. Dillie answered a million questions, with Rupert protectively at her side.

The lone silver lining was that Campbell had been spared the gruesome discovery of his beloved nanny and friend. Nor did he seem afraid or troubled by the morning's commotion, indeed delighting in the grown-ups' attention. It was like an unexpected party. He need never know the truth, at least for years, if not decades.

The apartment building was temporarily condemned and evacuated, pending structural review of the pipes, water heaters, and smoke detectors. Lola's death was ruled a catastrophic accident, her autopsied remains returned to Jamaican relatives.

Rupert paid for the funeral and gifted the family a sizable annuity. The *Post* screamed another freak headline. Lawsuits against the building owner, if not criminal charges, were guaranteed.

Dillie and Campbell lingered at Victoria's for three numb days and, once cleared for travel by the authorities, promptly left town.

● ● ●

Winding past the dense cluster of live oaks, magnolias, and towering elms—still majestic in their post-fall slenderness—they targeted the distant plantation manor that emerged in the clearing. In profile, its backside was more prominent: the balcony that connected the upstairs bedrooms peeking over the fenced-in patio and garden flanked with evergreens. Far beyond, the fields seemed to vanish at the soldierlike trees framing the union of the Big Harpeth and West Harpeth Rivers, which begat the estate's name. The manor looked off-kilter but was positioned for maximum exposure to the waterways that wrapped around the property. The rivers came first.

Her father lightly honked a pattern as he rounded the mansion side—unnecessary but a habit—and circled the driveway loop, past Khaki's favorite elm, to the front entrance. Here was the grandeur, the calm beauty she'd always taken for granted but seemed especially glorious—gentle and welcoming—at this homecoming.

She drank it in anew: the three stories of weathered brick trimmed in new white, square and symmetric, with a pitched copper roof and nine bays of shutter-less, lead-pane windows. A two-level, raked portico marched from the middle, bolstered by Ionic columns and adorned with carved banister and swirling, plaster frieze. Two of the four chimneys streamed curled wisps into the sky. Inside, all lights blazed, the house aglow in the predusk gray.

The double front doors flew open. Vivian led the charge, clapping her palms in glee, her face wide with smile. Ever lean and tall, she wore her typical household uniform of oxford cloth button-down untucked over paint-smattered chinos, her upswept, silvery blond mane speared in a messy twist with a school pencil. The disheveled look seemed calculated to mask her Hollywood siren beauty but, like a born star, merely accentuated it. Only her jolt of fresh red lipstick betrayed a hint of vanity, an afterthought for a special occasion.

She strutted down the geometric brick sidewalk bordered with unkempt box hedges, neglected till the spring. Bypassing Dillie with a wink, she opened the back door. "*There's* my guy!" she teased, reaching in for the buckle.

Emma seemed inclined to honor, then dismissed, the private family moment as she hurried behind, brimming with joy. Her frosted hair was impeccably coiffed, per usual, in the Betty Crocker style that black women her age considered *au courant*. Her hug held an urgency and zeal that had always set her apart from the rest. Dillie clung tightly, comforted by her Norell perfume mixed with the burning oak in the crisp air. Booray bounded from the open car door and, remembering, dashed off to mark his favorite tree.

Khaki had dressed for the occasion, in a camel-hair suit of her own making, a fall paisley silk scarf tied and tucked down the front. Her white-laced hair was pulled back severely in a precise bun, makeup slight but meticulous. She paused on the top step, steadied on her painted cane, and for a moment Dillie feared she could no longer navigate the simple stairs. Khaki caught her concern and smiled. With spot-on timing and a matriarch's entitlement, she descended with ease—her cane a mere accessory—and maintained a spry and regal gait toward the drive. She could still upstage without saying a word.

She held Dillie's face with her hands and eyes before kissing her forehead in silence. To Campbell, she flashed a grin but declined to hold him. Later.

"Is our *Downton Abbey* arrival done?" Vivian asked, nosing her grandson. "Let's get you inside, where it's warm."

The family moved toward the door.

"Richard, stay useful," Vivian called back without looking. "Get the bags."

● ● ●

It was never meant to be her home.

Nor was it deeply ancestral. River Kiss had been the family compound only since World War II, when her great-grandfather, flush from the local dairy he'd founded, bought the crumbling estate from its tapped-out descendants. Khaki's husband joined the business and grew it into a regional empire before selling to a national brand shortly before his death. The windfall was enormous.

Teen Vivian harbored dreamy notions of an artist's apprenticeship in New York, Paris, or Florence but wound up a philosophy major and Tri-Delt at Vanderbilt. In her junior year, a blind date with a medical student eventually led to marriage and a newlywed apartment near the hospital, an easy jaunt for Richard's residency. Her surprise pregnancy—twins, no less—abruptly changed the equation.

Their move back out to the mansion was allegedly temporary, to cushion the shock of Vivian's young, double motherhood with Khaki's and Emma's helping hands. The stay wore on, delayed by one thing or another, primarily inertia. When Richard joined an ENT practice near downtown Nashville, he grew itchy, ostensibly for a shorter commute, but mostly to be man of his own house.

The tragedy of Adam's sudden illness changed everything again.

The fever claimed its victim within ten days; the family wound never healed. These were fuzzy times in Dillie's memory, but she was aware of grief and upheaval, her mother's black days and terrifying mood swings. She remembered her father having to take primary care of newborn Lance, sealing their bond as his favored child, even as she was shunted off to Khaki and Emma. Gloom darkened the home, it seemed, for years. Her grandfather's death when she was in kindergarten sealed their permanent residency. River Kiss became their home and refuge, their birthright.

The family's retreat into itself was near total. Once a debutante and country-club centerpiece, Vivian shrank back from the city's tentpole events—Symphony Ball, Frist Gala, even the Swan Ball—that merely increased their mystique among Nashville's aristocracy. She focused on the home, motherhood, and her art, well aware of but unfazed by their increasingly eccentric reputation. "All aboard the Bigfoot Express!" she'd call out before heading to town for errands. They weren't hermits, merely cloistered, freely mingling throughout Franklin and never missing a Sunday service at Saint Paul's Episcopal, third row from the front.

Not surprisingly, Dillie redoubled her efforts to excel at everything, particularly normalcy, which required separation. She was supposed to marry Clayton Whorly, join the Junior League, stay local. She did none of these.

"I think my proudest achievement," said a teary Vivian at Dillie's high school graduation from her own alma mater, Harpeth Hall, "is that you turned out so viable."

two

"In Christ's name we pray...," Richard said, wrapping up at the dinner table, their hands joined.

"Can I add something?" Vivian piped in, head down. "I think we still have Him," Richard answered.

Vivian looked up—around the table, toward the chandelier—and breathed in. "Just...thank you. For bringing them home. Safely. Where they're so very much loved." She paused, considering more, before an abrupt "Amen!" that spread through the room.

Dinner was an unusually sordid Southern feast, given the family had long since switched to healthier fare. Tonight, doctor's orders be damned. Everyone gravitated to their natural spots at the rectangular, polished oak table, set with Vivian's wedding china and silver. She'd even lit the ivory candles.

"Nobody makes corn bread up there like you, Emma," said Dillie, crumbling a golden muffin into chunks for Campbell, who palmed them into his mouth from his high chair tray. *Her* high chair.

"Did you think they would?" Emma said, lining up six pills of various shapes and colors on Khaki's bread plate. One by one, Khaki slipped them past her lips, a dainty swallow of water after each. The ritual seemed to dampen her mood. "Lotta sugar? Lotta butter?" Emma added, tucking away the pill caddy, one eye on the disappearing medication.

"You know it," said Dillie, cutting small pieces of glazed ham and scooping macaroni and cheese onto Campbell's plastic plate. She added a few green beans but skipped the collards; he wouldn't understand.

"That's not corn bread; that's cake." Emma *tsk*ed. "Poor Yankees."

Khaki had removed her silk scarf inside, revealing the jewel-studded cross pendant she always wore, an heirloom token of her deep but unobtrusive faith. It glimmered in the light as it had since Dillie's earliest memories. While her parents had never been devout—their church attendance and dinner prayer mostly rites of manners—Khaki maintained a strong spirituality and belief in the hereafter, especially following her husband's death. Dillie remembered stumbling upon her having heart-to-heart talks with him for years after. At the time she'd thought it creepy; in hindsight she found it beautiful.

Dillie gauged a slight change in her grandmother since her last visit; she'd always been soft-spoken but had quieted more over the past few years, as if she'd passed off her baton of wisdom to Vivian and only stepped in to clarify or correct her when off track. Tonight, however, she was a silent observer.

"We fixed Granddaddy's office up in the crow's nest," said Vivian, erect in her leafy tapestry dining room armchair with saddle leather seat. "New carpet, wiring, the Wi-Fi. You can get away from it all and do your writing."

"Oh," said Dillie. "Thank you."

"We've kept the landline and answering machine, too," Vivian added, nodding at Khaki and Emma across from her, "since the Pigeon Sisters refuse to get cell phones."

"They are bad for your brain," Emma insisted. "And other parts, apparently."

"And what, pray tell, would those parts be?" teased Vivian. "According to the sages of *Cosmopolitan?*"

"Hush now," Emma teased back, shaking her head. "I'd be ashamed."

Vivian glanced at her husband. "Let's not get vulgar," she told the ladies. "Richard might get the vapors." He swirled his wineglass on the table, ignoring her.

"Oh, and Lance called this morning," her mother went on. "He's hoping to come for Thanksgiving, if I can stand the *shock* of both my children home at the same time." She passed the corn bread basket without taking any. "I declare they work those residents too hard. When your father was at Vanderbilt, I felt like a war widow. No wonder Lance can't keep a girlfriend."

Boyfriend, thought Dillie, but let it drop. "No wonder...," she said, spooning macaroni off Campbell's bottom lip.

Booray stood at Dillie's side, expectantly wagging his tail as she ate.

"Now, now, Booray," Vivian chided with a playful tone. "No begging. Someone didn't teach you manners."

"I'm sorry. I can put him upstairs," said Dillie, but Vivian waved it off and said, "I bet we can teach him together." She sat forward in her seat, primed. "Campbell, would you help me? Can you say 'No, Booray'? 'No, Boo'?"

Campbell stared as his grandmother. She smiled at him, nodding encouragement.

"Is he still not talking?" she quizzed Dillie through her grin.

"Not really. Not yet."

Vivian stopped smiling, leaned back in her chair. "Well, I think that's odd. Do you read to him?"

"Yes, I read to him," Dillie said, gently pushing away Booray's probing snout.

"Even a parrot you have to *teach*," Vivian went on. "It's just odd for a child his age…"

"He's been through a lot lately…Boo! Sit!" She pushed harder.

"Aw, mean ol' Mommy," Vivian cooed, luring him with a piece of ham. "C'mere…" She stroked his head as he wolfed it down. Instant allies.

"Biscuit better watch out," Dillie said, feeding Campbell another spoonful. "He's not used to cats."

"Biscuit ran off a while back," Vivian said, picking through her dinner, eating little.

"Oh no. After all these years?"

Richard cleared his throat. "We have a slight…coyote problem these days."

"She ran away!" Vivian insisted, irritated. "Your father always defaults to the catastrophic. Sometimes cats just run away, do they not? I'm sure she found a good home."

"Coyotes?" said Dillie. "Since when?"

"They've always been up in the hills but moved closer the past couple years," Richard said, pouring another glass of wine, the lone drinker at the table. "Some idiot's probably feeding them."

Emma offered another muffin to Dillie. "Did you hear the Carneys' German shepherd ran away, and they think it actually joined their pack?" She shook her head in amused disbelief. "Can you imagine? They can't get the fool dog back!"

Richard toggled Khaki's hand. "You sit American sniper on the back rocker, and those critters won't stand a chance." Khaki, who'd been staring at her uneaten plate, perked a bit and said, "Bang."

The family laughed.

"Just keep an eye out," Richard added, nodding at his daughter.

Vivian glared at his emptying wineglass and dabbed her mouth. "Reminds me, I need to call the exterminator. Biscuit was so good with the mice. Emma, don't let me forget."

Dillie tried unsuccessfully to bait Campbell with another bite of ham. "I'll take your mice over my city rats any day. At night, they just take over...."

The family stared at her. Khaki started nibbling.

"Lots of rats in the big city," Vivian said after a pause. "I'm not at all surprised."

Emma joined in. "You remember that Broadway tour we took with the *Tennessean?*"

"Oh yes," Vivian said, fighting a squeamish giggle. "Yes!"

"That little park! From the Meg Ryan movie. By the statue, do you remember?"

Vivian squealed and flicked away the memory. "Rat park! Oh, my heavens. It was alive, just a writhing sea of rats!" She delighted in the revulsion before collecting herself. "Oh, not at supper..." She shuddered anew, her face comically sour.

"Did rats kill your nanny?" Khaki asked, focused on her place mat. The room silenced.

"Mother," Vivian whispered sharply. She glanced up at Dillie, rolled her eyes with the barest shake. *Ignore.*

Campbell pounded his tray for more macaroni and stared over Vivian's shoulder as he chewed. She brightened.

"Campbell has discovered the mural. Look at him!" The hand-painted tableau of the estate wrapped around them, having survived the decades with periodic restorations, the mansion, river, trees, and hills alive with color. Graceful palominos galloped the grounds, grazed on lawn. The rest of the family took it for granted, as lush and richly rendered as it was.

"When I was a little girl, I'd play in here for hours," Vivian went on, drinking it in anew. "I'd see the horses running through the fields and beg Daddy for one of my own. That certainly fell on deaf ears." She relished her grandson's fascination. "It *is* glorious, isn't it, little man? You really cannot find artists of this caliber anymore."

"It's not rats, of course," Khaki continued her thought, still into her plate. "It has returned."

Vivian, Richard, Emma sat tight, tolerant.

"What?" said Dillie. "What has?"

Khaki looked up at her, calm. "Our family trouble. It's back."

Vivian scratched behind her ear, as if bitten. And then sniffed the room. "Mercy, did we leave the pie in the oven?"

● ● ●

The kitchen, like the rest of the house, had been thoroughly updated while preserving its original flavor. The mansion was Vivian's largest canvas, which she constantly energized and fine-tuned with the help of *Architectural Digest* and her tireless—and grateful—interior designer. "Eclectic opulence," she called the seemingly haphazard, yet meticulously curated, mix of antique and modern. Hardly a museum relic, the estate was a fresh, magazine-worthy showplace, ever evolving. (Even as she declined repeated requests for magazine shoots of the house: "Why would I do that?")

The latest home improvement was invisible, high-tech, and slightly unnerving: a security system that spoke with a British, disinterested female voice each time a downstairs door or window opened. It multitasked as an intercom and wireless music system, which Vivian ran from her kitchen computer command post. They'd never had an alarm before, and Dillie chalked it up less to threat of intruders than to her father's longtime hobby of cutting-edge gadgetry. "Agatha," as her mother named her, would take some getting used to.

Vivian rinsed, Dillie dried.

"Why don't we redo your room, too?" Vivian said, sponging the Limoges dinner plates in the oversized farm sink in her blue rubber gloves. "I've been culling ideas from my magazines. Furniture, wallpaper, drapes. Spruce it up. Wouldn't that be fun?"

"I doubt we'll be here that long," Dillie said, gently handling the good china.

"Well, I hope through Campbell's birthday, at least. I've already planned it."

"Mom, I wish you wouldn't..."

"But it's the most important one!" Vivian insisted, passing off another. "The first is for the parents. The child is clueless, of course. But the second? He *knows*. I always regret we missed yours."

Dillie shrugged. "I survived," she said, instantly regretting her choice of words. Vivian ignored it, barreled on. "I hope Rupert will join us," she said.

"We'll see..."

Vivian shut off the water, turned. "Dillie, all men stray on occasion. It's the nature of the beast. And they are all beasts."

Dillie didn't want this talk. But still: "You're the last person I
would expect to defend him."

"A child changes everything," Vivian replied on cue.

"I don't know that he 'strayed,' as you put it," Dillie went on,
still uneasy. "I'm just not sure I can handle a life of suspicion."

Vivian cackled. "Trust me, it's the men who *never* stray you
gotta be leery of. Did I tell you about poor Cousin Ann's unsavory
discovery? Talk about humiliating…"

"What did Khaki mean?" Dillie interrupted.

Vivian handed off the final plate, sighed. "Oh, Khaki's getting
a little funny…."

Dillie turned with alarm. "Really? You mean she's…?"

Her mother shrugged, filling the casseroles to soak. "She's
eighty-two. It'd be funny if she *weren't* getting funny. She'll zone
out, say odd things she won't remember. Especially at night
when she's tired." She turned off the water, peeled off her gloves.
"'Sundowning,' they call it. And she's always had a mild form of
epilepsy, since she was a teenager, which you never knew. But it's
progressing." She dabbed her forehead with the back of her hand. "I
just hope we don't have to relocate her. That would gut me. We did
meet with the folks at Belmont Village in Green Hills, just in case."

Dillie dried the last copper pot. "When did this start? The
sundowning."

Vivian searched the air. "Couple years ago, I guess. Comes and
goes. We just smile and nod." She wiped her front with a bistro
towel and snorted a laugh. "Get used to it. You'll be doing it for me
before you know it. If you're not already."

The family migrated, on schedule, to the conservatory post-dinner—the tropical, glassed-over room off the patio that her mother called the Florida room when warm and the winter garden when not (as horribly energy inefficient as it was in the cold months). Team Vivian and Richard took on Khaki and Emma with their quietly heated hand of contract bridge, picking up from their last matchup the night before. The battle could creep on for weeks.

Dillie held Campbell in her lap, well past his bedtime, an exception for the night. She propped open the leather family album, thumbing through photos that stretched back long before her time. Vivian as a little girl, glittering debutante, young mother. Khaki, Richard, and Emma (and others) through the decades. Both were riveted.

"Campbell, honey, you know your numbers yet?" Vivian called out, scrutinizing her cards with a wink toward Khaki. "Come whisper what the dowager countess has got going on there."

Campbell looked up at the sound of his name, but Khaki raspberried. "Don't be teaching my grandson to cheat," she scolded.

"*Whose* grandson, old woman?" Vivian threw her card.

Dillie paused at her own childhood photos she hadn't seen in years. A single studio portrait of her and Adam dressed alike in boy/girl variations of blue gingham with duckling embroidery (courtesy, no doubt, of Khaki). The rest from this time frame were of Dillie solo, either beaming broadly at the camera or pouting on the verge of caterwaul. She smiled at her own extremes.

"I declare, Khaki's elm is looking a little jakey," Vivian mused, staring up at the tree that sprawled above the conservatory's glass roof. "Richard, you should have someone look at it." Long part of family lore, no one knew—or ever asked—how the ancient tree got its nickname, including her grandmother. "Did you hear me, Richard?" Vivian badgered.

Khaki played her card, scooped up the trick, added to her growing pile. Vivian groaned.

Baby Lance arrived on the facing page, Dillie's arms wrapped around him like the protective older sister she'd always been. Even his earliest photos hinted at the golden boy he would become. They were clearly the stars of the album; Adam was an asterisk.

"You remember Uncle Lance?" she asked Campbell, tapping. "That's him. Baby. And Mommy. Bigger. Like you."

Campbell patted the studio photo. "Uncle Adam," said Dillie, pointing upward. "In heaven."

The family focused on their next hand.

"Mom, do we have more pictures of Adam?"

Vivian studied her cards, ping-ponged her mouth. "Somewhere. Upstairs."

Campbell clawed the album pages backward. Dillie gently helped him, to prevent damage.

"Mom, look what he turned to," said Dillie, showing the wedding photos. Vivian glanced over and grimaced. "Oh Lord, who *is* that clueless dame in the white dress?"

Campbell zeroed in on the wedding party portrait, in full but fading color. His fingers clutched at the faces; she held him at bay.

Next to Richard, holding rabbit-ear fingers over his head, stood a tall, young joker, marring the formal photo with a goofy face. But a handsome one, in a carefree, rascal way. Sexy even, the more she studied him. Campbell leaned in, captivated.

"What is it, Campbell?" said Dillie, amused. "Dad, who's this fellow next to you?"

Richard looked over. "My best man. Bucky."

Dillie went to turn the page. Campbell resisted. She laughed. "Campbell's obsessed with him."

Vivian played a card. "Bucky would love that," she purred with disdain. "Quite the funster he was."

"Are you still friends with him?" Dillie asked her father.

Richard considered his next play. "Bucky died. A long time ago." He looked up to ponder. "Shortly after your first birthday, or thereabouts. You wouldn't remember him."

"DUI...,"Vivian elaborated, arching her eyebrows.

Richard said, "We don't know that," and Vivian said, "Malarkey. We know he drank a lot, drove a lot. We know his car didn't run itself off the road." She looked over. "And, Dillie, you wonder why I nagged you so about..."

Khaki, engrossed in her hand, started smacking her lips. Softly, then louder.

"Mother...,"Vivian called out over the noise. "*Mother!* Are you tired?"

Khaki looked up. "Not at all, Sister. Why?"

"You're making that ugly sound again."

"I am?" said Khaki, slightly chagrined. "Mercy."

Vivian exhaled, laid her cards facedown. "Perhaps you should complete our annihilation tomorrow night." Richard did the same, scooting back. "I have an early surgery in the morning." Emma followed suit, went to help Khaki up by the elbow. The party was over.

"We put the old crib in your room," said Vivian, kissing her grandson's forehead. "And a space heater. The furnace is on the blink again."

● ● ●

Her girlhood room didn't need refreshing, Vivian's insistence notwithstanding. It was perfectly spruced.

There had been a time—her teenage years of discontent—when she'd bridled at its frilly preciousness: the multi-pastel, climbing rose wallpaper that matched the drapes and the fringed canopy with shirt-stripe lining over her four-poster bed; the too-proper, wall-to-wall trellis Stark carpet. A "princess chamber," her mother called it, ever priming her for the role. No wonder Dillie had resisted. Now its classic luxury bolstered her.

Given the late hour, she would have skipped story time, had Vivian's needling not stuck in her head. She rocked the dead-asleep Campbell through the first half of *Guess How Much I Love You* before giving up. The day had been too much with him.

"I love you, Campbell," she whispered as she laid him in her old crib and tucked the blue blanket around him. "Right up to the moon and back."

Quietly, she unpacked the few toiletries she'd brought—mostly makeup and medications, her bathroom already stocked with her usuals—and on second thought hid her prescriptions back in her bag. She'd taper off the anxiety meds but allowed herself a Lunestra to take the edge off her travel day. After washing and brushing, she zipped her bag and hoisted it to the top shelf of her closet, far out of a toddler's reach. Her prep school kilts and debutante dresses, tissued and bagged, hung next to her teenage nightgown, which still fit almost perfectly.

Campbell chortled from his crib and scrunched into fetal position. She tweaked the blanket and smoothed his hair. "That's right," she told him. "You're safe here."

A chill breeze brushed her face. She turned to the French door to the balcony, ajar. She went to close it, paused, and then stepped outside into the still night, as she'd done hundreds of times.

In the silence, she could hear the river's familiar and gentle trickle just beyond the trees. The dark estate stretched out to abyss, delicately lit by the sliver moon glowing through thin cloud cover, teasing a late-fall storm. The fine, clean air smelled and felt like home. A yelp in the distance broke the spell.

Dillie listened. It sounded like a young dog. Another joined in, and then a pack. The yelps turned to overlapping, frantic squeals. Not dogs. The new coyote problem.

The manic chorus grew more fevered and hyenalike, triumphant. A fresh kill, of something. Dillie shivered. A timidly curious Booray joined her on the balcony, perked and sniffing. The shrieks abruptly stopped. Silence again.

"Come on, Boo," she said, pivoting back to the door. Movement caught her eye.

At the tree line on the river, almost blended in, stood an animal in silhouette. She squinted. Too large for a coyote, too small for a deer. Poised and still, it seemed to stare at her. Transfixed, she did the same. It moved two steps closer into the moonlight, stopped, one paw lifted.

The wind rustled the thicket behind it, highlighting the long, pointed ears atop its head. The Carneys' missing German shepherd?

Too late to call them tonight; she would alert them first thing in the morning. She peered into the darkness. It must have been the angle, or the distortion from such a long view, but the ears—the whole head, really—seemed a different species entirely.

Booray, who couldn't possibly see that far, caught its scent in the breeze and woofed a warning. Dillie palmed his head to quiet him and blocked his path to the fire escape down, lest he be tempted to give chase. When she looked back, the creature was gone. She scanned the length of the fields and trees, searching for movement. Nothing.

The space heater clanked. She ushered the excitable Booray inside, closed the door. An exhausted Campbell slept soundly.

"Go to bed, Boo," she ordered. He curled on the carpet, ears spiked, facing outward.

From down below drifted soft piano and a familiar tune. Dillie brightened at the nightly ritual, heartened by its endurance, and went for her slippers.

She found Khaki in the dark living room, at the rosewood Steinway, in her own nightgown. "Clair de Lune," as always at this hour, and ever flawless. Without turning or missing a note, Khaki slid a few inches, tipped her head in invitation. Dillie joined her on the padded bench, dangling her legs.

The piece ended. Khaki placed her hands in her lap and nodded at the keys.

Dillie set her fingers, paused, withdrew. "I've…forgotten," she stammered.

"You? Nonsense," Khaki said, still looking ahead. "You were my best pupil. Even better than your mother. So disciplined. Brave."

Dillie's sobs were instant, unleashed. She collapsed and heaved, as she hadn't in years and would never allow herself in front of anyone else, or even alone. Her pent-up shock and grief exploded with a force that trembled the piano bench. Khaki was already cradling and rocking her with power and force.

"I know, my girl," she said, stroking her hair. "I know."

"I didn't know where it would hit next," Dillie unloaded into her neck, arms wrapped around her thin, sturdy waist. "Why me?" she pleaded.

Khaki clutched her, nestling her cheek on her head, and waited for her to spend it all and settle. Then, tenderly: "But see, my girl, we would never learn to be brave if there were only joy in the world...." She pulled back and held her face. Dillie saw her own pain absorbed in Khaki's eyes, where it always ended up.

A grace note, then a chord and a riff. A new invitation as Khaki teased a jollier tune. Dillie's fingers knew this one, from her earliest lessons. Timid, then bolder, they were soon hammering out their showstopper, "Weeping Willow Rag," in seamless duet. A command performance.

A wind-driven tree branch scratched up against the window, which jolted and then tickled them, as they laughed and played through.

"Soft pedal, soft pedal," Khaki reminded her giggling pupil as she tipped her head upstairs. "We don't want a *scolding*."

three

Her mother was right: Things always seemed better in the morning. Especially this morning.

Maybe it was the sharp fall air, even more gem-edged today. Or the comforting medley of poached eggs, scratch biscuits, and fresh coffee wafting from Emma's breakfast kitchen.

Mostly it was the clear-headed distance from the assault of chaos over the past countless months, culminating in unthinkable tragedies that made her value the mercy of shock. Even days later, she could scarcely digest the calamity. Selfless Lola, she knew, would wish that blessing on those left behind, until they were ready to process it and move forward.

The mystery of Madeleine would likely never be solved. How a tourist from Manchester, England (with her family, no less), developed a sudden obsession with Rupert—how? from where?—was a tangle of absurdity overshadowed only by the catastrophe of her death, and her unborn child's. And how she ended up with his watch—or engraved an identical one, which spun a whole new web of questions—was impossible to explain, as even now she wondered where it was, whether it had ever been real, or just an imagined by-product of that confused week, that hazy, nightmarish evening in particular. Dillie refused to relive it. Irrelevant now. There was simply no sensical answer.

Her own relationship with Rupert was a different matter: equally confounding but hardly irrelevant. If Madeleine was a baffling enigma, then so was Dillie's mistrust and paranoia. But their hiatus was a good thing for now, as she sorted out whatever had plagued her for so long, among the stability and her-ness of home.

The serene delight in Campbell's face proved she'd made the right decision, in that first morning alone. His new discovery of the river and open spaces, the subtle but clear effect of fresh air and quiet, his comically gleeful introduction to honeydew melon (Vivian: "Why have you been depriving my grandson?"), all made her question the humanity of raising a child in the grime-and-noise-choked city. So becalmed he was, he didn't need his morning nap.

Mrs. Carney thanked her for her call—"We've pretty much given up on that dumb dog"—before launching a non sequitur ramble of her own self-improvements and "breakthroughs." Vivian, spooning out containers of Moe's BBQ at the kitchen counter, anticipated the deluge and twirled a "wrap it up."

"Brenda's been so taxing since taking up with that shrink of hers," she explained over pulled pork and potato salad. "The therapy curse. She thinks everyone's as fascinated by her life as the person she *pays* to be."

Khaki had reverted to pensive silence. After Vivian took Campbell outside for a post-lunch tutorial on the varieties of trees about the grounds, Dillie lingered to visit with her grandmother at the kitchen table. She regaled her with Manhattan updates of *Hamilton*, the latest Lela Rose sample sale, the Sarah Charlesworth exhibit at the New Museum. Khaki used to relish these insider tales of the vibrant, tuned-in metropolis she loved and would likely never visit again. Today she nodded with a polite smile but seemed unfocused, even non-comprehending. Dillie pivoted to silly gossip about her friends and their only-in-New-York lives, hoping for a laugh, a spark; the reaction was the same.

Theirs had always been a unique bond, distinct from the rest of the family. They shared the same name, although the origins of their nicknames were shrouded in family lore and had been accepted without questioning. At some point they'd simply landed and stuck. Whereas she got discipline from Vivian and steadiness from her father, she received nurturing and enlightenment from Khaki. Only after she'd left home for college did Dillie appreciate how lucky she was for the daily contact of a live-in grandmother, especially this one.

It was Khaki who taught her needlepoint and how to baste a skirt and buy a pocketbook; who took her to the symphony, the ballet, treated her with downtown excursions to the old Satsuma Tea Room for their hidden sandwich, spoon bread, and chocolate meringue pie on Fridays. Only Khaki could paint so magic a picture of the grand, long-gone department stores, like Harvey's and Cain-Sloan (especially their restaurant fashion shows and Bunnyland each spring), strolling Church Street like a well-heeled tour guide in her hat and white gloves. And only Khaki, forever tweaked by the ravages of the Great Depression, could convince her it was perfectly acceptable—even chic—to use the Sunday funnies as wrapping paper, no matter the occasion. Never preaching, rarely scolding, Khaki was always an effortless role model of flair, faith, vitality. And possessed of a wisdom that often bordered on clairvoyance.

So spotty glimpses of her mental decline—and potential illness—hit especially hard.

"Is everything all right?" Dillie asked, reaching out to palm her hand. "With you, I mean." She alone could ask her grandmother such a loaded question so directly.

It jolted Khaki, who seemed to debate her response.

"I'll fill you in on a little secret old people don't like to tell," she finally said: "When we seem distant, it doesn't always mean we're dotty. It's because we already know what you're going to say. What's new and exciting to you is yesterday's news. So while we try to hide it, the truth is—my love—you bore us." She grinned. "And yet we adore the effort."

Dillie laughed. For now, at least, Khaki was not to be counted out.

● ● ●

After the tree tour, Vivian revealed to Campbell the wonderland of her artist studio on the top floor. Here was her refuge, an erstwhile Parisian loft overlooking the estate, where she churned out astonishing abstract works, expert in all forms: charcoal, oil, acrylic, even dabblings in post-modern neon, mixed-media sculptures, and ceramics from her pottery wheel. As prolific as she was experimental, her art was brash and visceral, energized with an outsized passion that hovered this side of fury. Young Dillie always knew not to bother her when the door was closed.

More often than not, she destroyed her pieces when finished, although a few favorites lived throughout the house. She resisted all gallery offers, convinced they valued her social status over her talent, but donated a piece each Easter to the church's silent auction. Even Rupert marveled at her skill. There was no denying her gift, except Vivian herself.

Today she was a proud hostess, unveiling a miniature easel stocked with tablet, brushes, and a rainbow of watercolors. "VOC-free," she assured Dillie. "For my little Picasso."

Campbell ignored it all, more taken by her shelves lined with eerily lifelike dolls of baby boys in various outfits. Vivian had been collecting them longer than Dillie could remember, but guessed it started soon after Adam's death, an understandable yet eccentric form of coping. That it continued now was more curious. Perhaps Mrs. Carney could loan out her shrink for an exploratory session.

"No, no, don't touch," Vivian cooed, gently herding him away from her pricey collection. "My Linda Murray boys are not toys." Dillie remembered well.

Having skipped his morning nap and still adjusting to the time change, Campbell went down earlier than usual that afternoon. Emma pulled double duty as babysitter ("Such a treat to look after a little one again") while Dillie scoped out the attic office, testing the waters. It seemed silly to let it go to waste, and perhaps—after a while—she'd wade back into writing this or that, just to stay toned.

Other than her grandfather's desk, it was all new, just as her mother said: wallpaper, sisal carpet, ceiling fan. A cozy, serious workplace, with a feminine air and updated with the latest amenities, although the tube television and VCR parked in the corner harkened back to an earlier age. Tucked away, on top of the world, ready to go.

Dillie tested the Aeron desk chair, bounced on it. Caressed the leather blotter, repositioned the julep cups stocked with pens and pencils. Picked up the old-school, touch-dial phone. Dead. Clicked the receiver, useless.

The phone cord snaked down and behind her, underneath a little door to a cramped storage closet. Inside sat the culprit: a freezed-up modem and Wi-Fi router—equally modern and testy—which she rebooted. Lining the rest of the cubbylike space were remnants from the office renovation: paint cans with dried drips, leftover rolls of wallpaper, discarded snippets of cables and wiring.

Wedged against the back corner, alone and forgotten, sat a lidded cardboard office box, marked "family." It spilled over with glossy snapshots. Toddler Adam's smile greeted her, sticking out the top. On hands and knees, Dillie crawled toward it, minding her head of the sloped ceiling. She pushed the photos back in, dragged the box out.

It was a trove of family shots she'd never seen—still color-vibrant from being hidden away—organized in stacks whose rubber bands had worn out. Here was the Adam she'd been looking for.

They chronicled the family wonder of the firstborn: showing off at church and Easter brunch at Belle Meade Country Club; early, timid adventures in their old backyard pool; their first-birthday picnic at Percy Warner Park. Her mother never looked more joyful, cradling them in each arm. Dillie was struck how identical she and Adam were at this age, her own hair ribbons—a Vivian trademark—notwithstanding. Smiles came more naturally to her brother.

She didn't recognize most of the adults at this first party, likely her parents' contemporaries who'd moved on from their lives, making her wistful about her own New York friends whose paths were sure to diverge over time. Her eye shot to a handsome profile with swept-back hair and roguish grin, charming the young wives and mothers in the background. Over his shoulder, Vivian shot a wilting glare of disapproval.

It was Richard's best man, she deduced from the next photo. More mature and sedate than at the wedding, he still had a playful side, bouncing each hatted sibling on his knees. Adam beamed at the camera; young Dillie, like Campbell, seemed smitten by the man's effortless star quality. She didn't remember him but still felt his loss and wondered what he'd look like if alive today. Probably quite distinguished in a Robert Redford sort of way. She put the photo to the side.

The stack at the bottom revealed another birthday party, this one circus-themed with a teddy bear cake and balloon-filled, clear bubble umbrella hanging upside down from the dining room crystal chandelier (how did her mother ever permit that?). Dillie held the cake photo closer: The single candle was a large wax "2." The party Vivian regretted not having. Except she had.

The whole family was there, including her grandfather, who cradled infant Lance and barked orders at the camera, presumably the browbeaten Richard. In one almost comical study in contrasts, friends and neighbors clustered around the Vivian-assisted candle-blowing—Mrs. Carney's wild-eyed hysteria in the background suggested her new shrink was long overdue—while an oddly detached Khaki stood peering toward the foyer, arms folded in a tight clench. Emma, who no doubt had done the lion's share of the work, looked especially drawn and fretful behind her forced cheer. Lurking in the corner, dear Mr. Patterson, the church organist, caught it all live on a handheld camcorder. She'd almost forgotten about him.

She squinted at the picture and then at the others. The dining room mural looked different, although she couldn't pinpoint why.

Same fields and trees, mansion and river, and after shuffling through several from different angles, she realized she was merely accustomed to the brighter tones today, the result of expert restoration. Snapping a photo back up, she realized: horses. There were no galloping palominos, no horses at all, like the ones on the wall today and that her mother said she'd loved as a child. But they did not exist in the mural on Dillie's second birthday.

She pulled the photo. Searched the box for any videotape of the "never-happened" party, found none, and packed it back up. Opened the top desk drawer to squirrel away the pictures she'd saved.

Sitting inside, by itself and waiting, was a brown leather book with gold lettering: *OUR FAMILY TROUBLE: The BellWitch of Tennessee* by Charles Bailey Bell, a Descendant.

It was old, yet well preserved. She opened it carefully. Inside the front cover was an illustrated map: "Bell Family Farm—Adams, TN." Next, a black-and-white reproduction of a vintage oil portrait: "John and Lucy Bell, 1820." A humorless couple befitting their century.

Dillie leafed through the chapters more quickly. "The Spirit Makes Its Appearance" contained simple sketches of weird, fantastical animals: a large dog with the head of a rabbit, an enormous, black birdlike thing under the caption "The Witch Creatures."

Words leaped at her from the paragraphs as she thumbed through: "rats," "scratching...window," "gnawing...bedpost," and, repeatedly, "forbidden marriage."

The chapter "The Death of John Bell" offered "delusions," "gathering strength," and "possession."

The final chapter anchored her attention: "The Spirit's Promise to Return." She started to read....

"It wasn't a witch, of course," said Khaki at the doorway, in her overcoat and hat. "Not a ghost either. They weren't so lucky." Dillie, startled by her grandmother's effort to get to the top floor, held the book down. "The neighbors nicknamed it 'Kate,'" Khaki went on. "The family simply called it 'the Being.' And they never knew where it would hit next."

Dillie smiled at the reference, though not particularly funny. "I remember this from Girl Scouts. My troop went to the farm where it supposedly happened. Mom wouldn't let me, of course. She said it was..."

"...malarkey?"

Now Dillie chuckled. "And at slumber parties, they said if you chanted her name in the mirror, she would appear behind you. But she never did."

"This wasn't child's play," Khaki continued. "It tormented the Bell family. Psychologically, then physically, and then violently. Killed the father. And promised to return to the descendants." Dillie expected a wink, a grin. They didn't come.

"*Mother,*" Vivian called over the intercom. "*The Bigfoot Express is on the move. Where you be?*"

"Why," Dillie asked, "did you leave this for me?"

"Because my father wrote it," said Khaki. "The year it promised to return."

She reread the cover. "Your...father?"

Khaki nodded. Dillie laid the book on the desk, straightened it. "Did it...return?"

"Mother, are you way up here?" Vivian called out, ascending the back stairs. "We'll be late for your B-12 shot if we don't get a jig on."

"Don't let her see that," Khaki whispered, turning.

"You know I hear everything," said the arriving Vivian, dressed to leave. "Don't let me see what?" She stopped. Saw the book. Huffed a laugh. "Oh my word."

"Why didn't you tell me about this?" said Dillie, tapping it.

"I declare, Dillie, I most certainly did," Vivian insisted, smiling. "Somewhere in between Santa Claus and the Great Pumpkin." She turned to Khaki with a tease. "What the devil have you been putting in her head?"

"You never told me we were *descendants*."

Taken aback, Vivian scrutinized her. "Our family tree is no secret," she said, dialing back the humor. "But this legend is ridiculous. And quaintly embarrassing. I was not about to traffic lies to my children. Why would I?"

"But after all that's happened?"

Flummoxed, Vivian waited for the punchline. Then her caution turned to concern. She took a breath, pained at the damage she'd underestimated.

"Dillie, honey, what are you saying?" She held up her hand to halt a reply. Then, gingerly: "Sweetheart, listen to me. I cry every night over what you've been through. It's too much to fathom, to wrap one's mind around. It's unthinkable."

She stepped closer, sifting her thoughts with the same soothing intensity Dillie remembered from her first heartbreak. "Life can be tragic, devastating—you know how well I know this. But that's what family is for. To love, support, protect one another, in times like these most of all. So we can move on. And live. What choice do we have?"

She capped it off with a gentle rib. "Please do not turn to witches and spooks to explain away the chaos of life." Dipped her head in mild reproach. "Isn't that silly?"

Vivian let her lecture sink in before reaching for the book. With brisk finality, she carried it back toward the door. "Meet me in the car, old woman," she mock growled as she passed. "We'll get you a Ouija board on the way home."

Khaki turned to follow.

"Khaki…," Dillie said. "Do you…I mean, do you think this is real?"

Her grandmother faced back, unreadable. "Do you?"

Dillie stared at the photo of Adam's innocent smile. Tucked it away in the drawer before pushing back from the desk.

She checked the time and placed a call on her cell, hoping for a quick answer. Campbell was surely up by now.

four

It was preposterous, of course. Indeed, malarkey.

The Bell Witch was an urban myth, if that. It was more a curiosity, a quaint local nugget of nostalgia as extinct and fondly remembered as Opryland or Greer Stadium. But at least those were real.

This was simply a yarn—an ancient one—that had endured in the periphery mostly through campfires and annual Halloween refreshers on the local news. The legend was a jolly part of the state's heritage, nothing more.

And that her family were descendants of the original "victims" was a nifty morsel but hardly meaningful. Bell was a common name in Tennessee, if not worldwide. And "descendant" was a vague term. She doubted how direct they really were, as if it mattered.

"*Soup's on!*" Emma called over the intercom at six, gathering them 'round for a more sensible meal of grilled tilapia, steamed broccoli, and Khaki's tomato aspic, which Campbell promptly spat out. He stuck to his penne with cheese.

It was odd of Khaki to dangle this supernatural tale, relating it to what Dillie and Campbell had been through. She'd always had a latent and refreshingly mischievous side, but the past few weeks—two years, really—were nothing to make light of. From anyone else, it would have seemed offensive. But it was impossible that Khaki meant any disrespect, or to trivialize her ordeal.

Then again, she had her own health issues, including, according to Vivian, mental ones. Most unsettling of all would be if Khaki took it seriously.

"Pardon our iceless iced tea. The Sub-Zero is anything but today," Vivian said at the dinner table. "We've summoned the Wills Company for a morning repair. I declare this house alone put their kids through college." She glared at the wine ring dribbled from Richard's glass. "Imagine what we'd save if your father were handy."

More vexing to Dillie were the discrepancies—the untruths, really—in her mother's version of Adam's illness and death. At the very least, her timeline was off. Her whole life, Dillie had believed she'd caught it first—no one knew where—before passing it off to her brother. Dillie had bounced back with ease; Adam succumbed quickly. It struck just before their second birthday, which is why there was no party. Except there was, she now knew. Where they both looked happy and healthy. Within days, of course, Adam would be dead.

"*Side door open*," announced the security system with crisp diction when Richard went out for more firewood. "Roger that, Agatha!" Vivian replied from the kitchen sink. "I swear your father does that just to hear his new girlfriend."

But it was more than two decades ago, recalled through a filter of anguish that Dillie better understood as a young mother herself. It wasn't surprising Vivian mixed up some of her facts. Surely it wasn't intentional.

There was a cease-fire in tonight's bridge game. Vivian read to Campbell—slowly, deliberately—from a stack she'd collected. Khaki tacked a skirt, fishing pins from her felt tomato cushion.

Emma burrowed into her latest Nora Roberts, *tsk*ing at each plot twist.

Dillie studied her grandmother. "Sundowning" was the right term. Khaki seemed to crater after dusk. Tonight she was especially withdrawn, as if chastened, focused only on the simple task at hand. She'd eaten next to nothing at dinner and hadn't spoken to Dillie at all—not even eye contact—since the afternoon's revelation. Her mood swings were vexing.

Dillie's phone vibrated.

"Where are you going?" Vivian called as Dillie retreated to the breakfast room. "Is that Rupert? Tell him we fully expect a visit."

It was Lance, returning her call on a quick break at the hospital. She filled him in.

"Did you say Bell Witch? Us?" He spoke above the background din of beeps and chatter and crisis. "That's kinda cool, actually."

"Why did Mom keep it a secret?" Dillie peered out at the brick outline of the patio, converted from a swimming pool decades ago, after Vivian read that children who grew up with them had increased risk of skin cancer. On the edge stood the rusted iron dinner bell her mother used to summon young Dillie and Lance back from the fields at suppertime, or to remind them of chores. Or when she was lonely.

"Oh, I don't know," said Lance. "She never permitted unhappiness, acknowledged weakness, or tolerated failure. I guess the whole evil witch curse thing just never occurred to her. Are you okay?"

"Yes, it's just…I mean it's silly, except it's not." She took a breath. "Ever since Campbell was born, strange things have been happening. Awful things."

"I know, Dill. Shane and I are very sorry about all that, about everything. He sends his love, too."

She turned to look back at the family through the conservatory glass wall. "And you? Anything...?"

"Strange and awful? I'm an ER resident on the south side of Boston."

In the background, a spike of hospital chaos. Someone barked his name.

"Speaking of, I gotta bolt...."

"Lance, what are the symptoms of rheumatic fever?"

"Why? Are you worried about Campbell?"

"No, I'm just..."

"It's not genetic, Dill. It's weird enough that you and Adam caught it. It's like catching polio."

"Do you still have contacts at the Children's Hospital here?"

"Sure. Why?"

"Records department?"

He paused. "What are you looking for, Dill?"

● ● ●

Khaki and Emma had turned in for the night. Vivian carried a fading Campbell upstairs, as Dillie came back from the kitchen.

"I meant to tell you," her mother called down from the landing, "I found Campbell playing near the back door earlier. Don't you know you never take your eyes off a child, even for an instant?"

"Sorry. I must have lost track," said Dillie, going toward her. "Here, I can put him down."

"I'll do the honors tonight," Vivian said, book in hand, as she disappeared up. "We're at the *Runaway Bunny* cliffhanger. Campbell is dying to know the ending...."

Richard intercepted her in the foyer.

"Dillie," he said, fumbling, "your mother mentioned you were talking about...were curious about..."

"The Bell Witch?"

He chuckled. Nodded. "That legend, yes."

"I was curious that I'm a descendant of the family."

"I guess you are, yes. Among many others, of course."

"Direct descendant, apparently."

He changed tactics, lightening. "It was a running gag when I was dating your mother. Whenever she got mad at me...which was not uncommon...I'd blame it on the Bell Witch. It was a joke, you see."

Dillie stared, waiting. Clearly he'd been sent on a mission.

"A lot has happened to you...lately," he went on, gauging. "And I was thinking...I have friends at the hospital. Very smart people. Doctors, of course. And perhaps you could talk to them...."

"You think I've lost it," Dillie said, and Richard said, "Not at all, Dillie. But PTSD is a real condition. And quite treatable. I think you owe it to your son..."

"Campbell's just fine," she flared, regretting her tone. She softened. "And I'm pretty well covered in the doctor department." Booray whined at the mudroom door, having not yet figured out the old dog flap. "Hold up, Boo," she said, turning.

"I'm happy to go with you," Richard added. "It might...be a good thing for us to talk to them together. Like a family therapy sort of thing. It could even bring us...closer, in a way."

She wanted to tell him it was a bit late. That the fallout from his ghosting on the periphery of her life for so long was that his newfound concern—albeit sincere—felt static and staged. That her top priority was avoiding the same mistake with her own family, and that his should be figuring out what made him an outsider, a spectator, with his.

She said none of this. Instead, she rubbed his arm. "Thank you, Dad. I'll think about it. Love you." And with a kiss to his cheek, she hurried off.

The night had chilled quickly. Booray bounded off toward the tree line, finding his spot. "Make it snappy, sir," she called out. A strange glow past the trees caught her eye. An intense spot of moonlight reflected off the water and hit a clearing. She moved toward it.

On a tree stump, facing the river, sat a woman. Dillie crept closer. It was Khaki, bundled up over her nightgown against the sharp wind.

Four yelping shadows with doglike energy scampered in front of her, twirling, pawing. Three large, one smaller, all scrawny and agitated. Dillie squinted. Coyotes.

From a clear bag, Khaki hand-fed them table scraps, focusing on one at a time. Like pets.

"That's a good boy, Jerusalem," she said, beckoning the more skittish young pup with a leftover piece of tilapia. Head down, it darted up and back, sniffing. With a jolt of courage, it snatched the fillet in its mouth and retreated a step to wolf it down. "Careful now," she said with a laugh. "There's plenty."

The largest adult circled the pup, menacing. "No, Black Dog," Khaki warned, waving a roll. "This one's for you." Ignoring her, it lunged for the fish. The others joined in, shielding the pup. One attacked. A gnashing riot erupted, as the animals locked into one another by the throat.

Khaki leaned toward the shrieking fight. "Stop it!" she commanded, clapping her hands. "Enough!" She reached into the knotted snarl to break it up.

"Khaki, NO!" Dillie screamed, racing toward her.

The shadows vanished into the thicket. The moonlight faded behind a cloud. Khaki, in darkness, turned to her with surprise.

"Is something wrong, Dillie?" She was alert, enlivened.

"What are you doing out here?"

Her grandmother looked around at the obvious. "I'm sitting by the river, Dillie."

"This late?"

Khaki chortled. "Maybe it's past your bedtime, but not mine. I like to leave food for our fellow travelers, whoever they may be." She peered at her granddaughter. "Are you all right?"

"It's j-just...," Dillie stammered, on guard for the wild pack surely lurking. "Is it safe out here?" Booray romped to her side, oblivious.

Khaki stood, brushed her hands clean as she approached. "Safest place on earth, as far as I'm concerned. Clears my head." She inspected Dillie with mock disdain. "When did you become such a city mouse?" Then she put her arm around her, leading her back toward the mansion.

"Sorry to alarm you," she said, stifling her amusement. "Let's go in. You're shivering, my girl."

five

Her insurance declined the refill, so Dillie paid cash. She must have left her other Zoloft behind in New York; she couldn't possibly be running low.

"This is your last one," the pharmacist told her. "Shall I call your doctor for a new prescription?"

"No, thank you," said Dillie, smiling as she whisked the bag away. "Have a good day."

She'd hoped her temporary return home would reduce her anxiety, not heighten it; that was the whole point. River Kiss, and her family, always had a calming effect, a spindle-clearing of sorts. It was the perfect place to decompress from the mayhem of the big city.

But whatever peace she'd felt that first morning had quickly evaporated, leaving her coiled and on edge anew. Then again, she was recuperating from a far greater trauma than normal, as her father pointed out. She couldn't expect to bounce back to her normal, centered self so quickly.

Her family itself also seemed different this visit. Vivian's cheer was forced and more manic than typical, her father and Khaki especially withdrawn. Even Emma, the emotional center of the group, appeared to be playacting, her nurturing warmth only partially masking a simmering unease. Perhaps the family was on eggshells, not sure how to handle her in the wake of such a tragedy. Or they were acclimating to the sudden upheaval in their own lives at her return, especially with a toddler in tow. In spite of their insistence otherwise, it was a significant—and open-ended—disruption in their long-settled routine. It was likely Dillie's heightened state of awareness made her overly sensitive. But something, in general, felt off.

Thankfully, the medications did their job—keeping her steady-keeled, luring her to sleep—even as she worried about their side effects, most notably her slurry dreams, that, when recalled the next morning, blended the real with the fantastical. She *knew* Khaki had been sitting by the river, tossing table scraps, but in retrospect, she couldn't be certain now the coyotes had been there. It was dark and far, and it was possible she'd heard them distantly—like that first night—and assumed they'd been in the shadowy clearing. The moonlight and acoustics, and her own imagination, might have conjured a freakish scene that never happened. Indeed, Booray had paid no notice of them.

The easiest solution—simply asking Khaki—would reveal one of them as unstable. Vivian was already on high alert, it seemed, to both of them.

The drugs had to go eventually, but she couldn't repeat the crash landing when she stopped cold turkey. She'd wean herself off them gradually, and soon.

She knew Campbell was up from his morning nap even before she arrived back at the house. An ear-phone-wearing Khaki was out in the field on her makeshift shooting range with her father's Smith & Wesson, as she had been near daily since Dillie was a little girl. While gun-hating Vivian had prevented her from passing down the dread hobby to Dillie, she couldn't stop Khaki herself.

After all, it was her land. Khaki had, however, adjusted her target practice around Campbell's sleeping schedule.

If the pistol's kick was too much for her these days, it didn't flummox her aim, as the intruder silhouette inserts tacked to hay bales were decidedly blown through at the heads. Dillie waved as she drove past, and Khaki smiled as she blasted on. Few things in life seemed to give her such joy.

She'd left a message that morning for Lance's contact at the Children's Hospital. It was a vague message, not only because Dillie wasn't exactly sure the information she wanted—or if she was even allowed to get it—but also because she felt a bit sly, subversive really, going behind her mother's back. Her biggest fear was the hospital calling Vivian for permission to release it, blowing her cover. She'd figure it out when they called back.

Vivian was in full grandmother mode, demonstrating how to make cheese straws with a pastry gun to a rapt and enchanted Campbell in his high chair. While they baked, she dragged him to the wall calendar above her desk, where she kept track of her commitments (the bug man, upcoming PBS specials, Khaki's many doctor appointments). With a grand flourish, she marked a red *X* over the current day, counting down to his second birthday two weeks off, which she'd festooned with stars, exclamation points, and smiley faces. Clueless, he couldn't resist her infectious delight, squealing and clapping along with her. The joy was mutual; Vivian genuinely savored every moment with her grandson.

The FedEx truck came right before lunch. "Richard, your booze is here!" Vivian yelled upward. "Your father joined a wine club. I declare we could fill the storm cellar with all the bottles he orders in. The delivery man must think we stagger around the house all day."

There was also a box for Dillie, from Rupert. Her favorite winter clothes she'd left behind, forwarded mail, including invites to holiday parties, and most charmingly, a blond Steiff teddy bear for Campbell, red bow and all. She'd introduce them at bedtime.

She tripped carrying the box up, breaking her fall on the landing, and noticed for the first time the sturdiness of the staircase. No creaking, no give, like other old houses. Coming back down, she ran her hand along the banister, testing it. Solid, wobble-free. The mahogany was slightly worn from years of use, but not at all in tune with a mansion this age. She'd never paid attention to it before and wasn't sure why she was now.

That night's bee in Vivian's bonnet was plastic surgery, as she leafed through the latest *Nfocus* magazine's social pages. "They've all fiddled with their faces," she protested, showing off a recent black-tie event at the War Memorial downtown. "You expect it in Hollywood, but it's creeping into our dear old town, even among the quasi-young. Didn't that used to be Ilene's daughter? She looks like she's had a head transplant."

Dillie looked around the conservatory. A newer addition from the original house, she realized, although she didn't know when. It had been here her whole life, at least.

"Richard, do you remember the pictures from the Frist Gala?" her mother prattled on to a captive and wholly disinterested audience. "Wasn't that a shock to the system? It looked like planet of the...jaguars. That's what they were. Jaguars in ball gowns."

Or had it? The old photo she'd found upstairs showed young Vivian cavorting in the pool, a tot on each arm, with the house in the background. But a brick extension jutted from the side, not the glassed-in conservatory that sat there now. At some point, one had replaced the other. It must have been during Dillie's earliest years—certainly before she was four or so—as she had no memory of the demolition and construction.

"Oh, and here's Caitlin at the 'Toys for Tots' Mommy and Me," Vivian said, flipping pages. "Good grief, is that her little boy or the Duke of Cambridge? He's choking in that getup. See, this is a pitfall of having children too late in life." She tapped the photo for emphasis. "The mothers go haywire. They smother. I think it's an overcompensation thing." She flipped on. "Oh well. Not my circus, not my monkeys."

The conservatory, like the remodeled kitchen, was part of Vivian's never-ending "enrichment" of the manor, along with the staircase, the floors, and the moldings that seemed slightly at odds with the old mansion. Even the walls had a hollow-knock drywall feel, not the solid plaster she knew from tours of other antebellum homes. As if the whole interior had had a face-lift from the inside out.

"*Zoot alors!* Eloise at a party. Who'd a thunk it?" Vivian zeroed in on the magazine. "How many of those husbands do you think she's torn through? It must be nice to go through life with a self-cleaning conscience. And no, I won't add, 'bless her heart.'"

"Judge not," cautioned Emma, and Vivian said, "Hogwash. In my experience, the only ones who *don't* judge are simply too self-obsessed to pay attention to anyone else. Not you, of course. But yes, perhaps I put a little too much mustard on it."

Vivian tossed aside the magazine. The bridge game was back to full battle mode.

There was nothing strange about a renovation, Dillie knew. The house was more than two hundred years old. It had been through countless modernizations—electricity and plumbing, for starters—to keep it safe and standing. That Vivian had embarked on a massive redo in the window between Adam's death and Dillie's youngest memories was unusual timing, but her mother had always been her most frantic and productive under duress. It was her coping mechanism.

"I declare we need to put you out on the circuit," Vivian said as Khaki swept up another trick. "You could earn your keep around here."

But the dining room mural was a treasured artifact, to be protected at all cost. And it had been not just restored, but re-created. Only a crisis—total destruction—could have prompted that.

A cloudy memory dawned.

"It burned," said Dillie. "The house burned. Didn't it?"

Everyone but Khaki looked up at her from their hands.

"When I was very young," Dillie went on, searching. "After Adam died."

Vivian spoke up. "Why, yes, it did, Dillie. The house was gutted by fire."

"And you never told me."

Richard and Emma shrank back into their cards. Vivian sat taller. "Maybe, maybe not," she said, feigning a mental search. "I have no specific memory of sitting you down to explain the fire. Or plumbing backups or rapes or terrorists. How would you have preferred that I handle those things with a little girl?"

Dillie sat still, tensing. The foyer clock ticked.

"Did I do anything else wrong? Fail you in any way?" Vivian added with rising arch. "Won't you please keep a running tab of my shortcomings, so we can sort through them together?" She laid down her cards, stood up. "I look forward to learning from such an authority on perfect motherhood. I've long envied the stable and loving home you've created for your own family."

She knelt down to kiss Campbell on the floor. "Good night, little friend," she stage whispered. "Ask Mommy to tell you the story of your nanny. She's big on sharing.

"Sweet dreams," she called back, ascending the silent staircase. "Such a funny way to end the evening."

six

"I thought he could use another playmate down there." Rupert's voice still had the magic to calm her down, even against her will.

"He loves the bear, thank you," she said when he called back late that night. Her relief in talking to him was tempered by the frustration in tracking him down. He'd been traveling again, of course. She struggled to keep her suspicions in check.

She wanted to tell him about her persistent anxiety, Khaki's funny tale, the house-gutting fire her family had hidden from her. Instead, she shared Campbell's newfound love of green beans in ham hock, his delight in running through fields and discovering the wonders of the country. "And just today Booray learned to use Jasper's old dog door downstairs. He's already turned into a country hound," she said, opening the balcony door to let him in with his latest stick. It was almost like two proud and loving parents talking.

"Your mother wants me to come visit," he added casually. "For Campbell's birthday, if you're cool with that."

Dillie sharpened. "Wait, my *mother* called you? When?"

"She thinks it'd be good for you. And for us, as a family. As long as you're comfortable."

"Are you two talking behind my back?" she demanded. "Assessing me or something?"

"Don't be paranoid, Dill. We're just…keeping tabs. Because we love you."

"Keep tabs in front of my face, please. I have to go."

"Put Campbell on for a minute," he said quickly.

"It's almost midnight, Rupert," she said, ending the call. "Children sleep at that hour."

● ● ●

She shouldn't have mixed Zoloft with Lunestra. A "contraindication," her pharmacist called it. It had a squirrelly effect, keeping her both foggy and wired well into the night. At 2:43 a.m., she gave up on sleep.

Facebook, Twitter, Epicurious didn't hit the spot, as she sat on her bed, lights out, so as not to wake Campbell or encourage Booray. She plugged in her earbuds and considered Netflix; then, with the barest hesitation, her fingers typed and Googled "Bell Witch." There were hundreds of hits. She lingered on the list and clicked one near the top that seemed the most official.

It was a gimmicky fan site, slow-loading and springing with pop-up ads, which she batted away. "Pleasant dreams," it teased on the stark black welcome screen. She swirled the ghostly graphic floating in the center, clicked.

The home page listed the legend, characters, FAQ, and a genealogy. She went straight to the legend, nixing a pop-up for anti-aging serum.

There was a sketchy, abbreviated history of the haunting. "The spirit" first materialized in 1817 as a weak, invisible disruption—a weird nuisance, really—growing fiercer and ultimately catastrophic over a three-year, violent onslaught. There was no known reason why it targeted this nondescript family on their remote farm near the Kentucky border, but as its havoc intensified, so did its infamy, eventually spreading to European newspapers as a global sensation. Over time, the unwelcome guest found a voice—that of a prickly, middle-aged woman—taunting the Bells between physical assaults. It was particularly cruel toward the father and young daughter, more empathetic to the sons, and strangely doting of the beleaguered mother, even keeping a bedside vigil during one life-threatening illness and coaxing her back to health. The town nicknamed it "Kate," and its mercurial presence became a torturous constant in the Bells' lives.

Canceling out a "Best Handguns under $500" pop-up, Dillie moved on to the next page.

Kate vowed to kill the father, and when he died under suspicious circumstances, "the Being"—as the family called it—made its exit, promising to return to the family in seven years, in 107 years, and then again at a time of its choosing.

An ancient ghost story, she realized. Every town had one. This one simply had more sticking power.

When Dillie clicked on the genealogy tab, a "Have You Seen Me?" ad popped up, with photos of three missing children from various parts of the country. She lingered on the innocent smiles beaming at her—moved yet helpless—before squinting closer. They seemed from a different era: faded Kodachrome, buzz cuts, horn-rimmed glasses. She checked the fine print: last seen in the 1950s, cold cases to be sure. No one could possibly still be looking for them.

She closed it, and the ad sprang up with two more Depression-era children staring at her, missing. No. Relentless, the ad bounced back. Hollow-eyed youths in brown and white daguerreotypes from an earlier century, all obviously dead now regardless of their fate.

A blizzard of pop-ups lurked below, missing children stretching back through time. Dillie kept knocking them away. The last was the most stubborn: a frantic "Have You Seen Me?" across an empty frame, waiting to be filled. The site was haywire. Cancel, cancel, cancel.

A new window blocked her. "Are you sure you want to leave this page?" it asked. She did.

The Bell Witch website underneath went blank. "Error," it read. "Server not responding." Dillie closed her laptop, now groggy and over it. Her tutorial done for the night, she curled up under her covers, welcoming sleep.

Booray lifted himself off the floor and scampered toward the French door to the balcony, tail wagging. He looked up at it with expectation.

"Boo?" she whispered in the dark. "Don't tell me you need to go out."

He sat obediently, still facing the door, tail brushing the carpet. "What is it, Boo?"

He looked past the door's window, panting with excitement.

Dillie padded to him, followed his stare. With her nightgown sleeve she circled a clearing in the window's fog, peered out onto the balcony, the fire escape, and beyond. The night was dark and gusty, across the estate. Dense, moving clouds threatened a new storm.

Booray stood and pranced up and back, restless and eager. She checked his face for signs of illness, hoping he hadn't eaten something funny when she wasn't looking. All she saw was joy, his typical look after a long absence. But he wasn't looking at her at all.

"Go to bed," she ordered, and when he didn't hear, she gently pushed him. "Now, Booray!"

He glanced at her and then back, as if confused by conflicting instructions. She prodded him again, and relenting, he retreated to his spot on the floor.

Dillie turned the lock on the French door, untied the drapes, and pulled them closed. She peeked over at Campbell, mercifully still asleep in his crib. Booray shot up again, newly energized on his way to the balcony door, before changing his mind and abruptly returning.

"You're one strange dog, Boo," said Dillie. His bright eyes pivoted to her, tail thumping twice, then back to the door, ears hiked and alert. So sweet and strong, and stupid.

She crawled into bed, pulled the duvet to her chin, facing the French door herself. Campbell's early wake-up would come all too soon, and her pills were finally, belatedly, taking grasp. She breathed in, out, as the wind picked up outside.

There was a scratch on the French door window.

Dillie lurched up, listened. *Scratch-scratch-scratch*.

It stopped. Started again, in triplet rhythm.

She threw off the covers, to the door, flung open the drapes. *Scratch-scratch-scratch*.

The oak tree abutting the balcony, animated by the wind, scraped against the banister. *Scratch-scratch-scratch*. Booray, unconcerned, eyed her. She closed the drapes quietly, then tiptoed to Campbell's crib, in case her burst of energy had wakened him. It hadn't.

Scratch-scratch-scratch on the window, but not the window, of course. On the outside banister. Even the dog could tell the difference. She got back into bed, pulled the covers.

Something smallish scurried across the floor.

Dillie froze. Silence. She held still. Nothing.

A squirrel, a rodent, a critter on the roof, she realized. Not inside. The acoustics tricked her, exacerbated by the increasing, thrashing wind. She settled down.

It scampered from one corner to another. In the room. Too heavy for a mouse. A rat.

She jolted upright, reached past her pill bottles for the bedside lamp. Turned the switch. Turned it again. Nothing.

The rat darted under her bed. Dillie held her breath. It paused right below, foraging. Booray snored, oblivious. She needed to open the French door, to give it an escape route, but felt trapped in the bed, lest any movement dislodge it back into the open.

A second pattering ran across the room toward Campbell's crib. She sprang up, reached into her bedside drawer for the always-there flashlight, aimed it at the floor as she moved closer. On hands and knees, she scoured under and around the crib, finding nothing. Her target had taken cover, waiting her out. She stood, beaming around the room. A rustling in the corner drew her focus. She shined at it, and the noise dashed along the wall, under a chair, before scurrying on. She couldn't keep up.

Behind her, tiny teeth gnawed at the bedpost. She yanked around, dropping the flashlight. Booray perked up at the commotion, watched her. Dillie picked up the shattered light, shook it, useless.

The gnawing intensified and spread to all four bedposts, feasting in rhythm. Several more vermin scattered throughout the room, scratching, crawling on all sides. Dillie spun, surrounded in the darkness.

The assault multiplied and spread across the floor, inside the walls, along the molding. One ran across her foot, needly nails pricking her skin. She kicked, shrieked.

Silence. Dillie caught her breath, listened. As quickly as they had arrived, they were gone, back through whatever mysterious openings rats used. She exhaled, calmed herself. Exterminators, first thing in the morning. Then a new cat, or a pair. Booray would adjust. She tiptoed toward Campbell. He'd sleep with her tonight.

A swarm of hundreds descended, amassed, and targeted the crib. Armylike, they crawled up the posts, along the top rail, and between the slats, leaping into the bed. Dillie screamed, raced to rescue him.

They flooded under her nightgown, shimmied up her legs, silky fur tickling her calves and thighs, moving farther up her body. She lurched into the crib. It was too late: His blanket writhed with the nest underneath, his hair alive as they engulfed his face and scalp. She tore off the blanket, grabbed him, triggering a symphony of famished squeals.

"Help!" she cried out to the ceiling. "Help me!"

A game and delighted Booray lifted on back legs and woofed a playful bark.

Dillie hoisted a weighted-down Campbell, as the rats hung by claws and dropped away, furiously screeching. One gnarled in her hair; another clung under her nightgown, sinking teeth into the small of her back as she lunged toward the door, begging for help.

She turned the knob, and turned, spinning without catching. She clutched and shook her childhood door that had never failed her before. "Somebody help!" she screamed, as the rats crisscrossed her body, encircling her neck and climbing her ears.

The door thrust inward, knocking her back with a rush and a beam of light. Richard in T-shirt and faded boxers, Vivian in boyfriend pajamas and with a flashlight.

"What is it?" her father said. "What's going on?" her mother demanded, blinding her.

"Rats!" Dillie cried, flinging them from her face, chest, and back. But her fists were empty.

Vivian's flashlight scanned Dillie, the floor, the corners. "Rats?" she said. "Where?"

"Everywhere!" Dillie insisted, relieved and confused at their sudden disappearance. "And the lights don't work!" she added, and Richard said, "The power's out."

"The wind, Dillie," Vivian explained, as to a child. She pointed the light toward the window. "The wind."

A trembling Dillie stood staring at them, and around the room. At nothing.

Vivian tossed the flashlight on the bed, went to rescue Campbell from Dillie's tight clutch. "My sleepy boy," she said, cradling him. "Mommy's stirred up quite a commotion in the dead of night, hasn't she?"

"What's happened?" Emma burst into the room in her robe and curlers. "What's wrong?" Her bright, wild eyes stood out in the dark.

"Nothing, Emma," said Vivian with calm forbearance. "Delphine has had an episode, of sorts. Now, if we can all take a breath, perhaps we might restore order to the household."

"There *were* rats," Dillie said, certain and not. "In his crib. Everywhere."

"Emma, will you take Campbell?" Vivian ordered, holding him out. "Ferret him away from this room of crisis?"

"That's my boy," Emma cooed, scooping him into her arms with a toothy smile. "My, my, you're getting heavy. Such a big boy." She cupped his head, whisked him out.

"And let Mother know it's a false alarm," Vivian added. "And to stay in bed." Emma nodded, pulling the door closed behind her.

Vivian sighed, grabbed the flashlight again. It circled the room, past the bed, then shot back to the bedside table with targeted precision, training on the pill bottles. "Oh," she said with a sharp inhale. "Oh dear."

She moved toward them. "Trouble sleeping, Dill?" She picked up a bottle, squinted at the label. "Interesting side effects, I am sure. How long have you been on these?"

"I'm not *on* anything," said Dillie, bristling at her own lie.

"Oh?" Vivian repeated, turning it toward her. "What are these? Chiclets?" She inspected bottle after bottle, grimacing. "Who prescribed all these? Dr. Bombay?" She *tsk*ed, shaking her head. "I shudder to think of the New York quack who has you in his thrall."

"*She's* not a quack...."

"Quite a cocktail you've whipped up for yourself," Vivian barreled on, lining up the bottles in a straight row, edge to edge across the table. "Is this a nightly ritual these days? Your new normal?"

Vivian held up her hand to preempt Dillie's next protest. She nodded through an exhale, her mind ticking as she straightened with decision. She pointed at Richard—"Good cop"—then at herself: "And the real McCoy."

She leveled her stare. "Pills," she said. "Rats. Witches. Delphine, think of your *son*. This illness of yours is harming him, too, you know."

"I know what I saw," Dillie said, now doubting herself. "What I felt."

"At least Khaki has an excuse for her dementia. What's yours?"

"I'm not demented!" said Dillie, doubting anew.

"Rupert was *this close* to taking Campbell away from you!" Vivian spat. "For his own safety. Did you know that? I said, 'You can't do that.' But now I share his alarm." She stood back, letting it settle.

"I begged him for time," she added. "Time is up. *Capiche?*"

Stunned, Dillie drank in the dark room's post-chaos calm. The room without rats, where there hadn't been any, certainly not the hundreds that had never swarmed the floors, the walls, the gravity-defying *ceiling*, for God's sake. The crowd of pill bottles, her secret companions for nearly two years, distorting her mind and moods, growing larger until they could scarcely fit on the bedside table. The crib where her son had been peacefully asleep before she jerked him awake for a traumatizing—and false—terror.

Softening, Vivian perched on the bed, patted an invitation. Dillie sat in the well-worn spot from countless such talks over the years. "Honey, what did I always tell you?" soothed Vivian, caressing hair off her daughter's forehead. "If we ignore a problem, it doesn't go away. It only gets worse."

Dillie nodded. "Yes, ma'am." Booray nosed up under her palm, nestling on her knee.

Vivian wrapped around her, rocking head on head. The bedside lamp popped on, brightening the room. Vivian laughed. "Right on cue!" she cheered.

She leaned into Dillie's ear. "I'll call my doctor tomorrow," she whispered. "He makes you confront your demons, not drug yourself away from them. And no one need ever know...."

The intercom by the door popped a crackle of static, jolting them. "The system resets after an outage," said a weary Richard.

The static grew louder, needling. A shriek of audio feedback pierced through. "Good gravy," said Vivian, cupping her ears.

The crackling settled into a trickling stream, then a rushing river. Underneath blossomed the cries of an infant.

"What is that?" said Vivian. "Is that Campbell?"

"No," Dillie said.

Classical musical—Mozart? Brahms?—weaved in, a weird symphony growing louder.

"Richard, can you fix this, please?" Vivian snapped.

Mozart, Dillie realized. A sonata. From the children's DVD.

The noisy mix blared through the hallway as they descended the staircase, Booray on their trail. A panicked Emma followed, carrying a docile and newly wakened Campbell.

"I'll take him," said Dillie, lifting him to her in the foyer.

Richard opened the door to the concealed cubby under the stairs, where the security console lived. "It's never done this before," he shouted over the bedlam that reverberated through the walls and floors. He knelt down, flipping switches, turning knobs. Nothing.

"Mercy," said Emma, covering her ears.

Campbell pushed back from his mother's embrace, arched up, and with a giggle pointed over her shoulder toward the front door. "What is it, Campbell?" Dillie asked, turning.

The doorbell rang.

Everyone whirled to it. "What in heavens...?" Vivian said, and Richard called out from the cubby, "It's just a malfunction."

Booray scampered off toward the back French door, tail wagging.

The back door buzzer rang. And again.

"Mercy," Emma repeated, sidling against the wall. The music-river-crying baby grew deafening.

The security system chimed an alert, and Agatha said, "*The front door is open*," although it wasn't.

"Richard, turn the thing off!" Vivian ordered.

"*The back door is open*," Agatha warned calmly.

"I'm trying!" Richard shouted, punching all the buttons.

Campbell giggled again. Dillie hugged his head to her shoulder and peered around toward the back. Booray wagged his tail at dark nothingness beyond, yelping once.

"*Window six is open*," Agatha said, now louder. "*Motion detected hallway three.*"

Vivian looked up the stairs. "Mother?" she called. "Is that you up there?"

Agatha's voice grew deeper and distorted, rattling the house. "*Door DETECTED Motion FIVE WindowHallBackOPEN...*"

"Unplug the damn thing!" Vivian screeched, as the house alarm unleashed its siren.

Agatha screamed: "*FIRE! FIRE! FIRE! FI...!*"

Richard ripped the power source from the wall, falling backward. All went silent.

Emma clutched her chest, grappling for a full breath. "Are you okay?" Dillie asked, and Emma nodded through a forced smile. "Yes, dear. Oh yes." She looked older.

Vivian deflated, palming hair back from her forehead. She sank against the staircase. Richard sat flat on the floor, fist full of cords. "It's done," he said.

Dillie rocked a delighted Campbell in place. Her grip was trembling. Outside, the wind had calmed to stillness. Booray returned to her side.

"Monsieur Cooper appears to have sold us a lemon," said Vivian through a hard swallow, dismissing the faulty security console with a backhanded flick. "I look forward to *quizzing* him tomorrow."

Richard climbed to his feet, dropped the power cords, dusted off his hands. His face sagged. "Let's just go to bed," he said.

"Hear, hear," said Vivian, and Emma said, "Yes. Oh yes."

Dillie led the pilgrimage up the stairs. The others followed. They reached the landing.

The alarm screamed anew. Fresh chaos descended on the house, until dawn.

● ● ●

The next morning, after thirty-three years with the family, Emma retired, to spend more time with her own.

seven

Emma's daughter Jasmine was extended family, having grown up with Dillie like a slightly older and much admired cousin. "Jazz" was, and always had been, sharp, stylish, and stunning.

They chatted and caught up as they packed her minivan with Emma's belongings—beige Coleman luggage set, hugs of clothes on hangers, her special daylight reading lamp—and delighted in Campbell's arm's-length curiosity over Jasmine's girls, six and eight.

Emma was dressed for Sunday, although it wasn't. The family lined up for their goodbyes.

"It's Mt. Juliet, not Siberia," she told an antsy but composed Vivian. "I fully expect visits."

"Y'all sure you can manage without her?" Jazz joked, shoving a milk crate brimming with paperbacks and old videocassette movies into the trunk corner.

Emma *pooh-pooh*ed. "Of course they can. I haven't lifted a finger around here in ten years."

"I can vouch for that," Vivian said, and Emma said, "Hush your mouth," tightening her squeeze.

She moved on to Khaki with a more ginger but earnest embrace. "Don't forget your pills," she told her. Khaki chuckled and said, "Don't forget *yours*."

Emma halted at Dillie, her smile warm but hesitant as she held her face. "Take good care of them," she said. She stroked the top of Campbell's head before linking eyes again. "All of them."

She stayed locked on Dillie as the minivan pulled away. The smile was gone.

"We won't rent out your room!" Vivian called out, her wave frantic.

The family stood, watching them go.

"Mom, can I borrow your car for the day?" Dillie asked. "I have some research for a project."

"There's a spare key in the glovebox. I'll give you mine later," Vivian said, taking Campbell's hand. "Shall we finish our watercolor, little man? We're up to Mr. R. *Rabbit? Rooster?*"

● ● ●

Emma's retirement was hardly surprising. She'd been hinting at it for years. Why wouldn't she want to spend more time with her grandchildren, especially with Christmas around the corner? And her "temporary" residency with the family, after her husband's death, had stretched on far longer than anyone expected.

"*In one mile, take a right onto exit I-24…,*" the Volvo's GPS directed. American female. *Not* Agatha.

Dillie cracked the window for a brace of crisp air as she focused on the busy I-65. There'd been no sleep for anyone. She felt sorry for the patient going under her father's knife that morning.

The backup battery that fueled the false alarm through the night—and summoned the police, firemen—was sealed and unstoppable, a poorly designed system run amok. Its reign of terror finally gave out as the sun rose, and Vivian left three progressively hostile messages for the installer before breakfast. "They scramble to *sell* it but never to *fix* it," she stewed, pouring a rare cup of coffee.

Dillie passed over into Robertson County, a name she knew from local weather reports but didn't remember visiting before. Or having reason to.

"In two miles, take a right on exit nineteen." She checked her mirror; much clearer on the less-traveled I-24.

And while a faulty alarm to this extreme was certainly irregular, it wasn't unprecedented, or even inexplicable. Her own motion detector in New York had silently malfunctioned soon after they moved in, which triggered a menacing visit from New York's finest (and a four-hundred-dollar false-alarm fine). The higher the tech, the screwier the breakdowns.

The well maintained but lonely road was familiar and Tennessee-esque, although she'd forgotten how expansive and lovely her state was. The flatter vistas and lack of hills indicated the pull north toward the Kentucky border.

The Children's Hospital had called first thing that morning to inform her, rather brusquely, that Adam's medical records, like everyone's, were confidential. That she was his sister was irrelevant, as they could only be made available to the parent, another doctor, or by court order. Dillie thanked the surly administrator—likely a Yankee transplant—and left a message for Lance in Boston.

She slowed to thirty and passed a carved, wooden sign: "Welcome to City of Adams." Riding across the middle was a cartoonish, black-hatted witch on a broom, a full moon over her shoulder. Perfect for an amusement park, ridiculous for a proper town.

She knew where she was going but not what she was looking for. "Research," she'd told her mother. True, in a way.

The town was sparse, quiet; the road undulating but straight. Modest, well-kept houses, mostly brick in pale red or beige, circa 1950s and since. A few dogs ran free but kept to their unfenced yards. Mailboxes still had painted cylinder attachments for news-papers. The *Tennessean*, the *Leaf-Chronicle*.

"In one thousand feet, you have reached your destination."

The gray obelisk in the distance caught her eye first. It stood back from the road, quite tall, with a large globe perched on top. The centerpiece of what looked like a small park, it was enclosed by a matching gray low wall and guarded by a black iron gate, all backing up to a dense flank of trees just beyond. The park sat empty and removed and was weirdly out of place.

Just past was an enormous farm field that stretched to the ho-rizon, barren and unmolested behind its barbed-wire barrier. Past that, according to the Volvo, was Dillie's destination.

It was a red-brick, school-looking square building, older than the rest of the town. The weathered blue and white sign on the street read "Adams Antique Mall" in block letters, subtitled with "Home of the Bell Witch" in Gothic ones. A "Schoolhouse Tea Room" placard dangled from the bottom, swinging in the slight breeze. The multipurpose town hub, at least for visitors and tourists.

To the side, a smaller, paint-flecked yard sign hawked the "Bell Witch Opry" on Saturday night. *Every* Saturday night? she wondered.

The site marker closest to the street stood out for its familiarity and officialness: an engraved iron plaque from the Tennessee Historical Commission, crowned with the trio of stars from the state flag. Dillie had seen countless, at notable universities, Civil War battle sites, Andrew Jackson's homestead.

Dillie slowed to read the inscription:

BELL WITCH

To the north was the farm of John Bell. According to legend, his family was harried during the early 19th century by the famous Bell Witch. She kept the household in turmoil, assaulted Bell, and drove off Betsy Bell's suitor. Many visitors to the house saw the furniture crash about them and heard her shriek, sing, and curse.

Dillie bristled: It diminished her home state to equate a ghost story with other sites of true, historical importance. Disrespectful, silly, and embarrassing. Who approved this?

Simmer down, she scolded herself. What did it matter to her anyway?

The parking circle was nearly full, including two full-size tour buses she had to inch past. Surely this wasn't their destination; more likely a lunch stop at the tea room. But why were they passing through Adams? Dillie squeezed into a spot between a newish Cadillac and an aging Impala.

The "malarkey" field trip her mother had ridiculed and forbidden.

The tea room was indeed bustling. So was the Bell Witch gift shop, a homespun and decidedly quaint emporium of all things witch-branded: key chains, coffee mugs, refrigerator magnets, jars of preserves and molasses. More tasteful than she'd expected, the shop offered a children's corner with puzzles, witch dolls, and hats, and a sizable Christmas section—seasonal or year-round, hard to tell—with ornaments, glass-domed boysenberry candles, and cinnamon-scented decorative brooms. Wafting from the next-door kitchen were savory whiffs of ham, biscuits, coffee. The whole building was cozy and festive.

It was a cottage industry, cashing in on the state's most famous tall tale. Tennessee's Paul Bunyan.

She eavesdropped on the chatty customers, nearly all late-middle-aged women, either longtime friends or newly bonded through their spinster/divorcée/widowhoods. Rust-belt accents, far from home. Probably on a Music City tour and snookered into a tourist-trap lark to the middle of nowhere. She'd be ticked. But they were enthralled. Eager even.

Unless this was the main event, the whole reason for their trip down South. Not possible.

Dillie pondered a *Where's Waldo*-esque coloring book for Campbell—a hidden Bell Witch on every page—but he was too young, and Vivian too hostile. It'd blow the whistle on her secret excursion, as deliciously subversive as that might be.

A couple in the next aisle broke out in laughter. Cackled, really. Past them were the grown-up books on pine shelves against the wall.

Dillie waited in line, her arms full of paperbacks—from tiny, local presses, if not homemade. Behind the cashier hung two framed portraits, a man and a woman from a long-gone century: stern, inscrutable, quietly regal. The Bells, of course. Her ancestors, if Khaki and Vivian were to be believed. Overseeing the brisk business their torment had begat.

"Fall under Kate's spell, too?" asked the winking cashier with a well-rehearsed line.

Dillie smiled back with a shrug. "When in Rome," she said, unloading on the counter. She breezed a laugh. "Do you...believe all this?"

The woman leaned in with a playful secret. "Kate's ninety-five percent of my sales." She winked again. "I *believe*." On the counter were discount coupons to *Kate! The Musical*, performed monthly. Unlikely to reach the Shubert anytime soon but kept the local players in the spotlight.

The cashier started to ring up the paperbacks and Xeroxed pamphlets stapled together, then stopped. "I'm happy to take your money, sugar," she said, "but really all you need is this."

Reaching to a pyramid of autographed hardbacks by the counter—professionally designed, quality-bound—she added, "Hot off the press," and handed over a hefty book.

The Being: The Complete History of the Bell Witch Legend by Dr. Randall Grant. Dillie checked the spine. One of the big houses, clearly legit. The author's jacket photo—a late-middle-aged African-American gentleman—looked distinguished, not unhinged. A PhD had spent precious time on this; a major publisher was hawking it.

"I'll take them all," said Dillie, adding it to her pile. The wink needed to stop.

"Vanderbilt professor," the cashier went on, running her card as she tapped the book. "Got so obsessed, he actually bought the old place." She pointed to the vast, empty field out the window. "For a song, so I heard."

"Did he buy the park, too?" Dillie asked of the obelisk far beyond.

The woman looked confused, then frowned. "That's the Bell Memorial," she *tsk*ed. "Lotta descendants buried there."

Dillie nodded at Ma and Pa Bell looking down. "Including them?" She considered, then opted against, revealing her connection.

"Oh no. The victims are buried on the farm itself. With their children and slaves. A sacred spot."

"Where on the farm?"

The cashier grinned as she handed over the loaded bag. "It's private property, ma'am," she said, another well-worn line. "Closed to the public."

● ● ●

The iron gate, while imposing, was not locked. She pushed it open soundlessly.

Hidden from a distance, below the wall, were the precise rows of identical granite tombstones—carved, angular, modern—inside the Bell Memorial. Roughly forty markers in all, lined rigidly through the lush and manicured lawn, they reminded Dillie of fallen soldiers in a national cemetery. Adams's Arlington.

Here were Bell descendants stretching back to the 1800s— surely exhumed and reburied, the tombstones being so contemporary and pristine—up to the current time. Several plots were reserved for future residents, the names eerily earmarked, awaiting their arrival. There were Johns and Joels, Margarets and Roberts; doctors and lawyers, and a handful who'd died as children and young adults. Bells, all.

She found her great-grandfather, whom she knew nothing about, except that he was Khaki's father and had written his own witch account the year she was born. It dawned on her she knew nothing about any of her ancestors—her whole lineage a non-topic throughout her life—as if her family tree began with those still living. According to his tombstone, he was a doctor and died when Khaki was fifteen. She wondered if Khaki ever came to visit; if so, she kept it private.

Dillie looked around. The cemetery, while peaceful and lovely—stately, even—felt odd.

The obelisk stood sentry over it all. "GLORY BE TO GOD," it demanded in large engravings. She drew closer to the smaller inscription underneath: a memorial to John and Lucy Bell, "pioneer settlers" whose fabled ordeal two centuries ago still filled the gift shop and tea room, spawned books and websites, and kept the tour buses coming on this random, pre-winter weekday.

The memorial left out their ordeal, and the witch, but it listed their children and, bizarrely, cryptic directions to their own grave sites: "267 Rods N 18° E From Here."

She hadn't brought a compass, not expecting a scavenger hunt. She'd never seen a memorial tease out map clues like a video game. No wonder her family had moved away decades ago; the relatives were batty.

Dillie peered out at the adjacent farmland. Wind rustled the dense thicket of oaks behind the cemetery, one towering above the rest in the middle. A high, chain-link fence stood between them. Clues notwithstanding, any sacred burial spot wouldn't be left exposed in the open field where crops once grew. It would be sheltered, protected, the site chosen for privacy and quiet contemplation. Most likely near the grandest tree.

On the horizon, at what must have been the edge of the property, a two-story log cabin spiraled smoke from its chimney.

Between the distance and the shield of trees, she could barely see it; they couldn't possibly see her.

The signs were nonnegotiable: "PRIVATE PROPERTY," "NO TRESPASSING," "VIOLATORS WILL BE PROSECUTED." The fence itself, though high, hardly an obstacle. No city mouse, she.

Dillie periscoped. There was no one around. She tested the chain-link, sturdy enough. Eminently climbable.

She wouldn't steal or break anything. She'd be in and out without a trace. The obelisk's tease was practically an invitation.

And after all, she *was* kin.

● ● ●

The sprint to the thicket was longer than it seemed, the folly of her quest more pronounced with each stride.

The cluster was larger and denser than it appeared from a distance, too. Winded, she charged into the thick tangle and stopped to catch her breath. It was darker inside, and silent. She vowed to get back to the gym soon; her heart shouldn't be pounding so hard.

Stepping carefully on the spongelike ground, padded over with decades of natural compost, she worked her way deeper into the dim forest. She'd lost the great oak she was targeting, disoriented at close range, so she searched for the thickest trunk.

She knew what she was looking for but didn't know why. It was more than mere curiosity, or skepticism; she didn't doubt the graves existed, or that they contained the people who had birthed the legend on this very land. Finding them wouldn't make her believe any more, or less (if that were possible). But seeing for herself would, on a gut level, help discern whether they were perpetrators of an inexplicable hoax, victims of a contagious delusion, or merely a superstitious family trying to explain away life's hardships. It would make them, in some way, fathomable.

A rustling to her right. Dillie froze. Too distinct and deliberate for the wind. A skunk, chipmunk, God forbid a rattlesnake—a woodland creature on its home turf. Unfazed, she crept on.

Bending low-hanging limbs out of her way, she spied a clearing just ahead, in front of a brawny tree. The thick canopy above strangled what little light fought through. Senses prickling, she moved toward it. The ground opened underneath, swallowing her into the earth.

A sinkhole, up to her chest. Damp, moldy soil encased her. Her clothes ruined, she'd have to get new ones, or sneak back home without getting caught. Served her right.

It could have been worse, or deeper. The bottom of the hole was solid and stable, almost floorlike. She spread her hands out along the rim—add a manicure to her list—and drove herself to the surface. She crawled on her knees to clear the pit, looked up.

Inches away, at the base of the trunk, lay the Bells.

Nearly camouflaged, their rustic tombstones crumbling and moss-shrouded, the family fanned out. Just beyond, several shorter stubs slanted in all directions, like crooked teeth.

She crept to the closest, the largest in the center. Gently brushed debris from its ancient surface. "GLORY BE TO GOD," it echoed across the top. More brushing, just below: "JOHN BELL, SR. 1750–1820." Dillie pulled back. The patriarch.

She glanced back at the sinkhole that lined up with his marker and pushed away the thought that she had fallen into his grave, that his body had stopped her. She resisted the urge to check.

His wife, Lucy, rested beside him, having outlived him substantially. Others, presumably children, completed the family, with the second-tier slaves encircling behind. The earth around the tiny cemetery was eroded and uneven, either timeworn or intentionally disturbed and desecrated. Cathedral lighting through the branches above cast a focused glow on the rot and decay.

They were real, as Dillie knew they would be. Oddities and targets of snoops and trespassers and even grave robbers for nearly two hundred years. Like herself.

A louder rustling jarred the silence. Dillie spun to peer into the distance. A mother doe with two fawns poised nearby, eyeing her back with matching fear. With a bolt, they disappeared deeper into the thicket. She exhaled. A hand grabbed her from behind. Dillie screamed.

"Are those signs not big enough for you?" the man's voice boomed, releasing her.

She looked up at the African-American gentleman, instantly familiar—and livid.

"Sir, I'm so sorry. I didn't mean to—"

"There's not much left to steal," he barreled on. "Bones? Teeth? What kind of souvenir you looking for?"

"No! I'm not taking anything! I just wanted to see—"

"This family deserves more respect than vandals picking over their—"

"Dr. Grant, this *is* my family!" Dillie shouted, pointing.

The professor stopped cold at his name.

"*That's* what I'm looking for!" she added.

eight

"As far as I can tell, it was the most famous haunting in US history," Dr. Grant claimed, filling two mismatched mugs from the teakettle. "It certainly lasted the longest."

The log cabin was cozy, warm, bookish; her host gracious. They'd thawed to each other quickly, both embarrassed by their initial clash, which seemed, at this point, comical. Neither fit the profile of intruder or attack dog. Dillie had apologized profusely, which Dr. Grant waved off, intrigued to meet a descendant and instinctively appreciative of an overeager student. Plus, he shared her curiosity.

"World's greatest unexplained phenomenon, they called it," he went on, showing off digital clippings from vintage newspapers in various languages, including exotic, Far-Eastern ones. "It wasn't just some spook floating around. This demon broke through in a violent reign of terror, with an erratic, psychotic personality. Intelligent, crafty, relentless. At least, that was the reporting." She scrolled through his laptop on the knotty kitchen table, while the dryer tumbled in the nearby laundry room. The headlines across decades and continents were bland but enticing: "Retracing the Eerie Steps of the Bell Witch," "Unlocking the Bell Witch Riddle."

Tweedy and learned—with a casual air of esteem—Dr. Grant reminded Dillie of various tenured professors she'd had in college, although his topic was certainly unorthodox. But his passion and expertise were genuine, and the book scholarly enough to justify his year's sabbatical for research and writing.

"It loved the mother, ignored the son, attacked the daughter, and murdered the father," he continued. "No rhyme or reason, just deadly results. Only time in history a spirit is believed to have killed a person."

"How?" she asked, swimming in the navy sweatpants she'd borrowed while her damp jeans dried. Dr. Grant's demeanor triggered a forgotten SAT word she thought she'd never use: *avuncular*. But there was also a hip, old-school coolness about him, the kind of professor his students would invite to the bar.

He yo-yo'd his tea bag, swirled it. "That's always been the mystery. Did the spirit kill him itself? Possess a family member to do it? Or was the family so tormented that they killed him just to make it go away? We'll never know."

The pristine and well-appointed home mirrored the fastidiousness of its owner. There was no sign of a wife or family other than framed photos on the hearth: toddlers, probably grandchildren, a few years older than Campbell. They warmed the room.

"What did it want?" asked Dillie.

"Apparently one thing: to stop the Bell daughter from marrying Joshua Gardner, a family friend. Warned all hell would break loose if they disobeyed. Killed the father, since he was pushing them to go ahead with it. That stopped the marriage, to be sure."

With his measured, academic tone, he might have been giving a lecture about the Continental Congress, the Bay of Pigs Invasion. But he wasn't. It was a fairy tale.

"It all sounds…quaint," said Dillie, and he said with a chuckle, "I doubt your ancestors would agree. Some parapsychologists think it forbade the mixing of their gene pools as part of its prophecy."

She ignored the absurdity of "parapsychologist," whatever that was, but said, "What prophecy?"

Dr. Grant twinkled a touch. "After the murder, it disappeared for seven years—to the West Indies, it said. Then returned to predict what we now know as the Civil War, both World Wars…and eventually the end of civilization. It claimed a Bell/Gardner offspring would be the catalyst. And it vowed to come back one last time, to prevent the Armageddon."

Could it get more ridiculous? she thought, waiting for him to crack a smile, which he didn't. "So how did they stop it?" she asked.

"How do you stop a hurricane?" he asked back. "Spells, charms, they tried everything—all useless gimmicks against this force of super nature."

"No…silver bullet?"

He shook his head. "The spirit dangled misleading clues about how to get rid of it. Either for torment or just to give the family peace of mind. That they'd tried their best against the inevitable outcome. After the murder, they simply obeyed. To this day, the Bells and Gardners have stayed far apart. The penalty is too high."

She peered at him. "You take this quite seriously, don't you?" she teased.

Dr. Grant finally laughed a healthy one. "Oh, it's a fascinating folk legend," he said. "With loads of naysayers, conflicting reports, so much evidence disputed or discredited. And yet it lives on." He searched for a thought. "Either everybody was lying, or plain crazy. Or something *did* happen on this land so many years ago. Guess we'll never know."

She almost didn't, but then: "Have you...seen it?"

He hiked his eyebrow in mischief, then dropped the act. "The Bells abandoned this farm generations ago," he said, dismissing it. "I reckon Kate left with them. It's like they've always said: The *house* isn't haunted. The *family* is."

Dillie half smiled. The dryer buzzed.

"It's getting late," she said, the sky dimming outside.

She thanked him again—for his hospitality, the history lesson, the ride back to her car—as she buckled up in the Volvo by the obelisk cemetery. "And I can't wait to read your book," she added through her open window, her jeans still soiled but at least warm and dry.

"Oh, you have a copy?" he said, surprised. She shot a playful glare as she lifted it from the passenger seat. "Autographed," she boasted. "*Personalized?*" he asked, reaching for it.

"You know, Dillie," he went on, scribbling on the title page, "you're the first descendant willing to talk to me. The others couldn't be bothered. Some were downright hostile. Why are you so interested?"

Dillie shrugged. "Family history. Just curious, you know."

"Out of the blue?" He considered the possibility, bobbed his head. "I see..."

"And you? That book didn't write itself. You even bought the farm, so to speak."

He laughed. "You wouldn't believe the deals you get on haunted real estate." She laughed along, and waited.

"Nah," he finally said, handing the book back. "When my wife passed a few years ago, I just...went looking for my roots, I guess. So yeah. Family history."

She looked at him, puzzled.

"Oh yes," he said. "They lived here, too. They're buried on the property." He nodded at the towering oak in the forbidden thicket.

"Difference is," he added, "my family *was* the property."

● ● ●

What did it take to get a damn leaf?

She'd hurried back to Nashville, barely beating rush hour. After a quick stop at the Franklin Public Library—for new bedtime reading for Campbell, and copies from their records desk before they closed—she snuck in the mudroom door and changed clothes ("That you, Dill?" her mother called upstairs. "I was about to send out a search and rescue!"), bathed Campbell, and joined the family for dinner only slightly late, deflecting questions about her day's "research."

Vivian had already removed Emma's chair, her spot for more than two decades exorcised from the table, giving them more room and distance. "Don't forget your pills, Mother," said Vivian, nodding toward the bread plate. She'd gone all out with dinner and held court with redoubled gusto; Richard and Khaki ate softly. No one mentioned the previous night's turmoil.

Fortunately, Campbell was cranky, giving her an excuse to head up early. After rocking him to sleep over *Frances Fix-It*, she took her own nightly meds and went up farther, to the crow's nest office.

Ancestry.com was user-friendly, and she input all the data she had: names, birth dates and places for herself, her family, and

Rupert. She added whatever additional information she could think of—high schools, colleges, wedding anniversaries—plus genealogical traces she'd copied from the library's records department, hoping for an elusive leaf, the site's hint of a clue in the budding of her family tree. She'd been warned by friends in years past that it could be slow going.

While the website worked its magic, she flipped through Dr. Grant's book, highlighter in hand. *From one seeker to another*, he'd inscribed on the title page, above his autograph. Downstairs, doors closed and water ran, as the family turned in for the night.

The chapter "The Being Speaks" caught her eye. According to eyewitnesses, once Kate found her voice, she could get quite chatty. Naturally, the family wanted two answers: Why it had come and when would it leave. She held the book closer to the desk lamp:

> *Your human mind cannot comprehend what I do,*
> *when I do, why I do. Alas, those answers await in*
> *the beyond, where all will be made clear.*

Cryptic and irritating. Dillie's meds were kicking in, coaxing her to sleep. She focused.

> *After wearing down the family with false clues and futile*
> *searches, the Being confessed the truth: It could only be tamed*
> *by the red-cloaked hand of a houngan priest ordained in*
> *Dahomey. Even if they could decipher that riddle, the Being*
> *said such priests were long dead. Thus it was invincible.*
> *And so the torment continued.*

Torment, indeed. Confused and weary—and addicted—Dillie read on and on.

A coyote's howl woke her. She jerked her head off the desk and listened. Others joined, then the eerie symphony of yelps and shrieks, seemingly closer than nights past. Another kill.

"Did you find what you were looking for?" Khaki asked at the door.

Dillie jumped, then laughed. "I didn't hear you come up," she said, and added, "I hope I didn't wake you."

Khaki wore her long white nightgown, her silver hair brushed straight around her shoulders. She rarely, if ever, left her room this way. She stood in the darkened doorway, arms to her sides, unsmiling.

"It's very pretty out there, isn't it?" she said. "So remote and peaceful. But a waste of time, I think. You already know the answers." She was calm and alert, but her eyes were distant.

"What...do you mean?" asked Dillie, still fuzzy from dozing. It was her grandmother, but not. Vivian's warnings of dementia, thus far mild and spotty, leaped to the front.

Khaki cocked her head, disappointed. "Rheumatic fever? Think back. You were there."

Dillie tightened. "I don't understand."

Her grandmother took small, measured steps toward her. "And why you came back here, where I'm so much stronger? That was no accident, you know...."

She was clearly off. Sleepwalking, nothing more. Unless Dillie herself was still asleep, gauzy and under the influence. But this seemed too sharp, immediate, real. She should talk Khaki down, call for help. Instead: "Why I came back...?"

"I'm almost strong enough," the not-Khaki went on, drawing closer. "You're almost weak enough. Then I will leave you alone."

Maybe an epileptic episode, Dillie thought, remembering her mother's warning. Don't startle or wake her, lest she fall and hurt herself. Dillie felt cold sweat prickling her scalp. "Strong enough… for what?"

Now Khaki showed empathy. "Surely you know," she soothed. "I've come to fetch him. Your boy. It won't hurt. I promise. And I always keep my promises."

Dillie pushed back in her chair, trembling. "My God, what are you talking about?"

"He is an error," Khaki explained, with apology. "It's not your fault. A girl next time, trust me. I won't let this happen again."

"Khaki, why are you doing this?"

As she closed in, the lamp brightened her eyes and silver hair. "It can be easy. Or difficult. Do it yourself, if you wish. That's even better. But just like your brother, he must go back."

Dillie bolted up. "I don't know what is wrong with you, but I'm taking him away from here!"

"Now, now," she scolded pleasantly, rounding the desk. "Don't you know I can follow you anywhere? But surrounded by family, it will be so much easier on you. Just ask your mother."

"*Stop it!*" Dillie pleaded. "Snap *out* of it, Khaki!"

Khaki took a deep breath. "*Oh my dear,*" she said in Lola's unmistakable voice. "*I'm not Khaki.*"

Dillie backed farther. "Who…are you?"

"*I live in the woods, in the air, and in the water…,*" said Khaki-Lola, following. She inhaled. "*…in houses with people,*" she continued, morphing to Madeleine's crisp British diction. "*I live in heaven and hell.*"

Now a little boy Dillie instantly recognized but hadn't heard since her own young childhood: *"I am all things and anything I want to be...."*

It evolved to a genderless, clicking, non-human rasp struggling to find a voice: *"Now...don't you know what I am?"*

Khaki's eyes tilted up and back. Her mouth went slack as she staggered and collapsed against Dillie, brittle and spent. She gasped for a breath, her lungs rattling as Dillie lowered and held her.

"Dillie, I'm so sorry," Khaki murmured, disoriented and ashamed, clutching her granddaughter. "Did I...do something?"

"Khaki, *what is happening?*" Her shivering arms threatened to give way.

Through her exhaustion, Khaki's eyes sharpened. "Listen, my girl," she said. "Get your husband here. He needn't know why. But you need him...more than you know."

Dillie rocked her on the floor as her breathing settled.

"And for your boy's sake...please...," Khaki said into her neck, "beware of me."

● ● ●

Garland Lecture Hall was easy to find. The Vanderbilt campus, like the rest of the world, was already bedecked for Christmas, on the cusp of Thanksgiving.

"Turkey, dressing, finals," Dr. Grant told the student-filled room, wrapping up class. "The most wonderful time of the year!" They laughed, packing up bags. "Have a good break," he called out over the din. "See you next week."

Dillie made her way through the exodus, a bundled-up Campbell in her arms.

Dr. Grant smiled, though taken aback. "Dillie, what a surprise." He knelt down on the stage. "And my, who is…?"

"This is Campbell," she said, holding him to her. "It's come back to kill him."

nine

"**S**oon after I moved to the farm, I noticed a glow over the family cemetery," Dr. Grant said, back in his cluttered office. "I thought it was just the moon hitting at the right angle. But it was persistent, nightly. Two years ago, right around this time. Hasn't been back since. Now I know where it went."

Dillie had unloaded everything: the postpartum psychosis, the near miss on Campbell's first birthday, the Lola tragedy, Khaki's late-night possession—the cascade of torment since her son was born. She told him about Adam's death, the fire her family had hidden from her, the hallucinatory assault of rats. There was no one else to turn to. She feared he'd be off-put and skeptical, doubting her sanity. Instead, he took notes.

"Your book said it could be many places at once," she said, and he said, "Watching, yes. But it wasn't all-powerful. It started out weak, growing stronger by the day, year by year. And it seemed to channel its strength before…"

"Before attacking," she said. "What do I do?"

He stewed. "I just don't understand, after all this time, why it would…Have you checked your family tree?"

She nodded. "Two hundred years, three continents. No Gardners anywhere." The website had been sprouting leaves all night.

"And your husband?" he asked. Ditto, at least according to the information she had. She'd yet to reach out to Rupert for more, fearing the escalation. His son's mother chasing a demon would be, she knew, the last straw. He'd whisk Campbell away, with her own mother—and likely every judge—backing him up.

"Could it be punishing me?" she asked. "For the illness I passed on to my brother?"

Dr. Grant doubted it. "As ruthless as it was, it never seemed vindictive or petty. It only punished those who disobeyed, or disbelieved."

"My grandmother, or whoever it was, called Campbell 'an error.' And promised a girl next time. Does that mean anything to you?"

He shook his head. "Kate was infamous for giving false clues about why she came, to keep everyone in turmoil. And then she'd give real ones. She was endlessly mercurial."

"But assuming all this is true—and I'm not saying otherwise," he went on, rubbing one eye under his glasses, "something must have triggered it."

"I don't give a damn what triggered it," Dillie said. "How do I stop it?"

His forehead bunched. "I'm not a paranormalist, but according to its history…" He paused. "You can't."

Her eyes pleaded, the sleeping Campbell against her. "He's all I have."

Dr. Grant grappled. "Those who ignore the past are doomed to repeat it…," he said, more to himself. Then he rose from his chair.

"Find out everything about your brother's death. It might be coincidence he died around the same age as—" He stopped himself, but Dillie nodded and said, "...as Campbell is now. Everything might be a coincidence, but I'm done explaining it all away." She got up to leave.

"And, Dillie," he added with care, "you're sure all this research, and my book, hasn't just ignited your imagination? Gotten you carried away? That's happened before, with others."

"You mean am I nuts?" she said. "I hope so. My son would be safer that way."

At the door, she turned back. "And I think your book is missing a chapter. Who is Jerusalem?"

Dr. Grant tensed. "That's the most mysterious part of the legend. Kate's split personalities, of sorts: Jerusalem, Black Dog, Cryptography, and Mathematics. I uncovered the names after my book went to press. How did you find out about them?"

"They found me. My grandmother, actually."

"They could assume any form, man or beast. Kate sent them first to soften the target, before her arrival. Have they shown up?"

"As beasts. Coyotes. Nightly."

"Then Kate is circling," he said, absorbing it all. "If any of this is real, if any of it means anything...then she's on her way."

Lance called on her way home. He'd pulled strings at the Children's Hospital, which was fruitless, as Adam had never been admitted there, or anywhere else. But more digging had led him down unexpected paths toward Adam's death certificate.

"You ready for this, Dill?" he said.

● ● ●

She found her mother out back, returning from the field with basket and clippers in one hand and a merry wave in the other. The frozen grass crunched under her.

"This snap frost seems to have *offed* Khaki's elm," Vivian called out as she crossed the patio, ringing the old farm bell for good measure. "Luckily I found some leftover leaves for the cornucopia...."

"How did Adam die?" Dillie demanded.

Vivian missed a stride, but just barely. "You know how," she growled, moving past her toward the door.

"His death certificate doesn't agree!" said Dillie, and pointed down to the bricks framing the center of the patio. "Why did you fill in the pool?"

Vivian whirled, looked, and threw down the basket. "Yes, Dillie. That's right. He drowned! Right here!" She feigned confusion, and then clarification, pinpointing the exact spot. "No, I'm sorry. Here! Against the edge!"

She tapped her foot on the cement. "His little head was butting against the wall, just under the pool cover that had come loose. Facedown, a drowned body assumes that position. But when we dragged him out, I said, 'That's not my boy! My boy has rosy cheeks and bright blue eyes, and his hair is clean and golden. I just washed and brushed it. But this one is ashen and bloated, his eyes are swollen and dull, and the hair, oh, the hair is clumped and matted with leaves and moss.'"

She paced a few steps back and pointed down. "And I rocked him right here and called to him, and Richard pried him away while I screamed, because I was holding too tight. I was crushing him, you see, I was trying to squeeze him back to life, but I was crushing him instead."

Palming strands back from her eyes, she scoured her memory and nodded in satisfaction. "So yes, Dillie, that's how your brother died. The blow-by-blow, as best I remember. My noggin was a little overtaxed, you know." She smiled and flicked open her palms. "Ta-da."

Dillie held her ground. "Why did you lie to me?"

The question baffled Vivian. "And raise you with that guilt?"

"What…guilt?"

"It was all your fault, you see," explained Vivian pleasantly. "Your second birthday—and *yes*, we had a party—when you fell and skinned your knee in the dining room. Such a meltdown, a tantrum really, not in the normal way a toddler bounces back to join the fun. No, it was in your nature for screeching melodrama, a narcissist even then. Demanding all our attention. And we gave it to you. You drove us to *distraction*."

Vivian looked around theatrically. "But where's Adam? Did he wander outside? To the river he loved so? Who was looking after him while we hovered over you?" She shrugged. "All night long, searching the grounds in total darkness. Only to find him"—she tapped her foot again—"right here!"

"Why didn't you tell me?"

"Burden you with his violent death?" She shot a dismissive glare. "We thought the fever story the lesser of two evils. But now you're snooping for death certificates with a fellow spy—I wonder who *that* could be? Now you want the truth, and now you have the truth. And still"—she periscoped—"no Adam! Thank you so much for the trip down memory lane."

Dillie swallowed. "Is there anything else I need to know?"

Vivian stared, darkening.

"Tell her," said Khaki from the back door. She stepped toward them.

Vivian sighed, without looking. "*Et tu*, Mother?" She seemed spent. "Has my entire family gone mad?" Then, turning: "You first. Go on. I've waited twenty-five years for your version of that night. We're all ears."

Khaki looked stoic and helpless.

"I thought not," said Vivian. "How convenient. I guess your mind was on the fritz even then." She called up to the sky. "This isn't what I had in mind, you know. We've all fallen so short." Back at Dillie, with pity. "Especially you. A broken marriage. A remedial child. And you're practically a junkie. God help us all."

The oven timer beeped in the kitchen. Deflated, Vivian headed toward the door. "Come help with the turkey, old woman." She extended her hand. "Here, watch your step. The ice beneath you is very thin.

"Oh, Dillie?" she called back at the threshold sweetly. "Since we're spilling secrets? You can tell your fag brother it's lucky he didn't come home for Thanksgiving. He *ruins* my appetite."

She passed Campbell standing just inside and patted his head on the way. As the French door swung shut, the reflection caught the strange creature—half dog, half rabbit—poised behind Dillie. She spun to it: a potted shrub next to a wagging Booray. She turned back to the reflection, just that.

The grinning Campbell caressed the windowpane in a gentle wave. His mother went to him, forcing good cheer, and ushered him in.

● ● ●

The pinks, yellows, and blues swirled prettily together. Dillie stirred faster until the pills disintegrated in the vortex of the bucket. With the back of the wooden spoon, she pressed chunks against the side, breaking them into smaller bits that dissolved with the others.

In the moonlight, she poured the milky liquid around the base of Khaki's elm and covered it over with clumps of dirt and leaves. She packed it down tight, a danger to no one.

Into the rolling trash can by the garage she tossed the knotted bag of prescription bottles, empty other than their rattling desiccants left behind.

She touched a kiss to Campbell's head, then logged in from her laptop on the bed. The tree had doubled in size; she clicked on the newest leaf and began her night.

ten

"In the last hundred years, three Bell descendants, all male, have died on their birthdays," said Dillie, showing her laptop and a spread of printouts to Dr. Grant, who huddled beside her.

The downtown Nashville library had a vastly more extensive public records department, especially for longtime local families, sharing a database with the city and state governments. Through a combination of typed ledgers, files converted online, and even old-fashioned microfilm, she'd pieced together a thin trail, of sorts.

"Ages twelve, thirty-three, and Adam, on his second. Our second," she continued. "Other than Adam, I don't know how they died, or if it's a coincidence. And maybe there are more. There are thousands of descendants, dispersed through the country. The world, probably."

"Ancient mystics believed the soul, the psyche, was its most vulnerable on the anniversary of birth," said Dr. Grant in a hushed tone, more out of habit than courtesy, as the cavernous reading room was largely deserted on a holiday weekend. "Some claim that's how the birthday party tradition began, like a rite of passage. To surround and bolster a person at their weakest psychic point. The older I get, the more I understand. When's his birthday?"

"In five days," she said.

Campbell, mesmerized by the chandeliers and high ceiling, sat quietly. An angel.

"These others were so long ago," said a frustrated Dillie, circling dates. "There's no one left to ask."

Dr. Grant leaned in. "Dillie, your family's been through this before. Ask *them*."

"They think I'm losing it. Including my husband. And I can't blame them." She drummed her fingers along her stack. "To them, Adam's death was a horrible tragedy, but a natural occurrence. Same with all my problems. The breakdowns, freak accidents. It's just life. My mother is in total denial that anything *un*natural could be behind it."

He grimaced. "Kate saved her greatest wrath for those."

"My father follows her lead, my brother was a newborn, but my grandmother...if she could remember anything...if her memory could even be trusted." She shook her head, sat back. "There's just no one else...." Then she lurched forward again.

She bolted up, packed her papers and laptop, lifted Campbell, who protested only slightly.

"And if *you* think I'm nuts," she told Dr. Grant with a surprise kiss to the top of his head, "we'd make a killing in Vegas. You've got the best poker face in the game."

● ● ●

The choir was joyous and rowdy, their syncopated claps of "Happy Day" ringing to the parking lot even before the doors opened.

By her car, Dillie watched the crowds file down the uneven stairs of Victory Southern Baptist Church, a lovingly maintained grande dame on the main drag. Traffic had been light, Mt. Juliet being a neglected suburb yet to succumb to sprawl.

She spied Emma first, splendid as ever in her Sunday's finest, but more effervescent and serene than she'd seemed in years. She'd rebloomed in just days of retirement, hugging old friends like a family reunion.

Holding her hat against the wind, Emma shook hands with the preacher, herded her grandchildren, and by chance glanced Dillie's way. The smile was instant and surprised but melted quickly. She inspected Dillie and Campbell and with a slow nod waved them closer.

"You were much too young to remember the chaos," she said in Jasmine's living room shortly after, pouring coffee into the good china with a slight tremble. "Your mother on edge, more than usual, the whole family toxic. I can't describe how…poisonous the air was in that house, for weeks before."

Campbell had warmed up to the older girls, who showed off the glass Christmas ornaments unpacked on the kitchen tablecloth while Jasmine stirred lunch on the stove. She'd been cordial but flustered by the unexpected visit.

"But that was just a prelude to…" Emma scoured the air, seeking. "It was like a battlefield. Like we were caught between warring factions. You couldn't put your finger on it, and I'm not a superstitious person, but I do believe in good and evil. And I swear they were both there, fighting all around us." She put down her coffee, not wanting it. "But when Adam…passed on…it was over, immediately. As if he'd been the prize, and been won. And after that"—she shrugged—"peace. Calm. Until now. When I felt it stirring again."

"And that's why you left," said Dillie.

Emma struggled, as her granddaughters laughed in the next room. "I love you all so dearly. You know that.…"

"But it's our trouble," Dillie said, toggling her hand. "The house caught fire that night, didn't it?"

Emma nodded. "In the attic. Old wiring, they said later. Your grandmother was upstairs changing Adam." She hesitated. "She'd been so strange all evening. So...distant." Shook it off. "The smoke traveled downward, oddly enough, filling the rooms. Oh, it was terrible, and so fast."

Crossing her arms about her waist, she stared out the window. "We scarcely had time to gather you up and feel our way out the front door. Couldn't see a thing, you know. Couldn't *breathe*." Her eyes shrank against the memory. "We *knew* Khaki and Adam were right behind us. We heard them coming down. And she was faster then. Well, we all were.

"But...they never came. Your father had to stop your mother from rushing back in. She clawed at him, marred his face. I never understood...was Khaki disoriented? Lost in the smoke? What in God's name made her...?" There was a cascade of shatters from the kitchen, followed by Campbell's terrified squeal.

Across the floor lay shards of glass ornaments, the tablecloth yanked off.

"It was Campbell," said one girl. "Campbell did it," said the other.

"I'm so sorry. Let me help," Dillie said, but Jasmine had already grabbed the broom, the pan. "It's okay," she insisted unconvincingly, as she swept up their Christmas.

"Lunch is ready, Mother," Jasmine added, avoiding Dillie. "And then you need to lie down. Too much excitement for one morning, I think." She turned with a forced smile. "I'm sorry. I wasn't expecting guests."

"No, of course not," said Dillie, rounding up Campbell, who'd calmed quickly. "We were just going."

"Dillie, wait!" Emma called out, hurrying down the front steps as Dillie buckled him into his car seat. "Don't mind Jasmine. She just wants to keep me...away from it all."

"I understand," said Dillie. "Thanks for your help."

Emma pressed a videocassette to her hand, the case scribbled with Dillie's birthday.

"Khaki didn't know what she was doing," said Emma. "And she doesn't remember that night."

Dillie nodded, not understanding, and tucked the tape under her arm. Jasmine stood in the front doorway, waiting.

"If I've learned one thing in this old life, it's to accept the things you cannot change," Emma added, then got closer.

"It will kill anything in its way," she whispered.

● ● ●

Now she knew why her family rarely spoke about Adam; the loss of his beauty and innocence were unendurable, even to her watching that night.

She'd never seen him alive, in motion, at least that she could remember. His was that magic combination of wonderment, glee, and vulnerability that made a parent favor one child over another, even if they'd never admit it. Although Vivian had dressed them in variations of the same outfit, his intangible lure made him the focal point of their second birthday party. No wonder young Dillie looked sour.

She huddled close to the crow's nest TV/VCR, on earbuds so as not to disturb Campbell, sound asleep in the playpen. The snapshots she'd seen before came to life: the circus decorations and balloon umbrella, her long-gone grandfather bouncing baby Lance, the spastic Mrs. Carney, all caught on camera by Mr. Patterson. Adam's star wattage (she was biased but thought Campbell shared his gift) contrasted with the party's mood of angst. Vivian's frenzied cheer couldn't mask her stress that at moments smelled like doom; Emma's strain was more obvious in live action. Khaki looked glorious—the timeless beauty in the family—but seemed lost and stilted on the cusp of robotic.

The camera jump-cut to post-cake, pre-presents. It zoomed in on the sleeping Lance in Richard's arms, who waved it off, more in irritation than jest. Her grandfather held court about a business matter that interested no one, while Dillie banged on her tray, demanding release. Khaki and Adam were gone.

Ramped up on a sugar high, Dillie raced circles around the table, banged her knee on a chair leg—*at least this much is true,* now-Dillie thought—and face-planted hard. After a scant pause of shock and realization, her tantrum exploded in earnest. Vivian rushed to baby her, as black smoke wafted from the foyer.

Now the camera fell to the floor, its view tilted and voyeuristic. Smoke and panic overtook the room, as Richard grabbed Dillie and a choking Vivian screamed up the stairs. Khaki called back, hurrying down. Heavier plumes billowed into the main hall and out the front door, chasing after the family. A crisis averted, as everyone fled to safety beyond.

Except Khaki. Clutching Adam close, she stopped just shy of the door as it swung shut, from the wind, force of smoke, or an unseen push. Dillie drew closer to the television screen, head cocked to match the camera angle. She squinted through the swirling blackness.

Khaki held still, gasping in the clogged air. *Open the door*, Dillie urged. *Run through it.* Instead, as if puppeteered, she turned toward the back, set Adam on the floor, caressed his head. Adam looked up at her, then straight ahead. He cowered a bit, but Khaki gently prodded him on. Lifting his arms to a trusted figure, he shuffled forward, his grandmother right behind, until they both disappeared from camera.

There was nothing more, as smoke obscured the lens.

Dillie paused it, sat back.

Over her shoulder, Khaki stood at the office door, digesting it all. Her majestic face clouded with anguish, and she opened her mouth to speak, but then silently slipped back and away.

Dillie heard herself heave, having held her breath without knowing. She steadied herself, to keep from hyperventilating.

Her instinct was to flee: to pack up Campbell and whisk him from the house, the war zone that had claimed her brother and now targeted him. But where? New York was clearly no safer, as Lola—and Madeleine—could attest. By its own warning, it could follow them anywhere. "I am all things and anything I want to be," it had taunted in Adam's voice.

Except it hadn't taunted, or even threatened. It had simply explained, almost in apology, that her son was "an error," not her fault, and promised not to hurt him when it took him. There was no anger, just a gentle suggestion she'd weather the loss more easily surrounded by her family. It seemed, in a twisted way, to care about her.

Madness. A force that could kill a child was the definition of evil.

Why not just strike and be done with it, if that was its plan? Instead, it spoon-fed clues, bided time, seemed to coax her to understand its mystery better. Dr. Grant claimed it was neither petty nor vindictive. Maybe it could be reasoned with.

"He's my universe," she said out loud. "Take anything else. Take me." Startled by her own pleading, she continued. "Whatever the reason, please find another way out." And then: "I'm begging you, Kate."

The room sat silent. Campbell clucked uncomfortably, needing his real bed. She went to him.

Her laptop dinged a notification on the website.

Her family tree had exploded with sickening branches.

eleven

Franklin's Main Street at Christmastime had always been one of her favorite places. Not this year.

"Did you hear they found the Carney dog?" said Vivian, weaving Campbell through the crowded sidewalk in his stroller. "Rabid. *Bang!* Merry Christmas!" She knuckle-rapped a lamppost papered over with signs for missing dogs and cats. "The city should really do something about our coyote onslaught," she said. "You locked Booray inside, right?"

Dillie and Khaki trailed behind, both immune to the festive, kickoff spirit of the shopping season. Even the Dickensian carolers grated.

They'd recovered from Vivian's flame-up a few days ago. The family was used to them, although this last had been unusually gutting. She'd glossed it over with a double-dose frenzy of holiday cheer amid preparations for her grandson's imminent birthday. "Just family, don't you think?" she'd said, plotting the party. "It's such a harried time of year for everyone."

Dillie had slept little, and fitfully, after combing through old news reports the website had unearthed. The family horrors stretched far beyond the state line.

"Oh look, Carol told me these were coming!" said Vivian, gawking at the Avec Moi shop window, packed with flickering candles. "You'd never know these were fake, would you? Carol says they're Disneyland technology. Aren't they something?"

In 1944, Sarabeth Blackwell drowned her infant son in a neighbor's creek outside Oxford, Mississippi, while her husband was stationed overseas. Detroit's Judith Kingston fired a pistol in her mouth in 1956, but not before a single shot to her teenage son's forehead.

"If anyone's curious," Vivian prattled on, "Carol knows what's on my Christmas wish list." She pointed at a strange contraption in the far window. "It's called a mangle. It presses napkins. Have you ever seen such a silly, wondrous thing? Why didn't I invent that?"

Imogene Willard, who in 1968 asphyxiated little Malcolm outside Trenton, argued, unsuccessfully, that she'd been cast under a spell by a Wiccan cult. By 1986, postpartum depression was a disease and a defense, but it didn't save Rosemary Danforth—who roasted her nine-month-old boy in the oven—from lethal injection in Carson City, Nevada. Distant relatives and Bell descendants, all. And probably many more.

"I always tell your father, don't shop for me, you'll screw it up," said Vivian, moving on. "Just go ask Carol. And he does." She snorted a laugh. "If I'm not careful, they'll take up together."

The only thing the new leaves proved was that the Bell women had a rich history of insanity. Ancestry.com wouldn't put them in ads anytime soon.

Separated by decades and geography—and likely unaware of any connection to the Bell Witch legend—these past-the-breaking-point mothers were guilty of atrocities far worse than anything Kate had been accused of.

"I declare," Vivian said, perusing the Parnassus bookmobile parked in the town square. "Did they pass a law that every thriller must have 'girl' in the title? Mother, have you read the new Lauren Groff?"

Then it hit her: Maybe there was no Kate. Never had been.

How much easier—for the Bells, for anyone—to pass blame to an unprovable myth than face their birthright of mental disease. Why not turn to superstition to explain away life's misery and shame? That's why so little of Kate made sense, why her clues ran in circles and hit countless dead ends. There was nothing to stop. She could be whatever they needed her to be, because they created her.

"Dillie, you remember Madame Fifi, that lady magician from your birthday parties?" Vivian asked, charging ahead. "Her number doesn't work. Do you think she retired? Or croaked?"

From the beginning, Kate had been a desperate figment of their imagination, the go-to scapegoat for the family's unfathomable secret: that psychosis coursed their bloodline. Their real family trouble.

Dillie dabbed sweat from her neck with her scarf. It dripped cold down her back.

It infected those who, like her, hadn't even known they were descendants. Nothing had triggered Kate, because Dillie had been born with her. How much of what she'd seen and heard was real, and what was delusion? Especially given the mishmash of meds she'd been taking so long, overprescribed by that quack in New York.

The fear and paranoia—her imagination run amok—were merely her subconscious warning that something worse was brewing. An early cry for help.

"Ruh-roh, don't look now," Vivian purred, flinching from another mother-daughter-grandtoddler trio across the street. "Three generations of Thurmans. The full catastrophe." She waved quickly and lurched into overdrive.

It was a more believable explanation than an otherworldly poltergeist descending to destroy her New York life and lure her back to its base of power, in order to snuff out the Great Destroyer posing as a two-year-old. With a corny tale of forbidden marriage straight from the Dark Ages. Such nonsense might have passed muster in the 1820s but was farcical today.

And it was something she could control. Unlike the other descendants whose illness crept up on them unawares, Dillie was on alert. With the right doctor and treatment, with the *acceptance* of the problem, it was a manageable condition. By knowing her history, she wasn't doomed to repeat it.

Vivian stopped outside the big-top-themed Main Street Toys. "Oh, look! Linda Murray has a new boy! Isn't he darling?" In the window corner sat one of the disturbingly lifelike dolls she'd collected for decades. The blond toddler looked like he'd been abandoned in the store. "I'm stocking up for my granddaughter," she said, a playful elbow to Dillie. "No pressure, of course."

But a mental illness couldn't explain Lola or Madeleine. Or Khaki's split-personality possession in the crow's nest office. Or Dillie's woes that precisely mimicked a legend she hadn't even known about when they began.

Unless she was that far gone. Would she even know? Did anyone?

Her mind churned.

"And Santa!" Vivian added, peering deeper. "I daresay Campbell needs to whisper in his ear." With a pivot, she zoomed his stroller through the door.

Khaki held Dillie back. She'd been silent all morning.

"I was twelve," she said simply. "Playing by the river, like I always did. When the river...stopped flowing. And changed direction. I was mesmerized. And then I woke up, right there on the bank, a different person." She stared ahead, grappling. "They called it epilepsy, said I'd had a seizure. But I knew better. It had returned, you see. Just like it promised. No one else knew, but I did. And I've felt it inside every day, spinning. And waiting." She was fully lucid.

"What happened outside that night?" Dillie said. "My birthday party."

Khaki struggled. "I...don't know. They found me unconscious on the patio. Smoke inhalation, they said. And then Adam..." She trailed off.

Dillie was afraid to ask, had to. "Khaki...did you...?"

Khaki faced her. "I'd rather kill myself. And I would, if that would stop it. But it won't, of course."

Through the window, Vivian sat a game Campbell on Santa's lap, laughing and waving them inside.

"You're both my little girls," Khaki went on. "Don't blame her for denying something this horrible, whatever it is. Deep down, she knows the truth. And she'll do everything she can to protect him."

"How can I protect him?" Dillie said.

"It's splintering the family, wearing us down, like it did before. It struck at our lowest ebb," Khaki said. "But a mother's love is fierce. So is a father's. Get him here. Surrounding your boy with family is our best hope."

Dillie nodded. "You know, Emma told me to accept..."

"...the things we cannot change?" Khaki's nose flared disapproval. "I don't know about you, Dillie," she said, straightening. "But I've had just about enough of that."

● ● ●

Her mental illness theory made sense to Dr. Grant.

"Many skeptics have suggested the same thing," he said, taking a welcome break from building exam questions in his office. "At least those who didn't charge outright fraud from the family. But I've never seen as much evidence as what you've been bringing me. For any of it."

"I'd give anything for fraud," said Dillie, pacing the room while Campbell toyed with the new Slinky Dr. Grant had bought for him. "At least that would make sense." She dabbed sweat from her forehead.

"But I know I've done nothing to trigger Kate," she went on, walking faster. "So what else could it be? And what difference does it make? All that matters is keeping him safe, today, tomorrow, as long as I live. Whatever it takes."

She crisscrossed the room, wall to wall. "I remember Lola said—God, Lola was right all along, but I wasn't ready; I didn't *get* it—she said the *ang* protecting him needs help. That's 'angel,' I looked it up, and I've never believed in that stuff before." She wiped her cheeks. It was broiling in here, especially with the weird weather outside. "Angels and demons, and Emma talks about good and evil, and Khaki says to surround him with family, as messed up as we are, that it's our only hope, but it didn't save Adam, did it?"

She swatted a gnat, or something, on her neck. "But I'm doing it. Lance is stuck at work. He can't get away. And I haven't explained all of this to him yet. I wouldn't even know how, really. But Rupert is coming for the birthday. He has no clue the minefield he's walking into, the loony bin really, the mess his wife has become, but he's all I've got!" She paused to settle a twitch in her mouth. "And you, of course. You're the only person I can talk to about all this, except my grandmother, and her mind, her memory, is so unreliable, like she can't remember it all, or is holding something back. Honestly, if it weren't for you, I'd have already..."

"Are you okay?" Dr. Grant said, inspecting from a distance.

"I've got two days!" she said in outburst. Campbell looked up. She calmed, patted his head, animated the Slinky to distract him.

And took a breath and a seat, knuckling the arms. "What would you do?" she said quietly. "You've got grandchildren, right? I hope I'm wrong, that this is all crazy, and in a couple days we celebrate that it's nothing. I would *love* a good laugh over this. Until then, what would you do?"

Dr. Grant leaned back in his chair. "In all my research on this thing, this phenomenon, I never expected to meet someone who was confronting it now. It was academic, you see. It was history." He pondered his words. "So if it is a medical condition...and you're off your meds, right?"

She nodded. "They were making things worse."

He questioned the wisdom but dropped it. "Then that's one thing. And you can fix that. But if not..."

Pen in mouth, he spun to stare out the window. "Tell me, Dillie. How did you feel? The day Campbell was born."

"How...did I feel?"

"Greatest day of your life?" he said. "Everything you've always wanted?"

She hemmed, off guard. "Yes, of course. But surprised. We were expecting a girl, you see. All the tests showed..."

"Anxious? Depressed?"

"But...that's normal. And I was determined to be a better mother than..."

He turned back to her. "One thing I've learned, through all my research, is a respect for Kate. Violent, yes. Sometimes deadly. But not spiteful, or random. She had a master plan, gave warning, and then cushioned the blow." He leaned in gingerly. "The family was devastated yet so relieved once the storm had passed. And lived long, happy lives. All they had to do...was give Kate what she wanted. And trust her for understanding more than they ever could."

"What...are you saying?"

"Maybe she doesn't want to take him. Maybe she *has* to."

Dillie waited for him to correct, rephrase, retract. He didn't. "Then she'll have to take me first," she said, bolting for the stroller. "And you can write another book. Thanks for your help."

"Dillie," he started, rising. "I'm only trying to..."

She turned on him. "This isn't academic, Dr. Grant. It's not some 'fascinating legend' to me. It's about one thing." She tucked a coat around the dozing Campbell. "*Him.*" Wheeled him to the door, opened it. "Of all people, I trusted you to know the difference."

Traffic was heavy as she drove in silence. The white sky grayed along the way. Dusk fell so early this time of year.

twelve

"My plane is due around nine, assuming I beat the storm to New York first," said Rupert, calling from his Minneapolis hotel that night. "I have to run by the office before I head down. Hope you won't get sick of me."

Dillie was struck how settled she became at his voice: strong, reasonable, excited. And unsuspecting. "Rupert, we'd never get sick of you. How long can you stay?"

Tell him, she thought. *Tell him everything.*

"I was thinking a month," he said.

With the intercom still kaput, Vivian blared Christmas CDs on the downstairs Sony, although she was waiting until after the party to put up the holiday decorations. ("One birthday at a time," she'd decreed.) Dillie closed her bedroom door to silence Louis and Ella.

"I'm sorry, did you say a month?" she said.

"And there's that vacation I owe you," he went on. "Martha's Vineyard's a bit chilly this time of year. How 'bout a cruise? All three of us. Hell, even Booray, if they'll let us."

"You can take that much time off?"

"Oh, didn't I tell you?" he said. "The reason I'm running by my office is to clean it out. For good."

"You...quit?"

"My bonus will tide us over for a while. Eventually I'll land on something a little more family friendly."

Dillie swallowed her joy. "But how will you buy more paintings?" she teased.

"Don't worry. I'll be hawking you out as soon as we get back to the city," he sparred back. "We're starting over, Dill. From scratch."

Explain it all. He'll understand.

She heard his other line beeping in. "Do you need to get that?" she asked, stalling.

"Nope," he said. "I'm answering to only one boss. Is he there? Can you put him on?"

"He'd love that," she said, turning to his play area by the crib, strewn with his newest books and toys. "Campbell honey, it's Daddy."

She looked around the room, the bathroom. "Hold a sec," she told Rupert, putting down the phone. "He was just here."

He wasn't in the hallway either.

"Mom," she called down over the music. "Do you have Campbell?"

"I do not," she called back. "Is my little man at large?"

Senses spiking, she scoured the staircase, the hallway room to room. Booray followed.

"Campbell?" she called out. "Campbell sweetie?"

Back to her room, to the crib. She looked around, felt a sharp breeze. The French door to the balcony swung to and fro.

She bolted outside, calling his name.

The glow by the river caught her eye, its orb hovering above the clearing near the bank. It centered on Campbell, far off, in silhouette against the water. Scampering around him was a puppy, each playfully curious about the other. She squinted. A young coyote.

"Campbell!" she yelled, racing down the fire escape stairs at the balcony edge.

The pup lowered on its haunches, sprang up and back, tail a-wag. It darted around him, front and side, yelping an invitation. Campbell turned to face it, giggling.

"Shoo!" she screamed, cross-waving her arms high as she tore across the field. "Go away!"

An adult coyote emerged from the darkness, scrawny but agile. Two more followed, slightly smaller. They encircled Campbell and the pup from different directions. Spooked, he backed away from them, as they herded him toward the water.

"NO!" Dillie shrieked, getting closer.

Booray rushed up from behind, howling an alarm as he flew past her. The clash was instant, silent. On hind legs, he locked throats with the largest. They thrashed side to side as the others guided Campbell closer to the river.

Dillie sprinted toward him, but a coyote lunged and snapped its fangs, blocking her. She reared back and struck, knocking it across the snout. It fell backward but poised to strike anew.

Bang!

Khaki pointed her pistol in the air, moving toward them in her robe. She fired again, piercing the sky.

The pack regrouped and turned, forming a barrier against Campbell, with the pup on the far flank. Khaki lowered her gun, aimed at the cluster.

"Khaki, stop!" Dillie yelled, in the crosshairs.

She pivoted a few degrees, fired. The pup blew back in a clean shot.

The pack sprang off into the thicket and disappeared in the darkness. Booray followed, warning them away. The orb of light went out.

Dillie scooped Campbell into her arms, kissing and soothing him. He was shaken but sturdy, hugging her neck.

Khaki hurried to them at water's edge, tossing her gun aside on the ground. "It's starting," she said. "It will soon hit from all directions."

"*Why is this happening to him?*" said Dillie, choking back fury.

"Mother! Mother! What's all the racket?" Vivian cried out from the patio, coming toward them with Richard right behind. "Why are you shooting this late at night?"

"Just a fright, Sister! Nothing more," Khaki called back, waving them away. "Warding off some vermin."

She turned back to Dillie, held her face. "Be brave, my girl," she said closely, her eyes alive. "We'll fight it together this time."

Khaki led them briskly back toward the house, the wind picking up. "Stop scowling, Vivian," she said as she passed. "You'll get lines."

• • •

Vivian dabbed moisturizer on her forehead, eyes, and neck. With her little finger, she patted lightly, watching herself in her dressing table mirror, as if entranced. Her finger trembled, smearing out of bounds. She grasped her hand to hold it steady, gave up.

"Lock the gun cabinet, Richard," she said over his electric toothbrush whir in the bathroom. She brushed her hair, eyeing him in the mirror. "Did you hear me?"

He rinsed, spat, padded out. "It's secure," he said. "And too high for Campbell to reach."

"I don't want Mother to reach it either. She's much too old. And too unstable, I think." She rotated her hands over each other to rub the lotion in. They still shook.

Richard sighed. "She's been shooting since she could walk," he said, laying his glasses on the bedside table. "And she'll probably outlive us all."

"*Lock it*, Richard."

She leaned on the French door, looking past the balcony across the estate. "I took poinsettias to Belmont Village today," she said, arms clutching her waist. "Mr. Burton's family was cleaning out his room." She ran her tongue over her upper teeth, sucked them once. "He died last Tuesday. Had you heard?"

"I had not," said Richard, switching off his reading lamp as he settled on his side, facing away. "I'm sorry to hear that. Good man. Good run."

Vivian nodded, still lost in thought. "It's a nice room," she mused, watching the night's clouds deepen across the grounds. "The whole place is mighty fine, really."

● ● ●

Dillie bathed and dressed Campbell in his plaid flannel footies. To hell with the guidelines: Tonight he would sleep in her bed.

He seemed surprised and thrilled by the unexpected slumber party. She read *Goodnight, Moon* aloud, as she had countless times before, it being his favorite from the beginning. She paused in the right spots, and he warbled an attempt (was that "cat"? "moon"?

not quite, but ever so closer), and by the time she wished good night to noises everywhere, he was sound asleep, thumb in mouth, finger over nose.

She switched off the lamp and coiled around him, stroking his hair as she sang Brahms' Lullaby just above a whisper. Tonight was for the classics.

Outside, the wind died down, the storm moving past. She needed to sleep. It wouldn't happen. Her brain spun, restless and on alert. It was a familiar, electric turmoil—not insomnia—that she remembered from milestone nights in her past when anxiety mixed with expectation about the next day's challenge: a big exam, a major job interview, a have-I-packed-everything move (but not before her wedding, when she'd slept deeply, confidently). Tonight the stakes were much higher.

Or were they? She didn't know.

Some families had a history of cancer, heart disease, ticking health bombs that might detonate, or not. Hers was hearty, long-living, but with an undercurrent of tragedy that most would insist was mere coincidence or bad luck. She didn't know.

In less than a day, her own family would be back together, on the road to healing with open forgiveness for past failings and joyful plans for birthdays and Christmases to come, bike rides and beach vacations and school applications and soccer games and piano recitals and his first crush and broken heart on his way to his own path that she would bolster and guide—but not meddle or intrude—to nurture the continuing growth of life that snored ever so gently in her arms right now.

She didn't know.

thirteen

"**B**ooray!" Dillie called out from the back patio. "Come, Booray!"

"Have you seen Booray?" she asked her father downstairs in the kitchen.

"Not since dinner, I don't think," Richard said, still in his bathrobe, late for a workday. "I thought he was with you."

"I assumed he'd let himself in downstairs. Has he been out all night?"

She'd slept better than she'd expected, dropping off shortly after the downstairs grandfather clock chimed twelve fifteen and waking surprisingly refreshed. She must have slept deeply to miss Booray's scratching at the balcony door. He was nothing if not persistent. But she never heard it. She hadn't, she now realized, seen him since he'd chased off the pack of coyotes.

Dillie searched the living and dining rooms, the mudroom, the garage. Even the sound of kibble hitting his bowl went unheeded. "Booray!" she called from the front door, bracing against the sharp wind that greeted the day.

"Biscuit would vanish for days on end, and then *voilà*," said Vivian, stirring Cream of Wheat for Campbell's breakfast. "Animals march to the beat of a different drummer."

"Thanks," said Dillie, well aware the cat had ultimately vanished for good.

"Do you smell gas?" Vivian asked Richard, sniffing around the burner. "Don't tell me we have a leak."

"Booray?" Dillie called through the upstairs hallway. "Here, boy!"

She looked through each open room. Rapped on Khaki's door.

"Khaki?" she said, listening. She knocked again, then turned the knob and peeked in. "Sorry, have you seen Booray anywhere...?"

Her first glimpse startled her. She opened the door to shock.

The room looked ransacked. Drawers pulled and emptied, the four-poster bed piled with dresses and suits on hangers, blouses and undergarments precisely folded, next to her tartan overnight suitcase, sitting open. Gone from the tables were framed photos of her grandfather, parents, herself. Even the tomato pin cushion and knitting kit, nowhere. This wasn't a cleaning; it was an exodus.

"Good morning, Dillie," said Khaki, emerging from her bathroom with a Ziploc bag stuffed with prescription bottles. "Is Booray AWOL?"

"You're running away," said Dillie. "Just like Emma."

Khaki tucked the bag into a suitcase pocket, reached back to unclasp her jewel-studded cross necklace. She circled it around Dillie's neck, hooked it. "From my mother. And hers." She straightened and patted it on Dillie's chest. "Yes," she said, twinkling at her. "It's time." With grace, she lit a soft kiss on her forehead. "You know I love you more than life itself."

"You said we would fight it together!"

"And we will," Khaki assured her through a comforting smile. "I won't be far. But it's safer this way. Rupert's coming tonight, is he not?"

"Khaki, you've always told me the truth. You know why all this is happening. Tell me!"

"The reasons don't matter," her grandmother said. "The family will protect him. His mother and father together."

"They couldn't save Adam!"

"But we'll be ready this time. Please, Dillie, let go of the other stuff. The family is strained enough."

"The family was together last time, and it didn't matter. Our mother was there. Our father was there!"

Khaki shook her head, shushing her. "Your father wasn't there." She finger-tipped Dillie's mouth.

"Yes, he was, Khaki! I've seen the tape."

"Your father is dead," said Khaki.

Dillie bristled. Her grandmother's dementia typically emerged at night; it was worsening at the worst time. "No, Khaki," she said, kind but firm. "Dad's not dead. He's downstairs, drinking coffee."

"Not really." Her eyes held a slight pity.

"Khaki, please listen. I just saw him."

"My girl, you saw your mother's husband."

Dillie froze, shrank back.

"Now, now," Khaki said.

"Oh…my God."

"Let it go, Dillie," Khaki warned. "*Please.*"

But Dillie had turned and fled the room.

● ● ●

The *Nashville Banner* Archive Room in the downtown public library was clubby and hushed. It sat on the far end of the special collections section, past white columns, a richly appointed and nostalgic museum of the long-defunct newspaper.

The kindly volunteer—a sixtysomething dandy—at the mahogany desk tried unsuccessfully to get a giggle out of Campbell, who'd turned moody on the drive into town, his midmorning playtime disrupted.

"Yes, that's all available," the bespectacled senior told Dillie, delighted to have a visitor. He led her across the geometric carpet, past the bronze paper boy sculpture and leather sofa, to a roomy table with a computer. "If you're looking for local stories, the *Banner* had better coverage than the state-wide *Tennessean*," he said. "Or maybe I'm just biased. Do you need a pencil and paper?"

"Yes, please," said Dillie. "I forgot mine."

"Do let me know if you have any questions," he said, with a final wink to Campbell on her lap.

She'd raced from Khaki's room, grabbing Campbell downstairs just as he was finishing a late breakfast. "What's wrong?"Vivian demanded, spoon in hand. "Where's the fire?" But Dillie was already out the door, buckling Campbell, still in his overalls and bib. She wiped his mouth, threw his orange parka around him, and sped off down the long driveway. Her mind ticked as she hurried into town, silently cursing the traffic that choked her once-drivable city. Everyone, it seemed, was on the road today.

Mercifully, the congestion eased downtown, as cars went against her. Almost evacuating, it felt like. Even the library parking structure had spots on the ground floor.

Dillie sat at the keyboard in the archive room, pad and pencil courtesy of the gentleman volunteer. The computerized archives were vast, not surprising for a daily paper with a hundred-plus-year legacy.

She typed in her mother's name, and her father's. Nothing came up. She asked the volunteer for help.

"Only the final ten years of the paper's records are text searchable," he told her. "We haven't had the funding for more. The rest are microfilm scans, if you know the date you're looking for."

"Thank you," said Dillie. She knew the month was June; the year was fuzzy. She counted backward and wrote down three options.

"No, Campbell," she said when he squirmed to get down. "Stay put, please."

It would be in the Sunday edition, she guessed. She couldn't find any. "The *Banner* didn't publish on Sundays," the man informed her when she asked for more guidance. "Check Thursdays. That's when Betty Banner held court."

She scanned the first year of Thursday Junes on her list, scrolling page by page. Then the second year. Bingo.

Vivian was unmistakable in her wedding gown, even in the smallish, black-and-white photo. "Vivian Goodman and Richard Parker," the announcement at the top of the page read. Not surprisingly, it was the social event of the week, if not the month, according to the paper's high-society chatterbox, the fictional Betty Banner. Held at River Kiss for roughly two hundred guests, the celebration had all the trappings one would expect for the dairy empire heiress, down to evening fireworks over the water.

Dillie sped past the dress description—illusion bodice, scalloped Venice lace, cathedral-length train—and the list of bridesmaids, former Harpeth Hall classmates and Tri-Delt sisters, to zero in on her father's section. Even Betty Banner couldn't mask his rather humble origins, although she trumped up his promise as a young doctor. Dillie found the full, proper name of his best man, Bucky, wrote it down on her pad.

"Just to let you know," the volunteer said, back from his desk, "I might be closing the room at lunchtime. I live in Donelson, and with the storm coming…"

"What storm?" said Dillie.

He seemed surprised. "Ice," he said. "Or so they say. It feels so mild, doesn't it? I just don't want to get stuck on I-40."

"Yes, of course," Dillie said, back to the keyboard. "I won't be long."

Her search intensified, starting with the day after her first birthday. She doubted it would be on the front page, or even the front section. It might not have been newsworthy at all. And yet, given his youth, good looks, the tragic waste of it all…

Campbell arched his back, straining for release. "Please, Campbell," she said, wrestling him. He warbled displeasure, threatening worse. "Ssh," she soothed, caressing his head, which felt warm. She hurried.

In the local sections, she skimmed past articles about city council shenanigans, the latest charity benefit at the Parthenon, detailed plans to renovate the Ryman. She moved quickly, speeding through the days and weeks.

Her phone sounded a strange buzzing pattern. She checked the screen for an emergency weather alert: a winter storm warning, on track that afternoon, with an advisement to check local media. She silenced it, went back to the keyboard.

TPAC's new Broadway series, a mayor's aide accused of brib-
ery, bulb-planting tips from Cheekwood's landscape designer.
Perhaps her father was wrong on his timeline. It was so long ago.
She scrolled faster and faster, testing Campbell's patience.

The headline flew past: "Waller Associate Killed in Car
Accident." She scrolled back.

The photo cinched it. A professional work shot, suit and tie,
but unmistakably the devilish, movie-star smile that charmed the
wives at her birthday party, captured her and Campbell's attention, and earned Vivian's jealous scorn. His mouth, forehead, nose
looked and felt so familiar. A promising young lawyer cut down
when his car hit a tree off Old Hickory Boulevard on a Thursday
night.

And her real father. This would eventually land harder, she
knew, but not now. There wasn't time.

"Thank you again," she told the volunteer, who seemed grateful that she was done. "Get home safely." He said, "You, too, miss.
You, too, little one."

The two-story window in the Grand Reading Room thrummed
with rain as she carried Campbell past the long tables of readers
and researchers, though many were packing their laptops and ma-
terials to leave. Campbell's forehead felt hotter, and he let out an
ornery yelp that pitched unusually high. It was nearly lunchtime,
he was restless, and she feared—with fresh alarm—that he was
coming down with something, on the day before his birthday. Of
all things, this hadn't occurred to her.

"We are closing soon," said the heavyset woman at the public
records counter, next to the stand-up, self-service computer station. "We're closing early." She already had her coat on.

"It won't take long," Dillie said, struggling to contain Campbell. She checked the list on the side of the screen, clicked on "Tennessee Birth Records." Propping him on one arm, she cap-typed the name from her scrap of paper: JOHN NORRIS. (*Dillie Norris*, she thought to herself, then pushed it away.) The computer toiled a few moments, then listed a dozen options of the same name. She checked the dates, did the math, eliminating the impossibles. Three-quarters of the way down the list, she found him. Her birth father.

His own parents' names branched off his. One was clickable, the other, not. She asked the all-set-to-leave woman behind the desk why.

"We only have records for those born in state," she said, making a show of cleaning up her station.

"Thank you," Dillie said. She clicked on the father, and the computer churned again.

The wind lashed rain sheets against the window. More visitors passed on their way out. The father's entry linked to his parents, both born in state. Dillie deflated. It would take hours, days, to check each branch, and the branches they spawned in myriad directions. Campbell arched his back and wailed.

"This department is closing now, actually," said the supervisor woman farther back. "We're shutting down the system. You'll need to come back tomorrow."

"It can't wait till tomorrow!" Dillie yelled, then calmed herself. "I'm sorry. It's something of an emergency. It's urgent. *Please.*"

Campbell squealed as she sat him on the counter. "He can't sit there," called the supervisor from her back desk. "Nobody can sit there." Dillie picked him up, held him to her side. He struck her in the shoulder. "No, honey," she said, grabbing his fist. "Don't hit Mommy."

She thought, clicked. The father (her great-grandfather—*stop it!*) was born in Shelby County, in the southwest corner. Her gut told her to head north, toward Kentucky. She clicked on the mother, born in Davidson, home of Nashville. Warmer.

There was an element of guesswork as she traced the bloodline upward. She could be completely on the wrong track—choosing the wrong parents when the right ones might be out of state records reach—but her fingers worked quickly, guided by instinct that felt more like impulse. If she didn't know better, she'd think something was leading her in the right direction. *Click, click, click.* Wilson, Sumner, Cheatham Counties, inching her way toward the Bell farm.

She hit a brick wall just as an ancestor led her to ground zero: Robertson County. The digital records stopped. The computer instructed her to see a library attendant for help.

"You'll need the paper records to trace back further," the woman said. She now wore her hat and a fed-up face. "Which would be possible if we weren't closing the library right now." Her supervisor seconded that from the back: "We are closed."

Campbell contorted, screamed anew. Dillie struggled to contain him and leaned over the desk. "I can't explain why this is so important, but you've got to believe me: It's life and death. Today. Now." She blinked back her desperation. "I am begging you."

The woman softened at Dillie's inexplicable crisis. "I'll be right back," she said with a sigh, disappearing into the stacks.

"No, no, no," the supervisor said, waving as she approached Dillie. "Miss, you need to evacuate the premises immediately." Dillie looked around. She was the last one left.

"Five minutes," Dillie pleaded. "That's all I need." Campbell, burning up, screeched and thrashed.

There would be nothing to find, Dillie knew. Only something to rule out, one less thing to worry about, to put her mind at ease on a day when Campbell, who was always healthy, was abruptly feverish, uncontrollable, and even violent. Now in full meltdown, he unleashed a piercing cry, as she rocked him standing up.

"Take your sweet boy home!" the supervisor said. "I will!" said Dillie, turning this way and that, trying to placate him.

The woman returned from the stacks with a thick brown ledger, embossed with "Birth and Death Records, Robertson County: 1800–1900" in gold.

"Anna, I said no," the supervisor said, and the woman told her, "You go on. I'll close up."

Dillie grabbed the vintage ledger, leaving them to quarrel. She checked the yellowing, typed index, found the name from her most recent clue, flipped to the right page. Back and forth, deeper in time.

Campbell screeched, kicked, and thrashed. Enraged, he pummeled his mother in the face. "Campbell, NO!" she shouted, restraining him. "Stop it!" He was broiling. In her frantic flipping, she ripped a brittle page down the middle.

"That's it!" the supervisor said, grabbing for the ledger. "You are defacing historical records." Dillie shoved her in the chest, shocking them all. "Get away!" she screamed as she yanked the book out of reach.

"Security!" the supervisor yelled out. "Security! We need some help over here."

The names were a blizzard: JonasBeatrice1896CasperShirley 1874...

Campbell twisted himself and unleashed a bizarre howl of fury. He'd gone feral.

"This way, ma'am," said the guard from behind, grabbing her elbow. "Time to go."

"Get off me!" Dillie screamed, shouldering him backward.

EzraDorothy1852—Campbell shrieked and clawed at her eyes, she held back his hands—RobertJezebel1823...

Dillie gasped and fell forward. She might have cried out. The guard seized her by both arms. It didn't matter. They were boneless.

The chaos around her fell silent and faded away. At the top of the page, sitting astride her family tree, Dillie found the other half of her bloodline:

JOSHUA WILLETT GARDNER
1800–1884

PART THREE

KATE

one

Vivian was blowing up balloons when Dillie stormed into the dining room, carrying Campbell.

"When were you going to tell me?" Dillie demanded. "When?!"

The table was laid out with jungle-themed paper plates and napkins of elephants, lions, and giraffes. The umbrella was opened and half filled with a rainbow of balloons. Vivian twisted a tie and beamed at her grandson. "Not yet, Campbell!" she said with cheer, taking him from Dillie. "You can't see your party room until tomorrow!" Then she called out, "Richard! Can you come, please?"

"Blaming me, telling me I'm crazy," Dillie said. "When you know this whole nightmare is all your fault!"

"Richard!" Vivian called louder. "I need you. Now!" She bounced Campbell, cooed at him. "Why the cranky face, little man? Did Mommy not feed you yet?"

If it weren't for the imminent storm—and the pitying intervention by her ally behind the desk—Dillie would have been arrested at the library. She apologized repeatedly and forced herself to normalcy. Her mind reeling, she assured them she was no danger to her child or herself, left her contact information, and promised to pay for any damage she'd caused. Mercifully, everyone was in a hurry to be done with it and leave.

The temperature had dropped drastically, although the rain was only starting to morph into sleet on the drive home. Campbell's tantrum had exhausted him, his fever fleeting and now gone. Spent, he slept the whole way through inching traffic as the city struggled to outrun the storm. Dillie's focus on the road helped temper her panic, though it flared anew as she turned in to River Kiss.

"Yes?" said a groggy Richard in cardigan and socks, descending the staircase, his nap disrupted.

"Run to Granddaddy!" Vivian said, gently prodding Campbell into the foyer. "That's a good boy." She swung the dining room doors shut, palmed back her hair. "Jeezus," she muttered to herself.

"Wake up, Mother! That's not his granddaddy!"

In one motion, Vivian whirled and smacked Dillie across the face. "Shut your goddamned mouth!" she roared, and then dropped an octave. "Don't spew your fucking poison in my house."

Dillie reeled from the strike and profanity, both firsts. She scarcely recognized the wounded lioness before her. "If you had told me," Dillie said, defiant. "If I had known..."

"Told you what, Dillie? Knew what?"

"Did you even know who Bucky's ancestors were?" Dillie said.

"Why the hell would I know that?" Vivian bellowed to the sky, arms open. "Why would anyone know that?"

She slammed her hands against her thighs and shook her head. "It's all so unhinged, Dillie. Don't you see how sick you've made yourself over this?"

"If you had told me what you'd done and what it meant," said Dillie. "That it had happened before and would happen again. If only you'd warned me..."

"You said he was a girl!" Vivian hissed. "Kate would have left us alone!" Dazed by her own outburst, she stumbled back and recovered with a pale laugh. "Christ almighty, it's catching. That sick old woman is getting to us all. My, my."

"Khaki's not the sick one, Mother. She told me the truth."

Vivian came at her. "She begged me to abort you! Did you know that? If she had her way, you wouldn't even be alive." Her hand shot to her mouth as she choked a breath. "God knows what she did to Adam that night. We'll never know, will we? We'll never know." She pointed upward. "To hell with the Bell Witch. *She's* our family trouble!"

"No, Mom," Dillie said. "My son is. And there's nothing I can do about it."

Vivian threw her arms around her daughter, collapsing into her. "She's ill, Dillie. You know she is," she whispered in her ear, a little-girl-secret. "You've seen it with your own eyes, haven't you? How I pray I'll never live to be this kind of burden on you. Won't you please help me help her? I'm at wit's end, honey. I'm out of options."

Dillie disentangled from her clutch, backed away. "I have to get Rupert."

Vivian held her face, her eyes desperate and wild. "It's getting ugly out," she said, a kiss to her hair. "Hurry back with him."

She leaned her head against the front window, watching Dillie and Campbell wind along the drive on their way to the airport. The heavy, gray clouds made it seem later than it was. The prickle of sleet grew louder on the quiet house.

"Do not go gentle...," she murmured softly. "Rage...*rage*..."

The Volvo disappeared over the horizon.

"Get the car, Richard," she said without looking. "It's time."

"Not today, Vivian," he pleaded with a sigh. "Tomorrow, the weekend. Not today."

She turned from the window, not hearing him. She straightened her oxford cloth shirt over her khakis, primped her hair. "Mother?" she singsonged. "Oh, Mother?"

The banister creaked as she pulled herself up the stairs. "These stories you tell. These *lies*," she called upward, one heavy step at a time. She marveled at the dilemma. "I just don't think you'll stop until you've destroyed this family. One by one, you seem determined to wreck us all. Your final mission. I can't have that, now, can I?

"Why, soon you'll be a danger to yourself," she went on, steadying herself down the hall. "And I'll be responsible, because I saw it coming and did nothing." She arrived at the door. "I'm so sorry, Mother. But you've left me with no choice...."

She turned the knob, pushed it open.

Khaki stood in her tweed suit and felt fedora, next to her tartan luggage in a neat row. Her room was empty and spotless.

"I'm ready, Sister," she said brightly. "Shall we?"

● ● ●

No more secrets, she vowed. She had to tell him all.

I-65 was a crawl from the moment she came down the ramp. Mere rain often crippled the town; sleet threw it into a tizzy.

"*...although the polar vortex's surprise dip south has caught Music City off guard, as residents hurry to...*" WLAC blathered on as she inched behind a white SUV, her windshield crackling with increasing pelts.

Rupert wouldn't understand everything and didn't need to. Even she was clueless about so many details, most of all what to expect when the clock ticked over to Campbell's birthday in a few hours. But at least she knew what had awakened Kate, the rule that had been broken so long ago, as wrong-headed as it was. She couldn't wrap her mind around the notion—from where? based on what?—that the innocent in the backseat, mesmerized by the blurred lights and thrumming sounds out the window, could be a potential threat to anyone, that his existence could conceivably jeopardize civilization. The idea was ludicrous, as was the concept of Kate herself at first blush. She'd eventually explain the whole saga to Rupert, calmly and convincingly, regardless of the fallout. But that could wait.

"The Highway Patrol urges extreme caution on icy surfaces and warns drivers to watch for downed trees and power lines..."

For tonight he need only grasp their son was in danger, as if a kidnapper were threatening him, and the police would be no help. Their best defense was to surround and protect him, ready for an unpredictable assault that just a few hours ago she still held out hope was imaginary but now realized was probable, if not inevitable. If past was prologue.

"BNA Air Traffic Control is scrambling to land approaching flights before the anticipated runway closing. All other flights have been diverted to alternate airports...."

Merging left onto I-24, her tires skidded, the Volvo gliding a few feet before she brought it back under control. God bless German engineering.

In the standstill, her mind churned around the fullness of the family revelations. It was just starting to land that her whole life had been a giant deception, hatched by her mother but conspired with them all, even Khaki. She wondered if her father knew, if that explained their distance. It certainly accounted for her parents' estrangement, which she'd grown up thinking was typical of long-time marriages. But it wasn't. It was the casualty of a lie.

Under normal circumstances, that would be damaging enough. And in any other situation, keeping the lie from her would be understandable, even expected. There'd have been no harm, not really, and little to gain by telling her the truth. But her current predicament was far from normal. Her family had just been unwilling to face it. Now Dillie had no choice.

Traffic stopped completely. An eighteen-wheeler up ahead had slid off the road, its semitrailer blocking a lane. She glanced in the mirror at Campbell, helpfully sound asleep, his nap schedule out of whack all day. One by one, cars tucked over to maneuver around the accident.

It struck her: Of all people, how had her mother fallen for a Gardner descendant? What were the odds? What chain of events—gravitational pull, really—had lured them together in the first place, with enough attraction and passion to jeopardize a close friendship and her young marriage? It was an inexplicable risk, a betrayal of such ruinous proportions with no possible good outcome. Careless, impulsive, selfish. And seemingly inescapable.

I-40 freed up a bit in the final stretch, as the rain changed sounds, growing denser even as it quieted. The ice had arrived.

She now felt more empathy than anger toward her mother, whose burden all these years must have been crippling. The loss of Adam was unimaginable, especially given the many layers of guilt she surely felt. No wonder she lashed out so viciously whenever cornered with the truth. The reality of what she'd done was damning, but the ramifications were catastrophic.

The airport was one mile ahead. She hit her blinker and worked over to the right lane. The interstate curved through the limestone bluffs already transforming into ice canyons.

And her mother knew the truth, of course, even if she couldn't own up to it. She'd admitted as much when she let it slip earlier about the gender confusion during Dillie's pregnancy. Had Vivian known Campbell would be a boy, she might have told her everything, to warn her against it. That mix-up, now that Dillie thought about it, was medically odd. It had even confounded her doctor. It almost seemed an intentional sleight, a last-minute switch to misdirect them all. But how, and why?

Even if Kate had that power, why would she trick them into having a child she'd forbidden?

She passed through the limestone cliffs. The airport exit came into sight.

Unless Kate herself had been tricked. By the *ang* Lola claimed was protecting him. The clash of good and evil that Emma vividly remembered from before. But which was which?

"Your boy is special," Lola had insisted shortly before she died. "That's why it wants him." The word had never given her such a chill before.

Dillie slowly forked off onto Terminal Drive. Campbell snored lightly. Even if she had all the answers, they wouldn't save him now.

She just had to get Rupert.

● ● ●

"Mrs. Delphine Goodman?"

The administrator, probably midfifties (it was hard to tell; women camouflaged their age so vigorously these days), stood in the doorway, rapping on the jamb. She wore a red, corporate suit and a will-this-day-never-end smile.

"Please," she told her, turning back from the window. "Call me Khaki."

The apartment was roomy and pleasant in an institutional way. Between the clubby sitting area, silk waterfall draperies, and faux antique mahogany furnishings, they'd made an effort to cushion the blow. Khaki laid her lamb suede gloves on the dresser and extended her hand.

She would have been happy to ride into town in silence, but Vivian had narrated the whole stretch of I-65, critiquing other drivers from the passenger seat and ticking off her to-do list before Campbell's birthday and Rupert's arrival. She was always the chattiest when under pressure, or feeling guilty. It was all so senseless. Richard said nothing, of course. Poor fellow. The drive, which normally would be thirty minutes, took more than an hour. The return, she knew, likely longer.

Belmont Village was familiar to her. She'd visited Abigail countless times in her final years and had only stopped looking in on dear, abandoned Dwight when he no longer recognized her. In hindsight, she regretted that. Couldn't even a stranger provide comfort and solace? Too late now. She'd find him on the other side, where they'd both be young and radiant again.

She'd insisted they drop her off with little fanfare and refused the wheelchair from the front door staff, although they carried her luggage behind. The common areas were largely deserted, the television at full blare with local weather reports. Even the parakeets in the gorgeous aviary had nested for the night. She'd like to have seen them in full flight.

Vivian inspected and approved the room, pointing out the scenic view of the nearby hills she'd demanded. "This is just a trial run, you know," she said. "If you're uncomfortable, we'll whisk you right back." Her tone had softened along the way, as Khaki had known it would. Under her tempest beat a golden heart. Always had.

Khaki embraced Richard, kissing the apology from his face. "I'm better than fine," she assured him. "Get home safely."

Vivian checked her watch nervously. "We'd better sally forth," she said. "The roads are worsening by the minute, I am sure."

"Goodbye, Sister," Khaki said in a tight hug. "I love you, my girl. Remember."

"See you tomorrow, Mother," Vivian said, battling emotion on her way out the door. "Get some sleep. Love you, too."

Khaki had just removed her overcoat and was watching the ice sheets out the window when the administrator arrived. She held a leather welcome packet with all the essentials. "You'll have to excuse us for being a bit short-staffed tonight," she said. "We weren't expecting new arrivals, especially with the weather and all."

Khaki nodded. "The conditions out are less than ideal. But don't worry about me. I'm quite self-sufficient."

"Has your family already left?" she asked, seemingly surprised.

"Yes," Khaki said. "They have guests arriving soon."

"There's a proper orientation in the morning, assuming our workers can make their way in," the woman said. "The kitchen is already closed for the evening, but I'm sure we can scare up something if you're hungry." She pointed to the amenity basket on the dresser, full of sweets and oddities.

"Not at all. But thank you."

The woman searched for a way to be useful. "I'm happy to send someone to help you unpack. Or to keep you company. Your first night and all. It can be a bit of an adjustment."

"That's very kind," said Khaki with a smile. "But it won't be necessary. I'm perfectly at ease."

two

Christmas was in the air at the airport. It felt out of sync. There was jolly music on the speakers and twinkling plastic garlands draped around the counters, but the mood was of confusion and helplessness. Lines stretched well past the ropes as passengers dealt with canceled flights. Fortunately, there didn't seem to be much anger. There was even, in some pockets, a crackle of snow-day excitement. This was weather, an act of God.

If they only knew.

Dillie checked her phone: 8:47. According to her flight tracker app, Rupert's plane, which had been delayed at LaGuardia, was still an hour away. She prayed they wouldn't divert to Memphis or Birmingham or God-knows-where. Surely they wouldn't have taken off if they didn't think they could land. She'd texted and called, but Rupert had already turned off his phone. He'd reply as soon as he could.

Dr. Grant had e-mailed her, apparently earlier in the day according to the time stamp, although it just now arrived. He didn't apologize or explain himself but offered his help in any way. That was her problem: There was no help to be had, no line of defense. And it was she who should apologize, as supportive and *believing* as he'd been from the start. He'd certainly been more of a rock than most of her own family. Her savior, really, for the past two weeks. She'd lashed out at him like a patient hearing a grim diagnosis. She couldn't bring herself to respond with an update on the truth of her bloodline. He couldn't fix it, and it wasn't his problem. She'd make amends eventually.

A policeman with a German shepherd sniffed past her seat in the outer lobby by the front doors. She longed to reach out for his protection but knew it futile. Instead, she said, "Look, Campbell. Look at the..." But Campbell was gone from the seat next to her.

"Campbell?" she called out, bolting up. "Campbell?!" She scanned the row, the crowds around the ticket counters. Nowhere.

Another group came in through the sliding glass doors just beyond. "Campbell!" she yelled and then asked them, "Did you see a little boy outside?" She palmed his height, they shook their heads but followed her out to the curb. "Campbell!" she cried, and the others did the same in all directions. "Orange jacket!" she told them.

Cars were clogged in stacks the length of the terminal, hovering just long enough to drop off or pick up. Several zoomed away, back into the icy night. She stooped to peer in windows, her panic spiking.

"Ma'am?" the K-9 policeman called to her from the door. "Is this your little guy?" He pointed.

Campbell stood right inside at the towering poinsettia tree, smitten. The dog could wait.

"Yes!" she said, running. She scooped him up, thanked the officer. "I just turned my back for a second," she explained, but he waved it off with a smile as the dog led him away.

"Don't touch," she said, pulling Campbell's hand back from the flowers. "They're poisonous."

He squirmed to be put down again. She couldn't risk another tantrum with more than an hour to kill. He needed food, but the pickings were slim in the main terminal. "Hold Mommy's hand," she said, clutching him as she targeted the swarmed Starbucks. "Stay close to Mommy until Daddy gets here."

● ● ●

"Nothing set me off, Richard," Vivian snapped. "We had to do it sooner or later, you know that."

I-65 had worsened on the way home, along with the storm. They were at a standstill. She parked her elbow on the windowsill, forehead to palm, looking out at fogged-over nothing. She wished for silence, and speed.

"We'd agreed to wait until after Christmas," said Richard, leaning forward at the wheel for a clearer view. He'd picked the wrong time to needle her. What else was new?

"So Rupert can see his in-laws in all their *deranged* glory?" she said, turning back just enough to hammer it home. "God knows what poppycock Mother would have put in his head. I'm trying to save that marriage. Is that too much for you to grasp?"

Vivian chewed her lip, cursing her dilemma: trapped in this car with a noodle who never knew the right thing to say. Or when to shut up.

She exhaled. God, she was a shrew sometimes. She rode him too hard, she knew. Always had. But he made it so easy. Irresistible, even. If only he'd strike back, the best defense against a bully. How could such an accomplished surgeon—and sturdy father, she had to admit—cower before his wife, decade after decade? Because he'd long ago tuned her out, she realized. Or else he just loved her too much, in spite of her best efforts. She'd become the comforting, ambient noise pollution in his life.

"Since when did saving marriages become a priority for you?" Richard mused under his breath, squinting through the wipers.

Zing! Well played, she thought. At least she had his attention.

"It's just assisted living, not a loony bin," she added, not taking the bait. "Not yet, at least."

They rolled a few yards, stopped. Again, creeping.

"And she's *my* mother," she barreled on. "Did you see her kicking and screaming? She knows it's for the best. For all of us."

In her periphery, she caught Richard's skeptical glance, which she ignored. She meant, of course, her mother's dementia and unpredictability, which took an increasing toll on them all. How long could they be expected to put up with it, as unqualified as they were? But if he thought, if he mentioned that witch—the stupid, nonexistent Bell Witch—she'd scream at the hopelessness of her entire family. For all his shortcomings, Richard had always been solidly sane.

She stared out at the jagged ice stalactites cascading down the limestone bluffs. Gorgeous, in a fairy tale way. They started flashing.

Up ahead, a red light swirled in the left lane, reflecting everywhere. Fire truck, ambulance, both. Traffic slowed even more.

"Oh God!" she said, hammering the armrest. "We can't be stuck here all night!"

"*Go straight, three miles,*" said the female GPS. Mercifully not-Agatha, but her equally disinterested American cousin.

Vivian twitched in frustration. "We've got to get home before they do!" she said. "Take the back roads."

"Too icy," he said, peering ahead. "The interstate is our safest bet."

Not just a noodle; an old bitty, as well.

"Do you need me to drive, Richard?" she said.

Richard hit the blinker, veered toward the next exit.

● ● ●

You could always judge the quality of a lodging by the bathroom. This one was superb.

Khaki stood at the sink mirror, freshly showered and in her nightgown, brushing her hair. The lighting forgave and flattered, another good sign. She looked young again. No one else would think so, but with her silver hair around her shoulders, she felt like a teenage girl. Right when it all began.

She debated pinning it up, but no. This was her natural state.

She'd packed her smaller suitcase carefully, only what she needed for the night. The rest of her luggage, just for show. After brushing her teeth and moisturizing—and with the barest hint of makeup—she tucked it all back into her toiletry kit, perched it by the faucet.

Her Bible held no sentimental value. Not an heirloom or anything inherited; just well made and in large print, in her preferred New American Standard. She'd worn out countless throughout her life, reading or simply holding in the privacy of her room. Like tonight.

The ice came down harder outside. It was surely crippling the city. Richard was an excellent driver—among other admirable, long-suffering qualities, God bless him—but she was worried.

The huge numbers on the old-person bedside clock blinked 9:53.

She settled upright into the striped recliner, paying attention and thinking. The weather was a curveball. Was it Kate? Khaki had thrown her own curveball, removing herself from the equation. Kate couldn't hijack and put her to use from so far away. But she would adapt, find a new way. Khaki listened, probed. Kate didn't tip her hand just yet. She would. She always did.

Dillie would be fine, for now. She and Rupert knew what to do, instinctively, to protect their boy. They'd make it home in time, where they'd be the safest. Especially with Vivian and Richard surrounding them. The readiness was all.

But still she fretted. Something felt off. Kate was surely stirring.

• • •

"Flight 551 from LaGuardia can claim their luggage on carousel three," announced the overhead woman. Even she sounded worn out.

Dillie stroked Campbell's hair, both pressed up against the glass-walled waiting pen. It was jammed with fellow waiters, restless but relieved the final flights of the night had made it safely. Mercifully, the live entertainment—a too-loud acoustic guitarist—had packed it in an hour ago. Instead, the television news panicked about the worsening weather.

She stared down the length of the terminal and its river of arriving passengers. "Look for Daddy," she said, on tiptoes. "He'll be coming." He'd be first off, she knew. Rupert always booked the bulkhead, for a speedy exit. She texted her location: "Welcome to Music City! We're here!" As an afterthought, she added a big smile emoji. Silly and endearing. The text didn't go through. She tried again.

The passengers were haggard but buoyant, some marching, some lumbering. There were hundreds, it seemed. A few darted in and out of the restrooms along the way. Dillie leaned in, searching. He'd wash his hands first, of course. He always did that right off a flight, knowing the germs on a plane. He'd splash his face, too, shiny and clean for their reunion after such a long absence. She checked her own dark circles in the glass. He'd have to cut her some slack tonight.

The initial wave passed, as the waiting room started to thin out. There were hugs and squeals from friends and family, the inevitable you-can't-believe-what-I've-been-through tales that drifted off as the throngs migrated toward the escalator to the baggage level. Dillie stroked and patted Campbell's head, standing beside her. She called Rupert, straight to voice mail even now. His recorded voice bolstered her, in spite of her irritation. *Turn on your damn phone*, she urged, unless the storm had knocked out reception. Naturally.

Only stragglers remained. A couple janitors. He might have stopped to pick up a gift—a plush for Campbell, Loveless jam for her—but the shops were dark and gated. The terminal grew quiet, the waiting pen dwindled to a handful. Dillie cupped her palms on the glass, leaving sweat prints.

Here he came from the distance! She'd know his gait anywhere, confident and brisk, but always unruffled. His typical sexy stride, head down, lost in thought. His hair looked shorter. "Daddy!" she said, grabbing Campbell's hand. She hurried out of the waiting room, stood behind the TSA agent at his station. "Long night," she said, and he nodded in agreement. She primped, useless as it was.

Rupert neared and lifted his head to greet them. But it wasn't Rupert. Another young Master of the Universe, but not her husband, obvious from fifty feet and more disheartening as he passed by. His wife/girlfriend threw her arms around his neck. And they were off.

Dillie looked around. She and Campbell stood alone.

"Are there any more flights?" she asked the TSA agent, fully aware he wouldn't know, and he didn't.

Campbell raised his arms to be lifted. He was winding down.

"He'll be here soon, honey," she said, lifting him. She peered down the deserted terminal one last time, then turned and walked away.

● ● ●

The noodle had picked the worst time to dig at old scabs.

"Be my guest, Richard," Vivian said, looking out her window, away from him. "Let's tell Dillie all about my neglectful husband and his attentive best friend. The water's under the bridge, and I really don't give a damn anymore. Spill all the beans you want."

Murray Lane was deserted, with good reason. It was typically a dependable cut-through; tonight, it was practically unpassable. Why had the GPS sent them this way, instead of the straighter, flatter Old Hickory Boulevard? And why had Richard listened? Still, his handling of the Range Rover was impressive. She'd give him that.

"She found out in the worst way," Richard said, navigating a curve with refreshing confidence. It was almost sexy. "You should have told her years ago. She'll never trust us again. Can't say I blame her."

His patronizing guilt trip fell on deaf ears. She'd long since forgiven herself and hadn't strayed since. For God's sake, she'd been just a girl. Lonely and restless and confused. Nothing to apologize for. "Never complain, never explain." If there were wiser words spoken, she hadn't heard them.

"*In one hundred yards, turn left onto Holly Tree Gap Road...,*" Ms. GPS instructed.

"Holly Tree's bound to be a nightmare," said Vivian. "Go straight to Hillsboro. Why is this thing even on? Your first time in Nashville, Richard?"

Richard slowed abruptly. Straight ahead, a massive downed oak blocked the road. One of its limbs threatened to topple a telephone pole with it.

"That's why it's on," he said, angling a careful left onto a darker street.

"These things know too much, really," Vivian groused, back to the window. The towering limestone canyon looked like ice castles climbing to the sky.

She'd almost forgotten, too, after all these years. Wasn't nearly three decades of responsible motherhood atonement enough? Why pollute their daughter with a secret that could only damage and destabilize? The whole family could have gone to their graves none the wiser were it not for the lunatic ghost tale dredged up from two centuries ago. Talk about ancient non-history.

"*Go straight two miles,*" said the GPS.

"Well, that's ridiculous!" Vivian cried out. "She's sending us back the wrong way. Turn the damn thing off!"

The road narrowed and snaked. It was a black sheet of ice.

"Take Hidden Valley to Lynwood; they can't be any worse," she said. Richard drove on, ignoring her.

"But don't for a second think I'm taking all the blame, mister," Vivian went on, arms folded, clutching her elbows. "It takes two to end up in our kind of mess, you know."

The car planed right, then left, Richard bringing it under control. "Jeezus!" Vivian screeched. "Get off this fucking road!"

"We're fine," he said, shaken but steady.

But she hadn't forgotten everything. Not Bucky. Her weakness, to be sure. A drug, really. She still remembered the high—no, the euphoria. Who was she kidding? The sheer, mind-blowing ecstasy, every bit worth the crash. She pitied the poor, uptight souls who went through life without tasting such an addiction. It shivered her even now.

Big, bright headlights rounded the curve ahead.

"*Take a left turn...,*" the GPS suggested.

"Where?" Vivian demanded of it. "Where?"

The lights barreled closer, refracting through the windshield. It blinded.

"Turn down your damn beams!" shouted Richard to the air.

"Left *right* NOW. *Turn* back...," the GPS begged.

"Shut it off, Richard!" said Vivian. "It's gone haywire."

He clamored at the console, as the oncoming truck veered into their lane.

"Richard!" screamed Vivian, lurching for the wheel.

But it was too late.

● ● ●

Khaki bolted forward in her chair with a gasp.

Her middle twisted. She knew the sensation. It was a taunt, a reminder of who was in charge. And a message that things had gone terribly awry.

It coiled tighter. Khaki breathed deeply, maternal instincts sharpening. The calamity came into focus.

Kate had flicked the first domino. Her show had begun.

three

He saw the light at the end of the tunnel, thank God. His shift, already two hours overtime, was wrapping up. With any luck, he'd be home by midnight. He'd never hated Christmas music so much.

The lines—mobs just an hour ago—had trickled to stranded travelers desperate for a hotel room (magical thinking) or crabby overnighters looking to vent to someone in uniform *as if he controlled the weather, the heavens, and the earth.* He couldn't say "I'm sorry" one more time. And he really had to get his real estate license, pronto.

The blond young woman, restless but polite, waited her turn until he beckoned her to the counter. He didn't need to force a smile at her and the sleeping child coiled around her neck; it came naturally, almost with pity.

"Can you tell me if my husband took a different flight?" she asked, leaning in. "His name is Rupert Pearce."

"I'm sorry, ma'am"—damn, there again—"but I can't give out passenger information."

"Well, he's my husband, you see," she said, slinging her purse around with one arm, fumbling for the zipper with her precarious phone hand. "I have my ID, but we have different last names, you know."

He patted back her effort. "It's airline policy," he said, with more apology. A sincere one.

Her boy lifted his head and yawned. She shifted him to her other side, hip out, off-kilter. "I understand that, but he's not picking up his phone," she said through her own strained smile. "I think some of the cells are down. Or something. And we're waiting for him. We really need to get him. Tonight."

He stared at her, grasping at civility, unlike the others from his hellish night. Worn down, stricken even, with an undercurrent of panic. And hardly a security threat.

She put her hand flat on the counter, by the luggage tag basket. It trembled. "It's critical," she pleaded with haunted eyes that seemed primed to burst.

He could ask his supervisor. Or risk it and speed up his real estate timetable. Either way, he had to escape before "Rudolph" looped around again.

"Could you spell the last name?" he said with a hush, clicking quickly. "Is that an 'i' or 'e'?"

● ● ●

The smell woke her first. Something was burning.

"Richard," she mumbled in her sleep. "Is the house on fire?"

A bitter, biting, electrical smell. A bad outlet, faulty wiring hidden in the walls. An emergency.

"Richard?" she slurred again, burrowing back into her pillow. Her panic was no match for her grogginess. She felt drugged, but that couldn't be. She never took anything, not even a sip of alcohol. It was poison.

She listened. No Richard. She felt his absence. He'd gotten out of bed, was on the case. He was good like that. Always had been.

She needed to wake the others. They should evacuate, like they'd done before when the house caught fire. But she couldn't move. Emma and Khaki would rescue the children: Adam, Dillie, and Lance. She'd join them as soon as she woke up.

She snapped to, seconds, hours later. This was a crisis. What was that incessant dinging? Too chimelike for a smoke detector, but not her alarm clock either, unless Richard had bought a new one. Her forehead throbbed on the right. She had to get up, escape the smoke. Her legs wouldn't budge, seemingly gripped from below.

Richard was close by, prattling on with great urgency. He'd handle it all. She was too weary. She leaned her face into the pillow, then yanked back with focus. It was an air bag.

● ● ●

"Canceled his flight?" she said, her voice pitching. "That's not possible. He would have called." Then: "Did he go anywhere else?"

Click, click, click. "He's not in our system at all. No further itinerary."

Her face quivered. He feared her arms would collapse.

He'd already broken one rule. What was another? "Let me check the other carriers," he said, working the keys. He squinted at the monitor with bleary eyes.

Her phone rang. She checked the screen, rushed it to her ear. "Rupert!" she said, newly brightened. "Where are...?" Listening, she gasped a laugh of joy. "Oh, thank God! Who's there with you...? Everyone?"

She winked and held up a be-right-there finger. "We're at the airport, waiting for you! No, I never got...Well never mind.

You're breaking up. Say again?" She shook her head. "I'm losing you. Just sit tight. And please tell Khaki we're on our way back. She worries so. Don't let Mom drive you crazy. Love you." She hung up, a different person.

"You've been so helpful," she said, brimming. "But he took an earlier flight. He's already back at the house."

"He is?" he said.

She zipped her bag, readjusted her sleeping boy. "Thank you. Thank you again. Merry Christmas!"

"Ma'am?" he said, looking up and back at his computer. "Ma'am?" he called again. But she'd already hurried across the lobby, through the sliding door into the night.

He must have typed in the last name wrong. He was so exhausted, he didn't trust himself. Rupert Pearce/Pierce was currently over the Atlantic Ocean, three hours shy of his London destination.

● ● ●

"They're on their way," Richard told her from outside the Range Rover. "Sit tight."

"As opposed to *what*, Richard?" she said, trapped in her crumpled seat, pinned against the limestone bluff.

It had all come back to her, sharply, as her brain woke up. The oncoming pickup truck, Richard's slam on the brakes launching the SUV into a spiral glide across the ice. The seconds unfolded in silence, until the skid off the road and crunching impact against the bluff that stopped everything. The right side of her head still ached from its smash against the doorframe before she blacked out. Her internal clock told her she hadn't been out long, more a daze than a loss of consciousness.

Fortunately, they'd been traveling at moderate speed, although the spin accelerated the collision, in that physics way. She could move her legs (thankfully unbroken), but the seat had slid forward and jammed in place, sandwiching her against the air bag and glove compartment. It was, she had to admit, not uncomfortable. Even the engine had stopped smoking, although the dashboard kept up its incessant dinging from the open driver door.

"This...is an unwelcome development," she said, looking right to the ice-jagged limestone looming out her window. "How's the other driver?"

"They're...it's gone," Richard said, and she nodded with a smile. "Yes, of course," she said. "Of course it is."

"They'll cut you out as soon as they get here," he added, stooped in his open door, as the ice fell around him. "I don't see any bleeding."

"No, I don't think so."

"Are you in any pain?"

"I'm right as rain," she said. "It's actually quite cozy."

"You'll be just fine," he said. From outside came a cracking of wood.

"What was that?" Vivian asked.

Richard paused and said, "We hit...a utility pole." She said, "Oh? We did?"

"It's leaning against the front of the car," he went on, nervously. "But it's holding."

"Oh?" she repeated. "And the power lines?"

"Just stretched some."

She said, "I see." She couldn't see anything, of course, except the air bags, the limestone dripping with ice, her shivering husband struggling to mask his panic on the deserted road. His was always such a steady hand.

She leaned over to peek between the bags through the caked windshield. Yes, there was the blurry pole, snapped at its base, tilting but seemingly suspended. The lines, glistening with ice, sagged in heavy arcs. Just beyond, the ice castles towered above and around her. The car had hit at an angle, her corner smashed against the wall.

So this was the way. Clever. Elegant, even.

"I do love you, you know," she said weakly, turning to him. "All of you."

He reached in over his seat to touch her shoulder. "We love you, too, Vivian."

"*Get back!*" she warned. "Stand away from the car, Richard." He withdrew.

She tipped back against the headrest, looking upward. "Life went terribly wrong, didn't it?" she said with a sigh. Then she sucked her front teeth, agitating.

"We're going to be okay," Richard soothed from the street, looking up and around. "They'll be here soon."

The pole splintered loudly near the ground, tipped over to crash into the bluff.

"I'm so sorry, Dillie," she said, looking upward. "I wanted to be there. You're on your own now, honey...."

Crack-crack-crack! Loosened rock and ice shards rained down on the windshield, bouncing off and scattering.

Vivian threw back her head and cackled. "There we go!" she said.

"*Go back one mile,*" said the GPS, reawakened.

SMASH! A large chunk landed, crackling the windshield into a web before rolling off the hood.

"That's right!" Vivian sneered at the air. "What are you waiting for?"

"*In two miles, turn left.*"

SMASH! Another fell, denting the windshield inward.

Richard stepped up and back from the open door, desperate. "We've got to get you out of there!" He reached in, but Vivian shoved him away. "Back!" she ordered.

"*In three hundred feet, bear right.*"

"You'd better be ready for me," she warned the sky through the moonroof. "'Cause I sure as hell am."

CRACK! A giant ice stalactite sliced the power lines, pierced through the windshield. Its stiletto tip popped the air bag, stopping inches from her heart. From its jagged edge dripped melting water that rolled down her chest.

"*Yes!*" Vivian cried in ecstasy, hammering the armrest with her fist. "Almost there, you fucking bitch!" The trickling drops ran further down her body, chilling her.

Just past the shattered windshield, an untethered power line snaked up and back and down and around, glancing off the street, the bluff, the Rover. It probed and flicked, buzzing with energy as it blindly sought its target.

Vivian clenched her teeth, shivering. "Do it!" she hissed, gripping both sides.

"*You have reached your destination.*"

The dancing, electric tentacle found the stalactite in the window, latched on and settled. The current warmed the trickle to a stream, jolting down Vivian's chest.

"And I will see you in hell...," she seethed, rattling.

The vibration sparked deep, radiating out. And all went white.

● ● ●

Khaki clutched her breast, the wind sucked out of her.

She crumpled to the floor, anchored by the dawning horror.

"No...," she whispered. All had been upended; everything was in play.

There'd be time for grieving later. Perhaps. Now straight action was critical. She racked her brain for any last line of defense.

Righting herself, she stood. Then she picked up the bedside telephone, punched three oversized digits.

four

Waze, while often quirky, had never led her on such a wild-goose chase before.

With I-65 at a crippling standstill, her GPS app had diverted Dillie to side streets she vaguely recalled from childhood. Treacherous, but at least open and headed in the right direction, in their roundabout way.

She'd hoped to maintain contact with Rupert on the drive home, but her calls were going to voice mail again. He'd likely left his phone upstairs in her room with his luggage, while her mother held him hostage in the conservatory, peppering him with questions about his future career plans. She smiled, feeling his pain. Hopefully her father had poured him a tall scotch, neat. The kitchen phone rang and rang, used to being ignored. She'd hung up as soon as the answering machine clicked on. There was no point in calling her parents' cells; she'd see them soon enough.

Murray Lane was icy but straight and a clear shot to Hillsboro Road. From there, she knew her way cold. Campbell was conked out again, his internal clock so far out of whack, it would take days to reset. She relished that challenge, after all this had passed. They'd both sleep for days.

The dashboard read 11:32. She rehearsed in her head how much she'd explain to Rupert, as there wasn't time for the full story. Khaki would chime in, backing her up in a calm, convincing tone. Vivian would rail in protest, but they'd ignore her. They had no choice.

Thank God Khaki had stayed put. She'd been packing that morning for parts unknown, which made no sense. Where did she expect to go on a night like this? And why? Her behavior—sometimes routine, sometimes inexplicable—was the most unsettling barometer of her worsening condition. In any event, Vivian must have held her at bay.

She slowed, headlights catching a downed tree blocking the road just ahead. Waze had missed this obstacle; a couple quick taps on her phone reported it. To her left, a side street branched off, heading in the right direction. Holly Tree Gap rang a bell; she'd once had a playmate who lived there, or maybe a Brownie troop. She carefully turned, winded along.

Campbell stirred from his car seat. "Ssh," she said, glancing back as he yawned and stretched. "We'll be home soon, honey." The road was pitch-black, streetlights out, the few houses dark. Neighbors stood in driveways, peering, chatting.

A swirl of red and blue clashed around the bend, dancing off the trees, the ice, the limestone bluff. She slowed, inching through the curve. Sparkling red flares dotted the road, braking her further. A policeman waving a lighted wand stopped her cold. Just beyond, a fire truck, ambulance, police car crowded around a portable white tent set up by the bluff. A toppled telephone pole leaned against it, power lines loose and dangling.

Under the tall tent, she glimpsed a large vehicle—a van or SUV—smashed against the limestone. A major accident. Police and EMTs milled about, passing time. There was no urgency; this wasn't a rescue. Hopefully the passengers were already safe. But the ambulance was still there. With the tent shrouding it all. She bristled.

It struck her: She should stay. Here were police with guns, firemen trained for emergencies and disasters. What could harm them? But it was a ridiculous idea. They'd never understand. And they were already dealing with an immediate crisis. A tangible one.

The officer with the wand held up his hand, spun it to send her back. A dead end. Another ambulance rolled up from the opposite direction. She squinted through her wipers: the coroner. She sank. The scene was tragic.

On edge, Dillie backed away, searching for an accessible driveway. Kindly neighbors guided her as she gingerly made her turn. Waze recalculated another byzantine and counterintuitive course. It rarely failed her twice.

The lights twirled in her mirror as she drove off. She said a quick prayer for the victim. *Godspeed*, she thought, *to all travelers on this terrible night.*

• • •

She never thought she'd say this, but thank God for *AARP* magazine. With the Internet, phone, and cable down (so much for the bundle), she'd raided the hairdresser's station down the hall. Cover girl Sally Field was even spunkier than she'd imagined.

Her floor quieted down early tonight, with dinner service moved up so the staff could outrun the storm. Her own graveyard shift was a skeleton crew, with most stranded at home. So far, the power held, although maintenance had readied the generator. She reminded Mrs. Dunbar and Mr. McGarrity to take their evening pills (she had; he was dicey) and gave Big Raymond a longer break, as there was nothing to do but sit out the silence. The attendant's station—the whole building—a fluorescent ghost town.

She was nodding along with Sally Field's guilt over neglecting her children, when a resident stormed up to the desk in panic.

"Please, can you help me?" said the elderly lady in her laced nightgown and robe, silver hair brushed down around her shoulders. She looked like an old little girl, and a lovely one. "My phone's not working."

"Yes, ma'am, they're down throughout the building," the attendant said, ransacking her brain before realizing she'd never seen her before.

"I need to make a call, you see," the woman went on, in clear distress. "To the police, firemen, anyone."

"Is something wrong? In your room?"

She shook her head. "And I need to warn my granddaughter, but I don't know her number. May I use your mobile phone? I'll send someone to the house."

"I'm sorry, ma'am, but I don't understand."

The woman grew more agitated, grasping at the desk edge. "Her husband didn't make it....I need to send the police to protect her." She seemed lost, helpless.

"I see. We'll take care of it, Mrs...."

"NO!" she said, slamming the surface. "Please don't humor me."

Raymond poked his head out from the break room down the hall. She nodded at him for help.

"There's...an intruder," the woman went on, calmer. "My granddaughter can't face it alone. It's waiting for her. And her boy."

She was nonsensical but so convinced that it was almost convincing. Raymond stepped in to take over.

"You remember me, Mrs. Goodman," he said in his smoothest bedside manner. "I brought your luggage in."

"It's taken her mother!" the woman insisted. "She's there alone!"

"This way, Mrs. Goodman," Raymond said, gently shepherding her away. "Everything's A-OK."

The attendant searched the name on her computer. New arrival. Probably off her medication. First nights were tough. She seemed like a dear, just disoriented.

She started to dial the family on her cell, then stopped; it was late and not wake-up worthy. Instead, she notated the episode in her file, with instructions to monitor her. Hopefully she'd acclimate in a few days. They usually did.

● ● ●

Waze nailed it this time. Franklin Road to Lynwood moved quickly, with few drivers left to slow her down. Even the ice had slacked off, her view clearer through the wipers. The Volvo drove as if it knew its way home.

The motorized gates to River Kiss stood open, either left by her parents for her return, or stuck from the weather. She worried the power was out, but not for long. As soon as she rolled through, the gates automatically swung shut. It was 11:51.

The mansion ablaze with lights was a welcome sight as she winded down the driveway. She knew her mother would have it lit up, especially for Rupert. None of the chimneys were going, but it was late, and her father likely had given up on the icy wood pile.

The ancient elms that canopied the drive hung heavy, their thick branches weighted down from the storm. She moved quickly under them with a spike of apprehension, relieved once she had passed.

A shadow crossed the downstairs French door off the foyer, her mother or Khaki keeping a lookout. Dillie beeped twice to signal her arrival as her heart ticked up a notch. They'd all made it back.

She parked in the driveway loop by the portico. "We're home, honey," she cooed to a now-awake Campbell, as she lifted him out of his seat. "You've been such a trooper all day. Guess who's inside? Mommy's got a surprise." A sharp wind had picked up, curving the tops of the trees. She shielded his head, burrowed it against her neck as she hurried to the front door. It would fling open any second for a joyous homecoming. She placed a mental bet on who would burst through first: her mother or Rupert.

They must not have seen her driving up, or heard her beeping, so engrossed in conversation they were. She knocked, waited. Peered through the side light windows encasing the door. Knocked again. Her mother's Christmas music was probably too loud. With one hand, she fished through her purse for the key.

"Anybody home?" she joked, swinging the door open with Vivian's standard entrance line. She closed it, stood in the foyer. The house sat silent. The grandfather clock ticked.

"Mom?" she called out. "Rupert? Khaki?"

She peeked in the dining room, carried Campbell through the living room into the conservatory. The sofa pillows were plumped, the lamps and chandeliers on, all set for guests. Beyond the glass walls, wind-driven leaves and debris danced across the patio.

They might be upstairs, either asleep or on their way, having waited up as long as they could. Rupert was bound to be exhausted and unaware of the need to stay awake and alert. She climbed the staircase to the landing, listened upward for voices, footsteps, running faucets. "Hello?" she said, sinking. "Rupert?"

She knew the stillness of her house when empty. More than silence; an absence of life.

Retreating backward down the stairs, hugging the wall, she thought of her last option but was resistant to check. She had no choice. Through the kitchen, into the garage. Empty. She closed and locked the door.

She stood by the refrigerator, its hum mixed with the gentle rhythm of the foyer clock pendulum. Campbell arched up to be released. "Ssh," she said softly, rocking him. Then she heard a low-toned beep.

On the kitchen cubby desk, next to her mother's computer, the vintage answering machine blinked red. The digital readout counted four messages. She hovered over it, not breathing. Her finger shot out, pressed "play."

"*Good morning, Mrs. Goodman. I'm calling from Dr. Vandeveter's office to confirm your appointment for Wednesday, October . . .*" A weeks-old message. Dillie hit "next."

The telltale pause of a telemarketer, then a droning: "*Hello? Hello? May I please speak to . . .*" Stop. Next. An overly perky recording about a Caribbean cruise they'd won. Next.

Another pause, against a background of commotion and crowds. "*Mrs. Parker, it's Rupert.*" She yanked back her hand. "*I've left Dillie messages, but can't reach her. My . . . father passed away this morning. We were expecting it, just not . . . yet.*" His voice was strong; only she would detect a crack of vulnerability. "*I should be back by Christmas, and I'll keep trying her. But could you pass along...?*"

Her cell vibrated in her purse. She fumbled for it with a trembling hand. Three missed calls and voice mails from Rupert, just now arriving. They mocked. She didn't need to listen.

In the foyer, the grandfather clock whirred. Its slow, full Westminster chime filled the house. It settled for a moment, then started to toll the midnight hour.

On the sixth, it stopped, its final clang hanging in the air. The pendulum was dead.

Dillie clutched her boy close to her chest. "Happy Birthday... Campbell," she whispered in his ear.

A tremor of wind rattled the walls, whistled under the front door.

Her head shot around. A dart of movement paced outside the fogged-up bay window. A second crisscrossed with a canine whimper, a scratch, a pawing. A third panted against the glass pane, with a flash of fangs.

five

Now he could surf Netflix guilt-free; Vanderbilt had just canceled classes for the next day, via text. His lecture prep could wait.

Dr. Grant had expected as much since the school's closing at noon but had stayed in town at his West End Avenue condo, just in case. The trek to Adams would have been hell in the storm. He'd deal with any damage to the cabin over the weekend, although the radar indicated northern Tennessee had been largely spared. Nashville and its suburbs were the bull's-eye.

His pied-à-terre near campus was convenient and serviceable, and could have been homey had he made an effort to mask its corporate-housing vibe. But his heart hadn't been in it, after selling the Acklen Avenue craftsman he'd shared with his wife for more than three decades. The furniture and sentimentals had gone to the farm, leaving him with Ikea basics and a few Pottery Barn flairs brought by his daughter. Framed photos of the grandchildren were a must—and aplenty—but he resisted adding more of his soul to such a temporary place. Retirement beckoned.

He scrolled, debating which episode of *Poirot* would lull him to sleep, when his cell buzzed on the bedside table. It was offensively late, and he checked the screen with annoyance. Then he snapped to.

"Dillie?" he said, sitting up against the headboard. The connection was lousy.

"*It's here, Dr. Grant!*" she said through waves of static. But her panic rang through clear.

"What's there?" he said. "Who?"

"*Kate, the Being, the BellWitch! It's here, at the door!*"

With the day's storm distraction, he'd forgotten about her imagined deadline. She'd tipped over to hysteria, right at midnight. Quitting meds cold turkey could be lethal, he knew. She shouldn't be alone, wherever she was. Especially with a child.

"Dillie, is your boy with you? Where's your family?"

"*Campbell and I are...ourselves...at the house,*" she warbled through broken reception. "*I don't...where everybody is.*" He heard her pull the phone away to soothe her son, futile as it was. Even through the spottiness, she was shattering. He should send the police, to protect them both, from her.

Swinging to the edge of the bed, his mind ticked. "Dillie, calm down, if you can. Are you sure it isn't just...?" A delusion? Final descent to madness? The question failed him.

"*It's come...take him!*" she insisted through increasing distortion. "*He's...Gardner!*"

Dr. Grant froze. "You're breaking up, Dillie. What did you say?"

"*Campbell is a Gardner and a Bell,*" she said through a clearer patch. "*Direct descendant, both sides.*"

"Are you sure, Dillie?" he said, halting. "How do you know?"

"*I found...records.*" She was weaving out again. "*...library.*"

Less hysterical. Calm. Convincing.

Her words came staccato. "*Can't...surrounded...I've got to...*"

The connection was lost. He redialed. Hopeless.

Dr. Grant stewed. River Kiss was thirty minutes away on a good day. Much longer with the storm. If what Dillie said was true—she'd been meticulous, *sensible* so far—her panic was understandable. Even justified. He struggled to digest the implications.

His keys sat on his bureau, next to photos of his daughter and grandchildren. They needed him, too. There wasn't time to weigh the risks.

Dr. Grant moved.

• • •

The 911 call center was overwhelmed, the hold made longer by the immediacy of her crisis. She let the kitchen phone dangle, one ear tuned. Thank God her mother had kept the landline.

The coyotes had left the window. They could be anywhere, even back in the woods. Perhaps they'd been curious, scrounging, looking for scraps. Like coyotes did.

And maybe Khaki had a medical scare—she'd had her share, usually false alarms and often at night—and out of an abundance of caution, they'd rushed her to the ER. Vivian had an itchy trigger finger when it came to her mother's health, much to Khaki's annoyance. They would have called, if they could get through. But she couldn't reach any of them either.

Even if that were true (she hated herself for wishing it so, but it was plausible, and Khaki would understand), they still shouldn't be in the house alone. They needed to surround themselves with others—the twenty-four-hour Kroger or CVS, even the all-night Waffle House—just in case. She gave one last listen to the hold announcement, then placed the receiver on the desk. Surely they'd trace the call and respond to the silence.

"Hold on to Mommy," she said, smiling at his confusion as she carried him back to the front door. "How 'bout a nighttime adventure? Do you want some ice cream?" She peered through the side lights, around and down. Listened. Then she slipped through the door, closed it behind her.

The sharp wind tore as she hurried down the steps, newly slick with fresh-fallen ice. Why didn't she have her keys in hand? Fingers probing, she dug through her purse as she kept watch, full circle— the shrubs, trees, fields. They came up empty, but the doors were still unlocked. She opened the back, placed Campbell in his seat. Still rummaging, she hopped in the front. Bingo. Keys into the ignition, doors locked.

The windshield had iced solid, wipers useless. Her mother always kept a scraper on hand. "Sit tight," she said, grabbing the key, jumping out, locking it behind her. She popped the trunk, clean and orderly, the scraper in its proper place.

Front and back, she chiseled out irregular patches big enough for her escape. The ice was falling steadily again, stinging her face and hands. Back inside, locked, coast clear. Her numb fingers dropped the key on the way to the ignition. It clattered to the floor. Groping on the rubber mat, she flicked them under the seat. With her head against the steering wheel, she contorted to reach them through the mystery of track and wires. Her middle finger brushed against the fob, and she strained to lure it closer. The horn sounded. She yanked back and up.

Dillie sat straight, calming her breath. The windows had fogged over. She looked to each, blind to the outside. Ice tickled the roof. She palmed dampness from her face.

The spare key. She flung open the glove compartment, tossed out the registration and leaflet maps, found the twin in the back. With a steady grip, she raced it to the ignition. By seeming miracle—though no reason to expect otherwise—the Volvo turned over smoothly and settled to a purr.

She smeared off the fog, front and side; the back could wait, although she hit the right buttons to speed it along. Ice had already started to reglaze. The wipers skidded and glanced but cleared a good enough view with the headlights. As she went for the gearshift, she remembered Campbell's seat belt.

"Let's buckle up," she told him, twisting over her seat. She hoisted him back and straight, wrapped his harness around. *Click*, the right and left straps together. The warming strips on the back window made slow progress. *Click*, the strap between his legs. *Please let Kroger be open in the storm.* She pulled on the tail to tighten.

THUD! A coyote slammed at the back window, jaws snapping against the ice. Dillie screamed. It lunged again, clawing at the glass.

She flipped back to the steering wheel. CRACK! A second attacked the windshield. Campbell cried out from his seat. A third gnashed at her window, pawing the sill. Surrounded. She tramped the brake, shifted to drive, gunned ahead.

The back coyote slid off the trunk. She slammed the brakes, threw into reverse. *Thump-crunch-squeal* as she crushed over it, back tire tilting. She braked again, the animal's convulsions thrumming the car underside, its desperate screeches pitching higher. The front coyote gripped the windshield, enraged.

Back in drive, she floored the gas, grinding the beast below. It fell silent. She circled the loop, her view blocked by fur, claws, teeth. The sharp turn around the conservatory came faster than expected. She hit the brakes, locking on the ice. The car fishtailed, slid. Khaki's elm came at her at an angle. The car skidded off the pavement, smashing into the tree. The impact dislodged the coyote, sent it tumbling off backward across the hood.

The engine kept humming. Back to reverse, nothing. She gassed harder. The engine roared; the tires spun and whined. The front of the car rocked, sinking deeper into the icy mud. Stuck.

Dillie looked and listened. Stillness. Peaceful, even. She exhaled in pent-up spurts. "Campbell honey?" she said, reaching back to caress the top of his head. He'd been shocked into silence, but his huffs signaled an outburst brewing. "Ssh, we're okay," she lied.

Where the hell were the police, firemen? Her family, most of all?

And the coyotes? Gone, for now. Maybe frightened off, like normal animals. These weren't normal. Nothing was.

The ice kept trickling. How long could they stay in the car? They wouldn't freeze, even if it ran out of gas. The most rabid, *abnormal* coyotes couldn't break through the glass. Until help arrived—and it would, had to—they were in the safest spot, tucked into the elm.

Her vision blurred, swam. She felt dizzy, on the cusp of nauseous. The overload of stress threatened her consciousness. And then—a tinge of gasoline. She sharpened. Not stress, but engine fumes, filling the car. She reached for the ignition, turned it off. The poison lingered and spread. She had to air it out, no matter the risk. Her brain clouded thicker, fumbling for the window buttons. Just an inch, front only. The cross breeze whooshed through the crevices, clearing out. The clean air braced, lifting her daze.

One eye on the windows, finger on the buttons, primed. Outside, the greenery waved in the gales.

BANG-SMASH! The car quaked, the roof collapsed inward, spraying glass. A giant limb landed down the middle, shattering through the windshield, demolishing the hood. It settled inches above Campbell's head, bisecting the car. The frame creaked, threatening a cave-in. The elm had more limbs high above: dead, heavy, ice-freighted. The wind gusted and shook; the elm groaned overhead. She reached back, unclipped Campbell's harness.

He cooperated as she lifted him, one hand shielding his head from a protruding branch. She slipped him through the front seats, onto her lap. As she bounced her knee, she searched her purse for the house key, grasped it. She checked through the windows.

Her door stuck, jammed from the collision. She rocked back and threw her shoulder against it, loosening its grip. Again. It cranked open enough for her to sidle out backward, hip first, lowering herself to the ground. She sprang up, reached in for Campbell, carefully maneuvered him out.

Dillie dashed around the conservatory and across the driveway, past the crumpled carcass, eyes flicking everywhere as she targeted the front door between the box hedges. Keys jangled as she slid the right one into the lock and turned.

Teeth sank into her calf, locked on. Jaws grabbed the middle of her spine, pulling her back and down.

The assault was silent. Dillie didn't cry out. She cushioned Campbell from the fall against her chest, lashed out with one arm. She struck scrawny ribs, a bony snout, felt a piercing yank-shake on her forearm. With an explosive scramble, she shook them off, sprang up and through the front door, slamming it behind.

On hind legs, the coyotes pawed at the side lights, fangs bared. "Go away!" she screamed, hyperventilating as she grabbed a knobby walking stick from the umbrella stand by the front door. Together, the animals dropped out of sight, disappeared.

A wet warmth on her calf, an odd sting. Teeth had ripped through her jeans, drawing blood. Her jacket was torn, too, her arm sore but protected. Campbell hung on tight. She'd run out of lies to soothe him.

Perry Como crooned to her. "Silver Bells" reverberated throughout the house. Her mother's favorite. The intercom lived again.

Help wasn't on the way. The hurricane had arrived.

A scrape on the dining room window: One coyote, now seemingly playful, yelped to be let in. A shaking from the back: The other scratched at the French door, rattling the hinges.

Campbell, beyond his limit, tucked into her neck. Her arms burned, about to give way. She moved toward the stairs; the coyote migrated to keep her in sight. She crept upward to the landing, her leg throbbing. The hinges shook again. Farther up to the second floor. If she could lay him in his crib for a few minutes, she'd figure out her next move.

At the end of the hallway, next to her father's study, light spilled from the stairwell to the crow's nest. A light that was never on unless someone was upstairs. But no one was. She listened for movement above, but all she heard was Perry Como. And scratches and whines from downstairs.

Dillie thought.

•　•　•

Though helpless, she refused to be useless.

Even if possible, there was no point summoning the authorities to the house, Khaki realized, once she'd settled down. They'd be ineffective, if not hostile at a false alarm. Either way, Kate would simply wait them out.

Back in her room—Raymond had kindly offered to stay; she'd politely declined—Khaki focused, surveying the crisis. Dillie and the boy were alive but in danger. Kate hovered nearby as Black Dog and Cryptography set out to bring back her prize. Her henchmen were obnoxious and deadly, to be sure, but simple. Dillie could outfox them, with a little guidance.

Toward the light, my girl, she urged, staring out her window. *Up, up.*

• • •

Hillsboro Road was a straight shot at this hour, but still slow with the ice. He reached forty-five only once, until he hit a slick patch on the dark stretch between Brentwood and Franklin. Fortunately, the street was empty, and he brought the pickup quickly under control.

Dr. Grant didn't know what he was doing or what to expect, but he couldn't ignore Dillie's hysteria, delusional as it may be. Surely by now her family had the situation in hand and would wonder about a strange man showing up in the middle of the night. His main concern was the boy.

He turned onto Berry's Chapel Road, off the main drag into a residential neighborhood. Here the streets were less traveled and icier. He slowed a bit.

Unless Dillie was right, about everything. His main concern was still the boy.

His shotgun was up at the farm, locked in the closet off his home office. He'd only used it to scare off the crows that infested the oak out his window, when their caws grew maddening and distracted him from his work. The lone other weapon he had—if you could call it that—was an old buck knife he kept at his condo for household chores. He'd grabbed it on his way out, just in case.

The houses on the street were mostly dark, families tucked in for the night. Sleds and other snow toys lay abandoned in Christmas-festive front yards, although a few young teens still made mischief ice-surfing down hills, long past their bedtime. Tomorrow was an unexpected holiday, and the parents were asleep.

His excitement grew, weirdly, the nearer he got. He scolded himself for the decidedly unacademic notion that a supernatural legend he'd studied for years could be real—and present—less than a mile away. It wasn't, of course. But Dillie's breakdown notwithstanding, he couldn't deny a perverse hope to encounter even a glimpse of the mystery that had confounded all seekers for so long.

The Gardner/Bell bloodline, if true, was a tantalizing new discovery. If the boy was a forbidden mix, it could fuel a new chapter for the paperback release, along with Dillie's temporary descent into madness that was perhaps Kate's most potent legacy for those who tried to untangle her riddle. He'd get Dillie's permission, of course, and change names to protect her family's identity. He looked back to the road just as the terrified girl in a pink parka waved frantically, smashed into the hood, the windshield, and up and over the top of the truck.

Brakes slammed, the truck spun a full rotation before careening sideways into the gully. Dr. Grant landed on his left shoulder; the pickup rocked and settled. He looked out the windshield at icy grass and ditch, up through the passenger window at dark sky. There wasn't time to shake it off. Unbuckling, he crawled from behind the wheel, forced the passenger door open, hoisted himself up to the side of the truck. He braced for what he'd find on the pavement. Even at moderate speed, the impact had been brutal. He looked in both directions.

"Hello!" he called out, lowering himself to the grass. He stumbled from the ditch to the road. "Can you hear me?" he shouted. Only the wind answered. He searched the trench on the other side. The girl was nowhere.

Back to the truck. The front was damaged from its landing, but the hood untouched where he'd struck her, the windshield and roof perfectly intact.

A light blinked on in the front of a house. He would have waited had there been anything to tell them, any help to ask for. But there was only a stranded professor, a disabled truck on an icy night, a phantom girl in a pink jacket who'd caused it all. If she'd ever been there.

Dr. Grant started running down the middle of the street, toward his destination.

six

Dillie laid him in his crib, facedown, the way he slept most soundly.

He still wore his orange jacket, overalls, even shoes. So out he was, his arms sat flat to his sides. She gingerly tucked them up to a more comfortable, natural position. Caressing his blond hair, she tilted his head to the side, facing away from her, so he wouldn't breathe into the mattress. She stepped back; he looked angelic in the dim light, like he always did when dead asleep.

As an afterthought, she quietly lowered the crib side, for quicker access.

Peeking through the closed drapes, she scanned the length of the balcony. Empty and still. She listened at the door—Bing Crosby had taken the microphone; she'd turned it down in her room—and then cracked it. Clutching the walking stick like a bat, she stepped into the hallway, closing the door firmly behind her.

The pawing and whining had been silent for a while—five minutes? ten?—which unsettled more than comforted. Perhaps they'd given up, frustrated by defeat and easily distracted, like wild animals were. They'd been too stupid to find the outside stairs up to the balcony, too dim-witted to follow their movements to the second floor. She creaked step by step down to the foyer, all senses peaking.

Wind swept around the house. "White Christmas" crooned to its end. A door flapped. Again. Again.

And nails clicking across the mudroom and kitchen floors. Dillie turned and bolted up.

They were on her by the time she reached the second floor. Teamlike, they darted at her from both sides, gnashing at an arm, a leg, her back. She swung the stick, battering across their muzzles. With a downward strike, she broke the stick on top of a head, sending the coyote backward. It shrieked and shook, dazed. Dillie raced on.

Into her father's study, door open. She targeted the glass-doored gun cabinet high in the corner. Grabbed the cabinet door. Locked.

The coyotes regrouped down the hall, scrambled closer. Dillie reared back, smashed through the glass door with her fist and half the stick, lacerating her hand. Dropped the stick, reached for a revolver. Turned as they rounded into the study.

BANG! A clean shot through the skull. The kick threw her back; she recovered to aim at the other. *Click. Click.* The trigger stuck, the gun jammed. Her hand throbbed, blood dripping down the handle onto the floor. In the instant she turned back to the cabinet—Khaki's second revolver was missing, and no time to load the shotgun, even if she knew how—the other coyote pounced.

She grabbed its neck, midair, as it flailed and snapped, claws shredding at her. With a burst, she threw it backward onto the carcass outside the doorway. It twisted itself over and quickly sprang to its feet. From down the hallway, a warning bark she knew, a familiar rhythm bounding closer. She rejoiced.

"Booray!" she cried in relief as he turned the corner. He dwarfed the scrawny creature he'd easily chased off the night before.

Booray stopped and stood shoulder to shoulder with the coyote, facing her. His ears were back and flat, brown eyes menacing and wild. His jaws dripped through curled lips. Froth. Together they blocked the door, growling at different pitches. A pack.

They would kill her, to start. Then they would find what they really wanted. They'd smell him, eventually hear him. They would find their way in.

Her dog led the attack as she burst through them, hurdling over the dead coyote. Her dog-not-her-dog reared up to topple her, instinctively knowing her center of gravity. He clamped on to the back of her thigh and thrashed his head as she struggled down the hallway on hands and knees. The coyote went for her throat as she swatted back. Dillie screamed, her pain and exhaustion erupting. Inch by inch, she clawed her way toward her bedroom door, against a chorus of snarls and yelps, a chaos of fangs. They would have to kill them together. Collapsing at the threshold, she reached up with one hand, grasped the knob, turned it.

They abandoned her instantly, bursting through the door as a team. Dillie crumpled to the hallway floor, defeated. The sounds were unimaginable, carnal: the dog's full-mouthed snarls and thrashing groans, the coyote's triumphant, high-pitched squeals. Quick, precise, primal. There was a lull, a moment's respite of panting, then an energetic thundering back toward her, paws on carpet.

She glanced up to a flash of orange jacket as the dog tore through the door, hauling a limp body by the neck, tiny shoes dragging. The coyote was fast behind, guarding the catch from the rear. Facedown, she breathed in the carpet runner, tracing the sounds of their path below. Across the foyer, the kitchen, to the mudroom, a confused pause, then a deliberate exit through the dog flap, followed by an impulsive one. The flap settled, and the house fell silent again.

Dillie lay still, listening. Then she gasped, heaved, flooding sobs into the floor.

● ● ●

The animals raced across the fields toward the tree line in the distance. The Labrador clutched the body more firmly in its jaws, dragging it along the ground, lifeless and slack. The coyote followed in its draft, shrieking conquest.

Springing over brush and tree stumps, the dog leaped at the water's edge into the river shallows. It broke through plates of ice that were slowly riding with the current. Belly deep off the bank, the dog submerged its capture in the frigid water and held it there. After moments, it released its prey, lifted its head to breathe again.

The coyote yelped from the side. The dog staggered back to land, unsteady. It growled, snapped at the coyote, scaring it off. Head hanging below its shoulders, its eyes cloudy, the dog seemed lost, disoriented. With heavy, rattling breaths, it zigzagged its way into the dense thicket, alone.

The small body resurfaced, facedown. It took its place amid the broken sheets of ice, bobbing against one, then another. The matted blond hair and orange jacket traveled with the river, into blackness.

● ● ●

Khaki grabbed her throat, cratering by the window. It was done. All their efforts for naught.

Then she cocked her head, absorbed it. With the slightest delay, a clearer picture came into focus. She breathed in relief. *Clever girl*, she thought, smiling with pride and more than a little admiration.

● ● ●

Dillie emptied out, her sobs settling. Forehead first, she pushed her way back to hands and knees. Her body ached—searing from the wounds on her hand, arms, thigh—but she rose and limped toward the staircase at the end of the hallway, leaning on the walls, then steady on her own.

She climbed the stairs with stronger purpose, ignoring the pain. Past the crow's nest office and storage closet, opening the door to Vivian's studio. There, under the easel and shelves of paint, brushes, and pastel chalks, sat Campbell in a circle playing with the other children. With a green marker, he slashed crooked lines across a tablet sheet, while babies and toddlers—some sitting tilted, others strewn on their side—watched the room with glassy, unfocused eyes. Campbell looked up at his mother with a self-satisfied smile, proud of his artistic creation. He wore his navy sweater, denim jeans, tiny peacoat with naval buttons.

"Mommy's back," she said, scooping him into her arms, abruptly pain-free. "You're safe now."

Another lie, of course. They'd realize the dupe and be back, likely soon. She grabbed a painter's rag to wrap her bleeding hand, stepped over her mother's eerie dolls and the ripped outfit from the one she'd sacrificed, and hurried Campbell from the studio.

She carried him down the back stairs, past the ground floor—
there wasn't time to barricade the flap, and she had a better
idea—to the basement cellar that had always doubled as the family's tornado shelter. After flipping the switch for the single bulb
that hung from the ceiling, she closed and bar-bolted the sturdy
door, navigated the rickety wooden stairs to the cement floor
belowground.

Leaning against the stone foundation walls were her girlhood
bicycle with the daisy basket, folded lawn chairs from long-ago
soccer games. In the far corner hulked the boxy furnace spawning
a metallic duct upward through the ceiling. Here they'd hunker
down until the storm had passed, the new day come. It was their
last refuge, the most impenetrable room in the house.

Dillie cranked open one of the chairs, held Campbell in her
lap. He curled into her. With her bandaged hand, she stroked his
head and back, sang "Frère Jacques," and listened to the furnace
hum, the wind whipping the grounds.

● ● ●

Ice floes linked across the river in bigger chunks traveling together. It looked almost passable, like a moving sidewalk of stepping
stones.

The jagged sheets slowed, as if forming a solid plane. The river
came to a crawl, then a standstill, seemingly frozen over. It sat,
pondlike.

Sheets cracked apart from an unseeable shift in tension.
Broken shards swirled in eddies around the edges of larger pieces.

The river stirred anew. Almost imperceptibly, the current changed direction, crawling back from where it came.

● ● ●

Temper, temper, Khaki thought with a scolding grin.

She'd held out hope—for no reason, just wishful thinking—that Dillie's stamina, endurance, *craftiness*, would impress, even soften. That Kate would give her a pass this time, to fight again another day. It wasn't to be. If Kate had any virtues at all, mercy wasn't one.

Dillie battled heroically but had reached her limit with this foe. There were no reinforcements to send, at least from this side. And the final assault was closing in.

Khaki surveyed herself in the bedroom mirror. Elderly, to be sure. She wore the decades well, with the grace and resilience that had served her through the full symphony of life. But the body was weak. Kate thought she was done with her. After all these years, maybe she was. But Khaki wasn't done with Kate, not quite.

She went to her smaller suitcase, still open on the luggage rack. Foraging to the back, she unzipped a tucked-away pocket, reached for the clear bag inside.

seven

Dillie dreamed of Martha's Vineyard—the East Beach that was Rupert's favorite, even if too touristy, the lighthouse fireworks he'd promised Campbell for next July Fourth (she felt he was still too young for all that noise)—when her shallow doze was jarred by an abrupt silence. The wind outside had stopped.

She leaned forward in the folding chair, cradling Campbell. Listened. It seemed the world had stalled.

The storm had moved on, as they always did. In a few hours, the sun would peek over the river and trees, lifting the darkness and, with it, the nightmare.

Campbell woke, pawed her chest. She bounced him twice.

Upstairs, a chime sounded. "*Front door open*," announced Agatha above. Dillie bolted up.

Campbell yawned loudly. She covered his mouth.

More stillness. Endless stillness.

The basement doorknob clicked, slowly turned. Gentle pressure on the door, pushing inward. The bar resisted. Again, lightly. Dillie backed a step, eyes on the door. The knob turned back, releasing. Fresh silence.

Campbell hugged his mother's neck, facing away.

Above, a dragging across the floor. Loud, heavy, effortless. A pause, then more dragging, in a different direction. Something tipped over, crashed. It got righted, easily, then dragged further, vibrating through the basement walls. The house furniture being moved, rearranged. Then nothing.

The overhead bulb went off. The room went black.

In the corner, the furnace cycled off, turning up the silence louder. And then a low hiss.

It grew stronger. And the punch of rotten eggs. Gas leaking through the basement.

Thick fumes mushroomed and spread. Dillie held Campbell's nose and mouth to her neck. Her brain started to cloud. She looked around the darkness, to the dim night glow through the small cellar window above. With one hand, she pulled the folding chair to the wall, stepped shakily onto it. She struggled for balance as she reached up to the dingy window with her fingertips, fumbling, pushing. It wouldn't budge.

Dillie swooned backward off the chair, sharply nauseous. She stumbled, caught herself, kept Campbell upright. The fumes gathered, overwhelmed. Campbell coughed. The room blurred and swam. She held her breath.

He could fit through the window. She had to break it. There was nothing, even if she had the strength. Campbell relaxed more. Both deadening.

She had no choice. She careened one way, then another, tripping on the bottom step. Loosely conscious, she staggered him upward, to the door at the top. With the last of her power, she forced the bar bolt open, leaned her head against the door. Exhaled.

"You are everything to me, Campbell," she whispered to her sleeping boy. "I love you." She kissed his forehead, lingering.

She groped for the knob, turned it.

● ● ●

"Mrs. Goodman?" The attendant knuckle-thrummed the door as she cracked it. "I'm just seeing how you're doing…." When there was no answer, she swung it open, peeked in on the new resident.

Fortunately, the crisis had passed, the panic attack over. The elderly woman lay in her nightgown, on top of the covers, Bible folded over her chest. Other than the rise and fall of her chest, she was perfectly still in slumber. Divine, really. Her tartan luggage, as yet unopened, lined up neatly by the door. They'd help her unpack tomorrow, to get her fully settled in.

She almost woke her to tuck her in properly, but she looked so peaceful. Deep, uninterrupted sleep was what she needed and had found. She'd check again at the end of her shift. Backing out, she dimmed the lights, pulled the door, soundlessly clicked it closed.

●　●　●

A soprano sang a cappella as soon as Dillie burst into the house. Her mournful, rustic voice filled the air.

"Softly and tenderly, Jesus is calling
Calling for you and for me"

Even in the dark blurriness, her home was unrecognizable. From the stairs, she took an immediate turn toward the mudroom. Blocking the door outside sat the kitchen refrigerator, ripped from the cabinetry and now unmovable. Dillie went the other way.

"See, on the portals He's waiting and watching
Watching for you and for me"

Through the kitchen, illuminated by the gas burners fired up high. All drawers and cabinets open; plates, cups, glasses perched in pyramids on the counter.

> *"Come home, come home*
> *Ye who are weary, come home"*

She stumbled into the foyer. The oil portraits hung upside down. A maze of upended furniture formed a byzantine path. Against the front door, the living room sofa, club chairs, grandfather clock teetered on top of one another, defying physics and gravity. She turned to the back door, barricaded by a mahogany highboy and entryway chest, both tilted at impossible angles. The clock tolled incessantly. The lantern chandelier spiraled in slow circles.

> *"Earnestly, tenderly, Jesus is calling,*
> *Calling, O sinner, come home!"*

The dining room door crept open, spilling a dance of light. Trancelike, Dillie moved toward it and inside. Dozens of white candles—votives, tapers, pillars, the whole arsenal—flickered on the far sideboard under the gold-leaf mirror. It was papered over with a ring of taped photos. She drew closer, winding around the dining table, past the muraled walls.

The photos were of Adam. Hypnotized, Dillie pulled in. She'd seen them all before: his birthday, the park, the family. Thrillingly alive. Smiling, always smiling at her. A glorious shrine, glimmering with light and love. A calm wrapped around her. He seemed to beckon her. He was okay. It was all okay. Come closer.

The soprano stopped, midverse. The clock fell silent. The house sat still.

Dillie breathed in, absorbing the beauty.

Movement in the mirror. Dillie spun, holding her boy. It shot across the table, upon her. She gasped.

● ● ●

Would it come? Had she taken enough? Surely so. Was she already there? No, she was still here.

But closer. She could feel the pull. A gentle tow, gliding her under. And her faith, which had gotten her this far. She leaned on it one last time, to get her where she needed to be.

It was tranquil, soothing. No surprise there. She gave over to it, wanting it to take her. But she kept a reservoir of strength, ready to summon. She'd need it immediately.

There was the light. It looked just as she expected. It brightened, growing wider. Others welcomed, shepherded her closer. She nodded in gratitude, grasped hands, but moved quickly past. Let's hurry.

On her bed, Khaki's breathing grew shallow, labored. She lifted her torso, eyes to the ceiling, then fell back. Her lids fluttered closed, mouth tensing, arms draped over to the sides. The Bible fell away off the bed, landed open on the floor.

● ● ●

The music box tinkled "Happy Birthday" just for her.

She sat at the end of the dining table, in Daddy's spot, although he wasn't there. Adam sat next to her, in his little blazer and striped tie, grinning at his sister. They were both in booster seats, ready for the party, but it wasn't theirs; it was hers alone.

The room was all circus and animals—plates, napkins, tablecloth. The clear umbrella hanging upside down from the chandelier brimmed over with colorful balloons. One fell and floated to the table, bouncing up toward her. She reached out to grab it, barely missing, launching it the other way.

Her mother—young and glimmering in a purple dress with lily corsage on this special day—hovered and scooted Dillie's chair closer to the table, so she wouldn't topple out. Bubbly, she leaned over to kiss the top of her head, said something she couldn't hear over the music box, and disappeared out into the kitchen, the door swinging behind her.

At the far end of the table, anchoring the other side, sat Bucky, handsome as ever in his dark suit. He waved and worked his eyebrows goofily, then blew her a kiss. She caught it and pitched one back. His mouth moved, but the tinkling drowned it out. She giggled anyway.

Lola was there, next to Adam, in a sunny yellow dress that offset her gorgeous braids entwined with a rainbow of beads. How strange and wonderful to see her dressed up, free of care, smiling broadly. Dillie was delighted she'd come to the party. It had been too long.

And even Madeleine, across the table, glowed with contentment and normalcy, so different from last time. She said something to Lola and rubbed the baby in her tummy, with a quick laugh to Bucky before turning back with bright eyes to the birthday girl.

Dillie clapped with glee, and they laughed and clapped with her, primed and expectant. She basked in the love of her new family.

The music box slowed, needing a windup.

The kitchen door swung toward them. Vivian backed into the room before twirling to unveil the homemade teddy bear cake, her favorite, with its big Oreo eyes and coconut fur dusted in chocolate. From its fat belly grew the flickering "2" candle, although she felt much bigger than that, especially in her booster seat, which made her grown-up height.

The music slowed to a crawl, each tinkle hanging.

Her mother lowered the cake over her head, set it on the table. Hands on knees, she crouched at her daughter's side, nodding encouragement with puckered lips. The others cheered her on, but she couldn't hear. They waved her closer. It was her time.

The music box stopped midnote.

Dillie took a deep breath, filled her cheeks, leaned in to the candle.

"*NO, Dillie, STOP!*"

Khaki stood in the foyer door, smacking palms to command attention. Late to the party, in her nightgown with her hair brushed to her shoulders, as if ready for bed. Dillie smiled at first, then stopped. Khaki never left her room this way. Her color was muted, like an old movie, pale against the vital brights of the others.

Dillie pulled back from the candle. Her grandmother said so.

With jerky, stop-motion movement, Khaki spirited closer in bursts. Door, window, wall, table, ignoring the others. At Dillie's face, holding it. Her eyes locked in, urgent and demanding.

"*Wake UP, my girl!*" she ordered. "*Help me now....*"

eight

Her eyes sprang open to a world upended.

It took a moment to get her bearings. She was groggy, lost. Her forehead throbbed. The wind had returned, fierce, but she was inside, dark and protected. She smelled gas.

Her cheek smushed up against a warm, hard surface. She focused on the wood parquet, up to the painted floorboard, the cream damask wallpaper. The foyer, facedown. Her head throbbed, too heavy to lift. Blood ran from the sting at her scalp line, dripped from the bridge of her nose. She didn't care. Exhausted and blurry, she could sleep here—for hours, days—but she mustn't. There was gas somewhere, everywhere.

Campbell. Where was Campbell? Her eyes rolled, looking. She reached out one arm, pawing for him. She tilted her eyes upward.

In a gauzy view, the conservatory on its side, through the sideways door, just beyond. The blurry blond hair, tiny peacoat and jeans—her boy—also sideways, except he wasn't. She was. She forced her head up.

Campbell stood past the sofa, the bridge table, near the French door, his back to her. Miles away.

"Campbell?" she crackled through a dry throat, swallowed, pushed harder. "Campbell!" she called louder.

He didn't hear her. The wind was too strong. But he paid attention to something, head up and listening. Maybe her mother,

Khaki, even Rupert, if he'd arrived after all. Campbell was mesmerized. She lifted up on her elbows, searching. Saw no one.

A wobble of dizziness. They had to get out; the air was poison.

"Here, honey!" she yelled, strengthening.

Campbell raised his hand, tentatively, as if reaching for someone. Trusting, his little fist grasped empty air, held on. He kept looking upward.

The French door to the patio blew open. Wind shot through the conservatory, the foyer, the house. Campbell bristled in the icy blast.

Dillie pushed herself upward, struggled to stand, but her legs were dead—asleep, paralyzed. She clawed her way toward the conservatory, fisting a rug, pulling. Inch by inch.

Campbell toddled toward the open door, led by an invisible presence of adult height.

"Campbell, NO!" Dillie cried out, straining into the conservatory.

He stopped, turned back to his mother, his face concerned, then frightened. He hung back, resisting. With steady, even pressure, his arm tugged him closer to the blackness outside.

Dillie lurched nearer, one hand shooting toward him. "Stop!" she said.

"MOMMY!" he called to her, brave but helpless.

"He's a BABY!" she screamed at the force trapping him. "LET HIM GO!"

The wind gusted harder. His feet planted but sliding, Campbell was dragged over the threshold toward the night.

A crack, a louder one, an instant's pause, a house-throttling smash.

Khaki's elm towering over the conservatory shook in the gales. A giant branch, ice-laden, broke away, plummeted, shattered through the glass roof. It landed explosively.

A fresh torrent of wind gushed in from above. It roared through the mansion, beastlike.

Dillie's legs awoke. She scrambled, sprang to her feet. Raced across the conservatory, grabbed up Campbell, newly freed from the clutch. The French door blew shut with sudden force, jolting her back.

The wind howled through the first floor, seemingly whisking her toward the front. Its fury knocked photos off their shelves, skewed portraits on the walls, ballooned draperies midair. With one arm, Dillie pulled on the grandfather clock that blocked the door, tipping it over to crash in the foyer. She reached for the upended sofa, straining.

A dueling gust tore through the dining room, flared the still-burning candles on the sideboard. They caught the air, found gas, ignited. The fireball burst and spread, quickly engulfed the table, mural, curtains. A river of flame flowed across the rug. Alarms squealed.

"*FIRE! FIRE!*" Agatha announced. "*FIRE! FIRE!*"

The inferno spread through the entryway. Gray and black smoke swelled to all corners, blinding and choking them both. One hand over Campbell's mouth, she pulled at the furniture blocking the front door. The flames arrived, licking up the sofa, quickly overtaking it. Dillie shot back as the heat blistered.

Oxygen dwindled. Disoriented in the thick darkness, she turned and turned, burrowing the listless Campbell against her neck. She crumpled, fading.

A double crash from somewhere. And then Agatha: "*The back door is open.*" Smoke whooshed past her, escaping. A fresh blast of wind smacked her face, filling her lungs with sharp air. She revived instantly.

The back door blown open, the force of wind knocking the barricade off its tilt. The outside welcomed her.

Dillie tore past the burning staircase and walls, through the door.

She ran across the patio, through the gate, ran and ran, across the fields, knees flashing as she ran faster, away from the burning house, toward the trees, the river, the water.

She collapsed on the frozen grass, her son in her arms. "I've got you, Campbell," she said to his soot-blackened face. Eyes closed. Unresponsive.

"Campbell!" she shouted, grabbing his cheeks, shaking his head. "Oh God, please…!"

Campbell huffed a little-boy cough, then yawned and opened his eyes. A moment's confusion before he found his mother, smiled.

Hyperventilating with relief, Dillie laughed and rocked him against her.

"Dillie!" A man in the distance, frantic.

She turned back. "Dr. Grant!" She waved as he called up toward the house, searching. He saw her, pivoted, rounded the fiery mansion, flames now consuming the upper floors. An explosion—then more—as if a battle raged inside. He ran toward them, keeping his distance from the inferno, overawed by the spectacle.

"We're here!" she said as he neared. "We're good." She stood, cradling her son.

"Are you okay?" he asked, reaching for her forehead. "You're bleeding."

She nodded, the pain from her gash reawakened but bearable. "I'll be fine," she said, wiping away a stream. A few stitches, nothing more.

A groaning from high up. The roof folded inward, collapsed down on the top floor. Flames shot skyward, outer walls caved. The house seemed to gnarl in climactic fury.

Dr. Grant herded them closer to the river, away from spiraling embers. "What the hell happened?" he said near the bank, catching his breath.

Later. For now: "We stopped her," she said simply. "We saved him."

"We?" he said.

Campbell sneezed, shivering. Dr. Grant ripped off his overcoat. "The child's freezing," he said, gently taking him into his arms. He swaddled the coat around him, held him close. Instant grandfather.

The fire, while still churning, had peaked. It settled into an even burn, having spent its fuel. Dillie watched the ongoing show. There was an odd beauty to it, a finality. Not bitter, just sweet. It was only an empty house.

A fresh breeze caressed her face and neck, lingered. It felt warmer, delicate but insistent. Dillie touched the jeweled cross resting against her chest. *Thank you, Khaki*, she thought. *I love you.*

Sirens whined in the distance, nearing. Red lights swirled from afar. Fire trucks. Ambulance. Help on the way.

Dillie turned. "We need to get him to the hospital...," she called out, then stopped, froze.

Dr. Grant stood knee-deep in the river, among the ice chunks, staring at her. The bundled Campbell slept over his shoulder, arms splayed peacefully.

"What are you...?" she said, and then, "No...No..."

"We need to trust her, Dillie," he said calmly. "We need to trust Kate."

He'd gone mad, didn't seem it.

Dillie crumbled. She couldn't. Not now.

Her mind spiraling, she stepped closer through the thicket. "Dr. Grant, please," she said, desperate to reason with him. "You're just... obsessed. With a legend. You've gotten carried away." She reached out both hands. "Please. Bring him back." His face didn't budge.

"Kate's prophecies always come true," he lectured, trembling with cold. "I've got family, too. Children, grandchildren. It's their world I'm worried about."

"But it's a myth!" she insisted. "It's not real!"

"We both know differently, Dillie," he said.

Men shouted orders to each other behind her. Full mobilization to combat the blaze far away. Red swam across the trees, the river.

Dr. Grant stepped back, slipped deeper in the water, caught himself. It reached his waist, rising. He held Campbell's neck against his shoulder. He could snap it so easily.

The swirling lights from behind caught a glint on the ground near her. She glanced down. Khaki's pistol she'd thrown off the night before, nesting on the grass. Dillie swooped to grab it, pointed it unsteadily toward the river. A warning.

But a toothless one, with Dr. Grant holding Campbell against him like a shield.

Dr. Grant shook his head in scold. "Please, Dillie. If you shoot us both, where does that get you?"

She aimed closer to him. And Campbell.

"You go ahead and have a long, happy life," he went on, shuddering in the freezing water. "Have more children, girls. You can, you know. I'll take the fall for this. Let me take the fall." He sounded so reasonable.

Campbell covered Dr. Grant from his shoulders to his chest, his little head tucked against his neck. Floating ice plates gathered around them.

"Hello there!" called a fireman from behind her, approaching. Then: "Oh my God!"

Her finger found the trigger. The gun wobbled in her hand. The shot was impossible.

"I need backup!" the fireman called to his crew. "Ma'am, put the gun down! Now!"

Helpless, impotent, Dillie lowered the gun, fighting sobs. The barrel quivered.

Dr. Grant pulled a buck knife from his waistband, flicked it open. Up to the back of Campbell's head, blade against his neck.

"Jesus Christ!" the fireman yelled.

Dr. Grant tensed the knife, readying. "Someday you'll thank me for this." He started to drag it across.

Dillie raised Khaki's gun with both hands. Trained it.

Dr. Grant's head. Campbell. The heavy ice chunks. She fingered the trigger.

The barrel steadied, tipped a degree up, a degree over.

Dillie fired.

NEW YORK

Epilogue

"**S**tay in the sandbox, honey," she called out from the park bench. "Did you hear me, Campbell?"

The little devil stopped himself midclimb, backed down. "Yes, Mommy," he said. "Stay in sandbox." He returned to the similar-age children, though apparently bored with them. The other playing areas—pyramid climber, tire swings—were for the bigger kids and required closer adult supervision. She needed a breather.

Her fearless adventurer. And quite the chatterbox lately, to hers and Rupert's relief. The dam had broken, after his late start. They found themselves censoring each other for the first time, lest he pick up and parrot the wrong things. She'd never realized how inappropriate they could be when they thought no one was listening. It was a challenging new game they relished, both fascinated by how much he absorbed and reflected.

"Campbell, honey," she said—one eye on him, the other on her iPad—"give the shovel back to her, please. You've got your own."

The twos were so far not too terrible. He was more active, to be sure. Bolder, too. The "mine-mine-mine" phase was in full gear, but Victoria said it would taper off in a few months. He'd certainly mastered "no," although rarely to his mother. He was good like that. Sly, even.

"Did you hear me?" She leaned forward, intervention ready. "Thank you," she said. "That's a good boy." And such a gentle, almost sheepish return. Quite the charmer, when he wanted to be. He knew how to play her.

His personality had exploded over the past few months. A blessed *joie de vivre,* which had always come in flashes but was now in full bloom since their return to the city. Nothing, it seemed, could dim his smile once he'd triggered it. That was her greatest relief. The trauma left no scar, at least not yet. If anything, it had unlocked his spirit. But she was on guard.

And he'd taught her how to laugh again.

Stability, normalcy, *calm*—she'd insisted on that in their new life here. For herself, as well. They cloistered. No galas, art openings, not even a nanny, for the time being. The family would take care of its own business, healing at its own pace. Rupert had put off committing to a new venture until the fall, freeing him up as a true coparent. He'd even learned to cook, at least the kid favorites (his Gruyère/mascarpone mac and cheese, while sinful, certainly outshone hers). They got their Netflix money's worth.

Their marriage—love, really—had strengthened, deepened from the crisis. It was the first time they'd actually depended on, instead of complemented, each other. And the first time they'd each taken the backseat. Rupert had offered to move anywhere she wanted. Dillie chose to stay in the city that had brought them together and where they'd built their lives. Somehow, its ambient chaos proved the perfect antidote—a distraction, if nothing else—to the horrors of last fall.

"Careful," she called out. "Don't kick sand at the little girl, please. That's not nice, is it?"

She'd avoided the local press reports about that night, as best she could. The deranged college professor so caught up in his book's subject that he'd snapped, targeting the family, shot by the mother in self-defense. All true. But not the whole truth. She kept that to herself alone. From the police, her family, her husband, her psychiatrist. She didn't lie, didn't have to. She simply withheld enough to wind the case down. There was no upside to full disclosure. In her mind, she'd written and rewritten a sympathy note to his daughter and grandchildren, one she knew she could never send.

The news stories omitted, mercifully, the deaths of her mother and grandmother on the same night. They received proper obituaries, without any connection to the other events. After all, there were none. One died peacefully in her sleep at a respectable age, the other in a traffic accident during a terrible storm when the city had dozens. That River Kiss was destroyed by fire was merely the latest sad end among the dwindling antebellum mansions that had met similar fates over the decades. Close friends gathered 'round to comfort them, but it was stilted and awkward. The collective calamity was simply too exhaustive. Freakishly, almost cursedly so.

The remaining family—all three of them—huddled and grieved. Lance was the most shell-shocked, Richard the most stoic. Dillie, at that point, largely numb. Together, they survived Christmas, handled all necessary affairs, and shortly after the New Year, migrated back to their separate lives.

But they kept in touch, more out of instinct than effort. Indeed, via phone and FaceTime, they stayed huddled. Lance managed a midweek trip in March and promised to bring Shane back for Pride weekend at the end of the month, his hospital schedule permitting. Richard, flirting with retirement, scaled back his practice and planned a July visit. She hoped he'd stay a while; there was plenty of room in their new place, and Campbell had grown increasingly attached to his sole grandfather through their weekly computer chats. Lance floated the rumor their father already had a new mystery "friend," although that felt uncharacteristically brazen. So far, he'd been mum; she'd wait for him to drop that morsel in his own time.

Even Emma, after much arm-twisting, agreed to bring Jasmine and the girls to the Big Apple for the Thanksgiving parade and Christmas kickoff (with a decided pass on "rat park"). She'd hold her to it.

"Campbell, do you need some water?" she asked, toggling the bottle to get his attention. "Tell me if you get thirsty, please." The playground was more crowded this week, with school freshly out for summer. Already a hot, steamy one. Off to the corner, pigeons clustered around a tyke sharing his popcorn.

She regretted—and always would—that her last memory of her mother and grandmother was of conflict and crisis. One rarely got to say goodbye, she knew, but at least one hoped for a final spirit of peace and love. The night's events had robbed her of that wished-for closure. It haunted her, even as she felt their presence, comforted by the faith that they were watching over her.

And life had smoothed out since Campbell's birthday. Immediately, like a switch that stayed off. Perhaps she'd grown more spiritual, but she had a sense/hope/belief that they—especially Khaki—were doing their part to keep it that way. And protect them. A year ago, she'd have laughed at the idea.

Dillie checked her watch and then Campbell's energy level, still unspent. He'd need his nap in an hour, when Rupert would be back from his squash game. She had her doctor's appointment at four, to check the effects of her new cocktail regimen, the dosage they were still adjusting. They helped, she felt. Fewer side effects,

less fogginess and unsettling dreams. Just a calm, centered stillness. And, with any luck, temporary. She yearned to be back in
charge of her own mind and moods.

"Campbell, no!" she said, bolting up. "Do *not* hit!"

There goes his impulsive flare of lashing out and bullying.
Then abruptly apologetic and adorable. Another phase, she knew.
Hoped.

"You're cool, Caitlin," said the young mother on the end of
the bench. "He's just wooing you, caveman style." Blonde, relaxed,
a tinge Bohemian, sipping coconut water to go with her Dave
Eggers paperback. Behind her sunglasses, she could almost pass
for the actress Nina Arianda. Surely not.

"I'm so sorry," said Dillie, but the probably-not-Nina shrugged
it off. "Just a love pat, really," she assured her. "She gets worse from
her brother. It's a regular MMA at our house."

Dillie laughed at her chill irreverence, sat back down.

"How old?" the mother asked. "Two and a half," said Dillie. The
mother nodded at hers and said, "Almost three."

Normally, a conversation with a stranger at a playground
would end on this pleasantry. But Dillie added, "They're quite adventurous at that age." The mother said, "It's why God invented
vodka. For us, I mean." They each put down their reading.

"This way!" Campbell ordered the other children around the
sandbox. "This way!" They followed.

"Quite the natural-born leader you got there," said the young
mother, and Dillie smiled and said, "My little overachiever. He
must get that from his father."

"Look out, world!" the mother announced, and they both
laughed at the procession. Dillie liked her, liked her daughter. So

did Campbell, in his caveman fashion. He needed new play dates, since his old ones still lived downtown. She could use one, too.

"You new here?" the mother asked.

"My husband and I just moved up the street. We were in SoHo. Well, Chinatown-adjacent." She left out their temporary midtown digs while house-hunting, as it never felt like home. "More family friendly up here, we think. And closer to the park, of course."

A welcome breeze buffeted her hair. She smoothed her bangs back over the scar on her forehead. Takako at Laicale had worked wonders with her new cut.

"What do you do?" said the mother, whipping off her sunglasses. Not Nina Arianda, clearly. But delightful. And sincerely interested.

"I'm a writer. I freelance for the *New Yorker.*" She paused and then added, "And I'm working on a book."

"Oooh," said the mother, turning closer. "So you're a *real* writer. What's it about?"

A harmless question, but one she avoided, for now. "It's just a...family history, in a way. I'm still figuring it out, really."

"I researched mine a little once. Off those sites. I just knew I'd find royalty, great leaders, hell, great *criminals!*" She shook her head. "Um...pizza maker. Tailor. Oh, and a bus mechanic in Yonkers. Don't get me wrong: Thank God for them. Just never felt so boring in my life."

Dillie smiled and said, "Nothing wrong with boring."

The mother shot out her hand. "I'm Monica."

They shook. "Delphine," said Dillie, not quite nickname-ready. "Very nice to meet you."

"Ditto. Always good to have a new friend to torture with stories about our children, right? God knows nobody else wants to hear them." Dillie laughed again at her verve and gusto.

Monica faced forward, opened her paperback. "Now get back to your book, or whatever you're doing. Don't wanna pester you."

"Not at all," said Dillie, back to her iPad. It was a good start. They'd run into each other here again, she was sure.

"Hey, where'd you get that necklace, by the way? If you don't mind."

Dillie touched the cross pendant without looking up. "It's my...was...my grandmother's. She passed away recently."

"I'm sorry," said Monica. "Thank you," said Dillie softly.

She read a sentence.

"I shouldn't have interfered," Monica added, abruptly earnest.

"No, that's okay," Dillie assured her. "It was several months ago...."

A smacking of lips. Again. Dillie tensed. Looked up and over to Monica, sitting tall against the bench, staring out straight ahead. She smacked twice more and stopped.

"I know that now," Monica said, measuring her words. "I know so much more now. And...what must happen." Her eyes were locked at a far distance.

Dillie pulled away. "What...do you mean?"

"She was right, you know. Kate. And you'll have to do it yourself this time. It's the only way to stop it. And it's...the right thing to do."

She knew the cadence, the rhythm. It had comforted her countless times, her whole life. Monica's voice, but not Monica.

"But I'll be with you, Dillie. I'll help you get through it. I'll always be with you."

Monica turned and gazed, her gentle eyes brimming.

"I'm sorry, my girl. I'm so sorry...."

Dillie spun to Campbell, still happily leading his playmates in the sandbox. Above his head, just beyond the playground, on a low tree branch, sat a large black bird. Perfectly still, it paid no notice of the noise and commotion. It stood sentry, focused on Campbell.

She rushed to the sandbox, took Campbell by the hand, led him past the playground gate.

He protested; she insisted.

The black bird took flight. A crow. Nothing more.

At the edge of the park, she picked him up, carried him past an ice cream cart, through a throng of tourists. She'd left her iPad, didn't care.

Scurried across Fifth Avenue, headed down Seventy-First. Past a dog walker, pulled by his menagerie.

The black bird waited atop the corner of the Frick Collection. Waited again on a spire of St. James' Church on Madison. On the traffic light at the Park Avenue median.

Much too big for a crow. A raven.

It couldn't be. Ravens didn't live in New York. Did they?

Too large for a raven.

The intersection teemed with pedestrians, crisscrossing under the giant bird of prey. One young woman, alone, wept for no apparent reason. Didn't the others see the monstrous creature? Didn't they?

"Look!" she said to the weeping woman, pointing up. "Look!" to the UPS man, to the elderly matriarch and her nurse companion. "Look!" to the uniformed doorman under his awning. No one listened.

Taxis blared at her, blocking the street. She darted around them to the far side.

The beast took flight again, circling, following.

Dillie clutched Campbell close, hurried on through the crowds.

Acknowledgments

As always, to my parents, sister, and family. My books baffle them, but they stay strong.

Special thanks for the moral support and encouragement of many kinds: Ryan Rayston, Jennifer Puryear, Pat O'Meara, Betsy Wills, Saralee Terry-Woods, Bridget Blaise-Shamai, Holly Bigham, Christina Evans, Marely Cheo-Bove, Terri Bond, Morgan Wills, Jacqueline Mazarella, and Owen Moogan. Big thanks to Stacey and Rob Goergen. They know why.

To those who were there right from the start: Jennifer Simpson, Tula Jeng, Holly Bario, Donna Langley, Wyck Godfrey, Marty Bowen, and Charlie Ferraro.

This book wouldn't have happened without the magic of my copyeditor, Penina Lopez, and cover designer, Steven Womack. Both wizards. Please live forever.

And I pity anyone who hasn't had lunch with my elegant and crackerjack book agent, Helen Breitwieser. Together, we've solved most of the world's problems. I've even learned to spell her last name. Next one's on me.

About the Author

DON WINSTON grew up in Nashville and graduated from Princeton University.

After a stint at Ralph Lauren headquarters in New York, he moved to Los Angeles to work in entertainment. His debut novel, *S'wanee: A Paranoid Thriller,* hit #3 in Kindle Suspense Fiction. His other novels include *The Union Club* and *The Gristmill Playhouse*.

He lives in Hollywood.

www.DonWinston.com

ALSO BY DON WINSTON :

THE GRISTMILL PLAYHOUSE

A NIGHTMARE IN THREE ACTS

DON WINSTON

Fame is a madness.

Betty Rose Milenski dreams of Broadway. Talented, ambitious, and obsessed, she was the biggest fish in college. But New York is a harsh wake-up. Unemployed and ignored, she faces a career as cocktail waitress instead of on the stage. And the clock is ticking.

She jumps at an internship at the country's most famous summer-stock playhouse, in spite of its bizarre, all-controlling reputation. There, she joins a family of eccentric and endearing fellow actors and bona fide stars, lorded over by the benevolent dictator Rex Terrell. With nonstop shows to sold-out crowds—tucked away in a charming, Americana village—the Gristmill Playhouse is every actor's summer dream.

But when a fellow intern mysteriously quits and warns her to flee, Betty Rose struggles to separate truth from make-believe even as she rises toward stardom. Is her growing terror and dementia a form of self-sabotage, or is the Gristmill grooming her for a final curtain call?

The Gristmill Playhouse. There's no business like it.

BOX OFFICE NOW OPEN.

ALSO BY DON WINSTON :

The Union Club

A SUBVERSIVE THRILLER

DON WINSTON

If these walls could talk, they'd scream.

College sweethearts Claire and Clay Willing are determined to start their married life independent of his rich and powerful West Coast family. But the tragic murder of Clay's older brother, coupled with his own stalled career, suddenly lures them to San Francisco and into the clutches of the Willing political dynasty.

Clay's parents welcome Claire with open arms and ensconce her in their exclusive private club atop Nob Hill, where she mingles with the eccentric Bay Area elite and struggles to maintain her identity in the all-controlling Willing clan.

But her in-laws are the least of Claire's worries as she unravels the freakish mystery of their son's assassination and uncovers the shocking reason they were brought back into the fold. With no way out alive.

The Union Club. Where evil has its privileges.

APPLY FOR MEMBERSHIP.

ALSO BY DON WINSTON :

The Top Five Kindle Suspense Thriller

S'WANEE

A PARANOID THRILLER

DON WINSTON

A spellbinding campus. A new family of friends. A semester of death.

High school senior Cody's prayers are answered when he's recruited on scholarship to the college of his dreams: a stunning and prestigious school tucked high in the Tennessee hills.

But the dream turns living nightmare when his classmates start to die off mysteriously. Is it Cody's imagination, or are his friends' tragic deaths a sinister legacy handed down through the generations? And is he next on the roll call?

A coming-of-age, paranoid thriller in the vein of Ira Levin, *S'wanee* weaves psychological suspense with dark humor in its brutal descent to a shocking climax.

S'wanee. Where old traditions die hard.

ENROLL NOW.

Made in the USA
San Bernardino, CA
17 January 2018